Louise
and
Vincent

A NOVEL

DIANE BYINGTON

Louise and Vincent
Red Adept Publishing, LLC
104 Bugenfield Court
Garner, NC 27529
https://RedAdeptPublishing.com/

Copyright © 2023 by Diane Byington. All rights reserved.
Cover Art by Streetlight Graphics[1]
Cover Image: Vincent van Gogh, Public domain, via Wikimedia Commons
No part of this book may be reproduced, scanned, or distributed in any printed or electronic form without permission. Please do not participate in or encourage piracy of copyrighted materials in violation of the author's rights. Thank you for respecting the hard work of this author.

This is a work of fiction. Names, characters, places, and incidents either are the product of the author's imagination or are used fictitiously, and any resemblance to locales, events, business establishments, or actual persons—living or dead—is entirely coincidental.

---

1.   http://StreetlightGraphics.com

*For Louise Beauchamp, who inspired me to write, and wasn't
at all like the Louise in this book.*

Chapter 1

New Orleans,
Louisiana, 10 July 1940

MY HEART LEAPS WHEN I hear the click of high heels ascending the rickety stairs to my apartment. It's surely the woman I've promised to speak with about Vincent. I've waited most of my life for someone to ask me about him, so I should be ecstatic. Yet now that the time has arrived, I'm terrified. I don't know if I'll be able to remember everything that happened and relate it to her without breaking down. Even more important, I fear I won't be believable. I have no proof to back up my version of events, so she might think I'm just an old kook.

Maybe I should let this opportunity go and take the secret to my grave. If I don't answer the door, perhaps she'll leave. But the day is hot and humid, typical for July in New Orleans, and my windows are open. An old box fan rattles away in one of them.

No, she'll know I'm here. Besides, I chose to do this. I'm the last person alive who knows the complete story, and I owe it to Vincent's memory to tell someone before I, too, pass beyond this life.

When I hear a knock, I struggle out of my chair and limp to the door, my joints complaining about the sudden movement. I pause with one hand on the knob and think about how I came to be in this situation.

A letter arrived from the Chicago Art Institute last week, forwarded by my publisher. In addition to writing a book, I've painted many pictures, so I tore open the letter, hands shaking with anticipation. Maybe the Institute wanted to buy something for their collection. But I quickly understood that the letter wasn't about my paintings. Instead, an art historian named Dr. Danielle Dupree asked if I was the Louise Ravoux who'd once lived in Auvers-sur-Oise, France. "If you are," she went on, "could I come and speak with you about your experiences there? I will explain more when we meet."

The only plausible reason she would track me down, fifty years after I fled to the States, would be to ask about Vincent. On my own, I'm not important, despite my book and my paintings that are only known locally. But Vincent certainly is, and he's growing more so as his paintings soar in value.

Without allowing myself to question my decision, I wrote back that I would see her.

And here she is, four days later.

I take a breath and open the door.

The young woman on the stoop appears to be in her midthirties—the same age as my grandson, William. Her brown hair hangs in frizzled waves to her shoulders, and her wrinkled gray suit has sweat stains under the arms. She must have walked directly from the train station in the midday sun. I'm impressed by this level of dedication.

I've chosen a light-blue cotton dress that was expensive when I bought it, back before the Depression wrecked my business and I lost all my money. With my shaky hands, I'd struggled to style my short white hair, but I eventually managed it. I've always liked to look as good as my situation will allow, but at eighty-five, *good* is a relative term.

Dr. Dupree smiles and introduces herself. I invite her in, and we sit on the hard wing chairs on either side of the sofa. If she sits there without complaints today, I might allow her to use the comfortable sofa on her next visit. I reserve it for friends and family, and at this point, she is neither.

The woman glances around the room at the many paintings hanging on the walls but doesn't inquire about them. She's polite—I'll give her that. She must be eager to ask who painted them. When—or if—I tell her, she'll probably be astonished.

She folds her hands on her lap, catches her breath, and begins. "Thank you for seeing me on such short notice. I wanted to speak with you for two reasons. One is professional and the other personal. I'll start with the professional reason." She pulls a folding fan from her pocketbook and waves it in front of her flushed face for a moment.

After so long in New Orleans, I no longer fight the heat. As I've aged, I've even grown to welcome it. Clearly, that is not the case with her. I will offer her something to drink after I hear what she has to say.

In a moment, she continues. "As you know, I'm an art historian. I specialize in the works of Vincent van Gogh, and I'm trying to put together the true story of his last days. Your name came up as someone I should interview."

She stares at me, waiting for my nod. When I finally give it to her, she continues. "I have looked for you for years, Mrs. Ravoux."

"I'm called Madame Ravoux, if you please, Dr. Dupree."

She starts and blushes. "Oh. Yes. I apologize, Madame Ravoux. And please call me Danielle."

I clear my throat. "How did you find me, Danielle? I lost touch with everyone in Auvers many years ago."

A twinkle lights up her eyes. "I happened upon a cookbook you wrote on French cooking. I didn't know if you were the person I sought, but since you had the same surname, I wrote to your publisher." She laughs. "You know the rest."

"Well." I nod. "And what do you want to know?"

"Were you really the proprietress of the Ravoux Inn in Auvers-sur-Oise while van Gogh was there?"

"I was one of the innkeepers, along with my husband, Arthur." I straighten in the chair and give her a tight smile. After all these years, I still dislike thinking about Arthur.

She lets out a breath. "I'm so happy to meet you, Madame Ravoux. I would love to hear anything you have to say about van Gogh."

"That's why I invited you. But first, I'd like to hear your personal reason for being here."

Her eyes fill with tears. "I'm named for my grandmother. She was Danielle Dubois, and I believe she was a friend of yours in Auvers."

My friend's face flashes before my eyes: vibrant, pretty, sassy. I peer at this young woman, but I don't see a resemblance.

Hesitantly, I nod. "Yes, she was my friend. She ran one of the other inns. But she moved to Paris to marry, and we lost touch. I haven't heard from her since I left France."

We sit in silence for a few moments, each with our own thoughts.

Finally, she says, "My parents are Cécile and Tomas Dupree. Do you remember Cécile, Danielle's daughter?"

I don't think of her often now, but I couldn't forget her if I tried. Cécile had a role in the tragedy that brought me to America. If she'd acted differently, Vincent might've been sitting here with me instead of moldering in his grave. But I don't need to mention that. I merely nod.

"My parents moved to Chicago when I was small, but as a teenager, I used to spend summers with my grandmother in Paris. Grandmère would take me to art museums, and we regularly visited the van Gogh paintings. She told me she'd been slightly acquainted with him in Auvers and that there was an important story about his time there that hadn't been told. She said it wasn't hers to tell, but if I found you, you might consent to relate it."

When I don't respond, Danielle goes on. "She would have loved to know I found you. Maman and Papa brought her over to Chicago two years ago, when the Nazis started gaining power in Europe. The move was hard for her, and I'm sad to say she passed away three weeks ago." She looks away, rubbing her eyes. After a moment, she continues, "When we cleared out her things, I found your cookbook. Inside was a recent note from Grandmére, instructing me to find out if the author was the woman she'd known. If so, I should meet with you as soon as possible." She pauses. "And here I am, madame."

I feel a momentary pang for my friend's passing. But too many friends have died for me to grieve someone I haven't seen for so long.

"I'm sorry she passed," I say politely. "What was the cause?"

"Breast cancer was the official diagnosis, but personally, I think she died from a broken heart, knowing the Nazis occupied her beloved Paris."

I understand that sentiment and share it. I wish that my elder daughter, Adeline, had been willing to leave Paris, or that I'd been healthy enough to go over there and bring her home when it was still possible. The worry and grief might cause my heart to break too.

But cancer... I lost my younger daughter, Germaine, to cancer ten years ago, and I wouldn't wish a death like that upon anyone.

I clear my throat. "Danielle was a good friend for a short time. I don't understand, though, why she was so insistent that you contact me."

After a moment, she replies, "I'm not sure, either, to be honest. Along with the cookbook and the note was a small package she insisted I give you but not until I'd heard your story about that time. Its contents are for your eyes only, and I was not to open it. I've done as she asked." She pauses. "But that's for later. For now, I'm eager to learn: did you know Vincent van Gogh well?"

I can't stall any longer, so I inhale deeply and respond. "Yes, I did. He stayed at our inn for the last seventy days of his life. He was my painting instructor, among other things. I remember those days fondly."

She leans forward. "Will you tell me about it?"

My heart lurches again. I grasp the arms of the chair and hold myself upright. "Yes. But you must allow me to recount it in my own way. Vincent's time in Auvers was inextricably bound up with my own, so you will need to hear my story first. And I have no tangible proof that any of what I'm about to tell you is true, other than my words. You'll have to make up your own mind. Is that agreeable to you?"

"Definitely. I want to know everything. Is it all right if I take notes?"

When I nod, she pulls out a notebook.

I clear my throat again and try to make my warbly old voice strong and confident. "I warn you—the Vincent I knew wasn't the madman people make him out to be. As far as I can tell, that's a tale someone made up to sell more paintings."

I shrug at her questioning look. "Oh, yes, he had spells of epilepsy or something similar for a year and a half before his death, starting when he mutilated his ear. I don't know if the doctors were ever certain what was wrong with him. But when he arrived at our little inn, Vincent was completely normal. He had just left the asylum where he'd lived for a year, so he was timid about being in regular society after so long, but for the time he stayed with us, I never had the slightest fear that he would harm himself or anyone else."

The lump in my throat has grown larger, so I cough to clear it. "Please bear with me as I arrange my thoughts." I lean back in the chair, welcoming its solidity. "I've never told the story to anyone."

Danielle's face lights up, although, to her credit, she tries to hide it. "You're fine. Start wherever you want."

This is all happening too quickly. Then I remember what I was going to do. "First, would you like some iced tea? It's a hot day and a long story, so I'll need to drink something so my voice stays strong. And I imagine you're thirsty after your long walk."

She nods. "Thank you. Shall I get it?"

"Yes, please. It's in the kitchen, just through there." I'm relieved to remain in my chair as I consider how to start. "And bring the canapés that are on the table."

When we are settled again, I allow the past to meet me, surround me, and carry me back into its warmth. The rattle of the fan, the stranger before me, and the weight of my old body disappear. I am thirty-three again, young and disillusioned about the future—until Vincent, the love of my life, changes everything.

Chapter 2
Auberge Ravoux, Auvers-sur-Oise, France, 20 May, 1890

THE DAY BEGAN LIKE many others, with a fight. I needed to pay the cook and the chambermaid, the only staff we could afford with business so slow, but when I opened the strongbox, the pile of francs had dwindled from the previous week. I counted the coins—definitely fewer. Sighing, I shook my head. I hadn't taken the money, so Arthur must have. We were the only ones who knew the combination to the lock.

Without thinking, I turned to my husband, who was dressing. "Have you taken some money from the box? There seems to be less than before."

He grunted. "No, of course not. It's not my fault you can't manage well enough."

I could manage fine if you didn't steal the money, I wanted to say. But I bit my tongue. Arguing with him gained me nothing but bruises. The previous September, when we first leased the inn, our funds

8

had stretched far enough to hire an extra chambermaid and a cook's helper, and I'd been able to feed our boarders good-sized servings of meat several times a week. But with money so tight recently, I had to be more creative with my offerings, serving more soups and less expensive cuts of meat. My heart sank at the prospect of decreasing portion size and quality, but that would be necessary if things didn't improve.

In the summer, Auvers-sur-Oise was popular with tourists from throughout Europe who came to see the town's historic château and the picturesque French countryside. Our landlord had assured us the inn would be quite popular then. The winter had been another story: long and grim, with few visitors. June had almost arrived, so we needed to hold on for just a little longer.

If Arthur took no more money, we would have enough to make the lease payment this month, but we might not manage it next month. I couldn't understand why people didn't flock to the inn, even in bad weather. Although our resources were limited, I was an excellent cook, we served good wine, and the rooms were clean and inexpensive. The scent of my desperation must have wafted throughout the village and frightened off potential boarders as well as restaurant customers.

Nagging Arthur was never wise, but I had to try one more time to find the answer. He'd finished shaving and was about to leave the bedroom.

"There is less money than last week," I said, trying to keep my voice steady. "I haven't taken it, and no one else has access. I had to let the extra chambermaid go—"

Before I finished speaking, he grabbed my upper arm and squeezed. The pain halted my words and brought tears to my eyes. I held my breath, waiting to see if he would stop there.

"Do not blame me because you aren't thrifty enough," he said between gritted teeth. "Are you so stupid that you don't know what's going on in your own home?" When I winced, he tightened his hold.

I tried to keep my voice from trembling. "Sorry, I must have been mistaken." I hated myself for apologizing, but that was the only way to keep the situation from escalating.

He released my arm and pushed me away then stalked out of the room, leaving me shaking. A new bruise had probably already blossomed in the same place as the last one.

Alone, I clenched my teeth to keep from screaming in frustration. *That vile man. Why did I ever marry him?* I knew why, of course. My dying father had arranged it, thinking I would be happy and well provided for. Fortunately, he hadn't lived to see how the marriage had turned out. I'd made a terrible mistake, but it was too late—far too late—to do anything about it.

Slowly, another thought crept into my consciousness. *Am I really as stupid as Arthur accuses me of being? Did I make a mistake?* I didn't think so. *But maybe...*

Enough. I took a deep breath and did my best to locate a sense of calm. Clearly, I would need to squirrel away a portion of our income in a place Arthur couldn't find. That way, if we failed at the inn, we might still have enough money to start anew somewhere else. Straightening my shoulders, I walked from the room.

Just before serving Arthur his morning coffee, I spat in his cup and stirred until the globule dissolved. He never noticed, but the minor rebellion carried me through the day with a smile on my lips. As usual, I managed the meals and the children and took care of the boarders' rooms, while Arthur served the bar customers and repaired things that broke. We barely spoke to each other, which was a blessing.

In midafternoon, I sat alone in the café, making flower arrangements for the tables and idly wondering how I might provide for myself and the children if I left my marriage. Unfortunately, divorce wasn't an option. Arthur wouldn't grant it—I'd already asked early in our marriage, when I realized things weren't going well—and even if he did, I had no way of earning a living without him. We weren't rich, but Arthur earned more than I could, alone and with two children to support. Nevertheless, I daydreamed about how wonderful my life would be without him. At times, I thought my fantasies were the only things keeping me sane.

I was startled when the door opened, and a stooped, bedraggled man walked in. He carried an easel on his back and painting supplies in his arms, along with a battered leather valise. Breathing heavily, he set everything down and wriggled out of the backpack then pulled a pipe from a pocket and stuck it in his mouth. He removed his straw hat and rolled his shoulders while looking around with a sharp gaze as though searching for someone or something.

I couldn't help but notice how much he resembled Denis, my first love—same red hair, bristly beard, and blue-green eyes. And he was also an artist. I hadn't seen Denis for fifteen years, not since he left me to move back to England. I didn't know this man at all, but the similarities made my heart pound as it hadn't in years.

He made no move to sit at a table, so he wasn't a restaurant customer. He probably wanted to rent a room. I loved when artists stayed with us. In my youth, before marriage and children intervened, I'd wanted to become a painter, so our boarders' sometimes loud and passionate arguments about art reminded me of the life that had passed me by. We currently had one room available, and I hoped he would take it.

The man was tall and had probably once been stocky, but he was far too thin now. His clean but wrinkled clothing hung on him, scarecrow-like. When he turned toward me, I saw the mangled ear. *Oh, the poor man. He must've had a hard life.*

Arthur, playing billiards in the back room, hadn't noticed the newcomer, so I stood and smoothed down my skirt. "Bonjour. May I help you, monsieur?"

He stood straight and smiled. "Bonjour. I'm looking for a room. Maybe for a few weeks, but I'm not sure." His voice was raspy, as though he didn't use it often. He spoke fluent French with what might have been a Dutch accent. After a moment, he lit his pipe and puffed on it, and a pleasant aroma of cherries permeated the room. And then he smiled, and the smile lit up his face like a sunrise.

I inhaled deeply while trying to ignore the magnetic draw of the man standing before me. "Uh, we have one on the second floor. Is that all right?"

He nodded, and his smile faded. Suddenly, he was just an ordinary man, inquiring about a room.

"Let me show you." I led him up the narrow stairway to room number five. It was small and sparsely furnished, and its only light entered through a small skylight.

"I'm sorry it's so minimally furnished. If you want the room, I can look for—"

"That won't be necessary. I left some furniture in Arles. If I take the room, I'll send for it straight away." He pursed his lips. "How much is it?"

Arthur usually handled these transactions, and he'd be angry if I interfered with his duties. We had agreed on the rates, though, so I knew what he'd probably say: three francs fifty a day for room and meals. Still, I needed to let him say it, or he'd make sure I regretted it later.

"You can talk with my husband about that," I said, rubbing my arm. "He'll give you the details."

Downstairs, I interrupted the billiards game. "Arthur Ravoux, this is..." I turned to the man. "I'm sorry for not asking your name. I'm Louise Ravoux."

"Vincent van Gogh."

I tried to repeat it, but the last sound stuck in my throat. "Sorry. I'll do my best. You're Dutch?"

"Yes. I know it's difficult. In France, most people just call me Monsieur Vincent. I'm happy to meet you, Madame Ravoux." He smiled, and his eyes shone.

He turned toward Arthur. "Monsieur Ravoux." They shook hands.

His manners showed he wasn't as rough as his appearance implied. I cleared my throat. "I shall leave the two of you to discuss the details of the arrangement, should it be suitable."

Returning to my table, I sank into the chair and watched Monsieur Vincent as he spoke with Arthur. I tried to remember if Denis's family had any Dutch relatives, but I didn't think so. Still, the two men could have been brothers. I pushed away thoughts of how that relationship had ended and focused instead on how much I'd loved his face, his hands, his body.

The men finished their discussion, and Arthur turned to me. "Monsieur Vincent will be staying with us for a while. Would you show him around?"

"Yes, certainly." I smiled as I walked over to him. "Let me show you the 'Artists' Room.' You may store your supplies there instead of carrying them all the way up the stairs. And your paintings can dry there if you'd like." I led him down the hall to the back room, where several of our other artists had set up easels.

Monsieur Vincent glanced at their paintings and grunted in a noncommittal way. Looking at me, he asked, "I can paint in here when it rains?"

"Most assuredly. This is your home now. Use it as you wish."

"Thank you, madame. Your husband said you have some other things to tell me?"

"Yes. I set breakfast out at seven, and you can help yourself. We serve lunch at noon and dinner at seven. I post the daily menus beside the front door. Please let me know if something isn't to your liking."

He nodded.

I led him to the counter to the right of the front door and gestured toward a stack of baskets. "You can place mail here for the letter carrier. He arrives around nine in the morning and again around four." I stumbled through some more instructions, but my voice faded away. Oh, something about the man flustered me, beyond how much he looked like Denis. Maybe it was his beautiful eyes or the way he paid attention, like nothing else in the world mattered but me. Looking away from him, I ran through the list of everything else I needed to say. "Unfortunately, we don't yet have indoor plumbing, so the privy is behind the building. The maid will empty your... necessity... container every morning." I faltered as he blushed. "Uh, here is a key for the back door in case you return after eleven, when we lock the front door. In terms of your rent, you will pay my husband in advance every week. He appreciates prompt payment." Relieved to be finished, I smiled. "Do you have questions?"

Suddenly, as if a tap had been turned off, his energy appeared to drain out of him. His shoulders slumped, and he seemed to find speaking hard. I didn't know how to respond. Something other than his ear might've been wrong with him.

He cleared his throat and rubbed his face. "No, madame. Thank you very much. I will retire to my room now." He stacked his artist supplies in the back room then slowly made his way up the narrow stairs, carrying his valise as though it held rocks.

"Oh, by the way..."

He turned.

"We have two daughters who usually run around in the inn. Adeline is thirteen and Germaine two. Please let me know if they are any bother."

His tired face brightened. "I love children. They will be a joy to me. My nephew is still a baby, but he's the apple of my eye. Thank you again, madame."

"Have a good rest, monsieur."

I DIDN'T SEE MONSIEUR Vincent again that evening, but we heard banging in his room for nearly half an hour. Arthur scowled at the sound but did nothing. After all, the artist had paid his rent, and I hadn't told him he *couldn't* hang pictures on his walls. He surely must've had a lot of them. Eventually, the sound stopped, and I relaxed. I'd been holding my breath as I prayed Arthur wouldn't go up to his room and confront him. We desperately needed the rent money, and the man would surely leave if he had to deal with Arthur's anger.

I understood my husband's anger better than anyone, having been the target of it more times than I cared to remember. Even though I often failed, I tried not to anger him, especially when he was already in a foul mood or had imbibed too much. Everyone benefitted when he was calm and performed the role of the jovial proprietor.

I set a place for Monsieur Vincent at a table in the back, but he didn't come down for dinner. Beyond our family, our only diners were the other boarders and a small group of townspeople. Weekends were our busy times, when Parisians arrived on the train to enjoy a day away from the city. On that slow Tuesday night, I'd made a delicious pea soup, but no one seemed to notice.

When the diners had left, I asked Arthur what I should do about Monsieur Vincent. "He seemed exhausted when he walked up the stairs. Maybe he's sick or something."

He shrugged. "You can take him a tray if you want."

I nodded, relieved that Arthur had suggested it instead of me. I carried a tray laden with food up to his door, which was closed. "Monsieur Vincent, are you all right?"

No answer.

Maybe he'd hurt himself with all the banging. I hesitated then cracked open his door so I could peek inside. The man was sitting on his bed with his head in his hands, rocking back and forth, and appeared to be lost in the throes of grief.

I eased the door shut, hoping he hadn't noticed the intrusion.

"Should I get a doctor, sir?" I whispered through the door, so as not to startle him.

Finally, a muffled voice said, "No. Please leave me be."

"I'll just place your meal outside your door." I hoped nothing was terribly wrong with our newest boarder. He seemed like a nice man, and I would enjoy having him around. Maybe he would smile again one day soon.

After a long pause, he replied, "Thank you, madame. Good night."

I set down his tray and tiptoed away. Apparently, we were both burdened by troubles.

Chapter 3

Nobody can in the beginning do as he wishes.
–Vincent van Gogh

MY FAVORITE DAY OF the week was Wednesday because I went to Paris on that day. For a few hours, I could rediscover the vital young woman I'd once been and enjoy the city of my birth.

The train left at eight, so I had no time to spare. After setting out breakfast, I dressed in my prettiest frock, put up my dark-brown hair, and pinned on the hat I'd found at a secondhand shop. I had stacked it high with feathers and ribbons, and when I wore it, I was a woman with prospects, not a worn-out wife, mother, and innkeeper. I dabbed a little color on my cheeks and lips, and I was ready.

On my way out the door, I noticed that all the boarders except Monsieur Vincent had gathered for breakfast. I'd picked up his empty dishes on the way to the kitchen, so I knew he'd eaten his dinner. *Should I take him breakfast? No.* I didn't have the time. Besides, Arthur might be angry if I gave the man special attention.

I kissed the girls, gave the cook some last-minute instructions, and said a frosty goodbye to Arthur. I wouldn't see him again for a few days, which was a relief. Our routine was that he managed the inn while I was gone, then he took the afternoon train into Paris, where he would stay until Friday evening, supervising the butcher shop he'd owned since before we were married. He worked hard while he was there, as far as I could tell, but he couldn't seem to hold on to his earnings, leaving us always on the brink of insolvency. I wondered what he actually did with his money, but asking wouldn't be worth the bruises I would get in return.

As I hurried toward the train station, I pulled my shawl tightly around my shoulders. The afternoon would probably be pleasantly warm, but the morning air was cool enough to make me shiver. I exchanged greetings with a few people also headed toward the station but wondered if I would ever feel at home in the small town.

Even though I anticipated a good day, gloom surrounded me like a blanket. I needed something besides a trip to Paris once a week to give my life meaning. Yes, my children brought me joy, but I shouldn't have to pay for that joy by being married to such a hateful man. Painting had once filled my empty spaces, but thanks to Arthur, I hadn't picked up a brush in years. I was only thirty-three, too young to be so empty. Many women had difficult husbands, and they found happiness in other ways. I wondered what was wrong with me.

My heart was empty, and so was my stomach, which growled loudly. I hadn't taken the time to eat breakfast, but after I visited with my mother, I would enjoy a pleasant lunch with my friend Hélène. We would eat our fill and talk until our voices were hoarse, then I would shop for things I couldn't buy in the village. Finally, I would take the afternoon train back to Auvers. For a few days afterward, the gloom would lift.

Sighing, I boarded the train with one minute to spare. Inside the second car, I found my new friend Danielle, who, along with her brother, owned one of the other inns in town. I slipped in beside her, and we air-kissed hello, happy that our trips to the city were coinciding again. We'd met at Mass on our first week in the village and hit it off immediately. Danielle had offered to be my guide.

"We innkeepers have to stick together," she'd said. "There are plenty of tourists for us all." And she'd laughed. Her laugh had lightened my heart that day and still did.

"How are you on this fine morning?" Danielle pulled a flask from her bag and handed it to me, smiling conspiratorially. "Let's celebrate our day of freedom, eh?"

I rarely drank in the morning, but I couldn't turn down her gift. I took the flask and swallowed a mouthful of fiery liquid before handing it back. "Thank you. A great way to start." I smoothed my skirt and smiled. "How has the past week been? I didn't see you in Mass on Sunday."

"Ah, I've been busy. So many guests and so many things to do. We had a wedding at our place on Saturday, and I lay in bed until noon on Sunday."

"Huh. It's been quieter at ours. We only got one new boarder this week. He came yesterday. A redheaded painter." I grinned at the memory.

"Oh, he was at our place first." Danielle laughed. "It was so odd. Dr. Gachet brought him in. You know Gachet, who has the big house just outside of town?"

I shook my head. That name sounded familiar, but we hadn't met.

"That's all right. You will. His wife died some years back, and he's been a little... unbalanced since then. Anyway, he brought in this painter, Monsieur van Gogh, as I remember, and registered him for room nine. They stayed and talked for a while, and then Gachet had to leave. As soon as he walked out the door, the painter picked up his things and headed for the door. Didn't say a word either." She laughed again. "My brother asked, 'Hey, where are you going, monsieur?'"

"'To someplace not so expensive,' he said. I don't know if he was going to tell us or not. We were only charging him six francs a night, which was a good rate, in deference to Dr. Gachet. But it was too much for him." She shrugged and sniffed. "I hope you enjoy his company."

I lifted my eyebrows. "He seems all right. Very concerned about money, as you say. But there's something unusual and interesting about him."

Danielle leaned forward and lowered her voice. "Yes, I'll tell you what I know. He's a crazy Dutch painter who's in Gachet's charge. You saw his ear, or lack of it, right?"

When I nodded, she continued.

"Poor man, he went mad and cut it off. And he's been in an asylum for a year. But he's the new darling of the Paris art scene. Perhaps he can stay sane long enough to enjoy his success."

I shuddered. *If Monsieur Vincent is so out of his mind that he would cut off his own ear, who knows what he might do if crossed?* I would watch him and do my best to keep the children out of his way, but truly, he seemed harmless. Whatever madness he'd exhibited that had put him in an asylum seemed to be cured. He was sad, I thought, but not insane.

"I was rather... taken... by his piercing eyes," I said softly, hoping I wasn't blushing.

Danielle's eyes twinkled as she grinned. "You know, a little flirting hurts no one." She'd been widowed for many years and enjoyed the occasional dalliance. "You don't need to take it beyond that if you don't want to. But flirting is fun." She then launched into a lengthy tale about her latest affair.

I listened with half a mind while the other half wondered what desiring someone and feeling desired in return would be like. I'd lost those feelings years before. Maybe that explained why I felt so empty.

Monsieur Vincent came to mind, and the thought sent a tingle to my belly. *Impossible.* He was a boarder, and I was married. Even mild flirting wasn't wise, given Arthur's temper. I tried to push away the memory of what had occurred the one and only time I'd flirted with a man, but it refused to go.

IT HAD HAPPENED JUST about a year before, when we still lived in Paris. Arthur and I had gone to a party hosted by one of his friends. I knew hardly anyone there, but I hit it off with a man I'd never met, and the two of us spent a pleasant quarter hour chatting and laughing in a corner of the room. Yes, I'd been flirting but only casually. I certainly wasn't interested in pursuing anything with him.

Before I knew it, Arthur was at my side, grabbing my arm and twisting. In a curt tone, he made our excuses and marched me from the room. Back at home, in the privacy of our bedroom, he whispered, "You embarrassed me with your flirting. You will take your punishment and not make a sound because I don't want to scare the girls. If you cry out, it will be worse for you."

Terrified at his bitter tone and the wild look in his eyes, I nodded. I expected a slap or two and resigned myself to putting up with it, as most women did. Instead of mild slaps, though, he repeatedly punched my face and body, bloodying my nose and mouth and loosening a tooth.

At first, I froze in fear. He'd never done anything like that before. I wanted to scream and curse and return his blows, but my body wouldn't move. So I silently endured the beating, the look on his face telling me he'd meant what he said about keeping quiet.

When he turned away to prepare another glass of absinthe, I hobbled out of the room and shook Adeline awake, then I picked up baby Germaine and rushed the three of us down the street to the apartment of my friends Hélène and Claude. I banged on their door in the middle of the night, praying they would answer.

Hélène opened the door and, after taking one look at my battered face, ushered us inside and put the girls to bed. Then she cleaned me up. My face was terribly bruised, and both eyes had swollen nearly shut, but my bones were intact, and I hoped the loose tooth would mend. Through chattering teeth, I told my friend what had happened. Hélène's expression was grim as she listened to my story.

Arthur showed up an hour or so later, still inebriated and yelling at me to get myself home before he killed me. Claude stepped outside while I peeked out the window.

"Go home," said Claude in a stern voice. "If you come back here again in this state and saying such things, we'll notify the police." He walked back inside and slammed the door.

To my vast relief, Arthur turned around and left when he heard an authoritative male voice. He was, at heart, a coward.

I stayed there for several days. Although Hélène urged me to stay longer, I knew I would have to return home. My friend's apartment was too small for all of us, and I had nowhere else to go. Before I returned home, though, I met with Arthur and exacted a promise from him, never to hit me again. So far, he'd kept his promise. Arm squeezes left bruises, but he must have thought they didn't count.

Regardless of his words, I would never trust him again. And I hated him even more than I had before.

That was what flirting had brought me.

I SHIVERED AT THE MEMORY but said nothing to Danielle. The conversation moved on to other topics, such as what meals we planned to serve in the next week and which market had the best prices and freshest produce.

Still, I couldn't keep Danielle's comment about flirting out of my mind. As a young woman, I'd enjoyed the pastime. Since my marriage, though, flirting hadn't been part of my repertoire—except for that one time—and I wondered if the skill was still inside me.

We changed trains at Pontoise and continued chatting. The Paris station came up more quickly than I'd expected, and we disembarked, knowing we'd likely see each other again in the afternoon.

I walked at a brisk pace to my aunt's apartment, where my mother had lived for the past year. While I walked, I watched people going about their daily activities: hanging laundry, playing chess in the park, laughing with neighbors. The sight of a young couple walking on the sidewalk, arms entwined, nearly brought me to tears. Even being in Paris didn't eliminate the blanket of loneliness that covered me.

To divert my mind from my troubles, I decided that, when I returned to Auvers, I would take a couple of hours every afternoon when things were calmest to go for a walk and get to know the area. By exploring it, perhaps I would come to love it a little. That would be something positive, anyway.

When I approached the apartment building, my aunt opened the door before I could knock. She pulled me into the vestibule and whispered, "I'm glad you're here. I want to call Dr. Garnier, but Claudia won't allow it. Maybe you can talk some sense into her."

Consumption was so pervasive in France that nearly everyone knew someone with it. Most of the sufferers went downhill slowly, over several years, before succumbing to the disease. A few patients lived, though, and I was sure my mother would be one of the fortunate few. Even though money was tight, if Maman needed a doctor, I would certainly get her one.

I nodded and rushed into the back salon where my mother was resting on a sofa. Her white hair was loose, and she looked paler than usual, but she smiled when I knelt beside her and kissed her cheek.

"How are you?"

She shrugged and looked away. "Ella tells me I'm worse, but I don't feel worse—just tired."

We both glanced at Aunt Ella, who bit her lip as though trying to hold back tears.

As I pulled up a chair, Maman handed me an envelope. "I received a letter from Émile yesterday. Here, you read it aloud."

My brother had immigrated to America ten years before, and his letters were always fascinating. In this one, he described his job at a hotel in New Orleans, where he'd just been promoted to general manager. He needed to hire a superb cook, and he wondered if I would be interested. "You could come, too, Maman," he wrote, "and we would be a family again. You could supervise from your bedroom overlooking the square. The French Quarter is so much like Paris that you might think you were still there."

Moving to America was impossible, of course. Arthur and I couldn't leave the inn until our lease was up in another year, and Maman's health wouldn't allow it. We laughed at the suggestion.

"He sounds happy," Maman said in a wistful tone.

"I love his letters." I shifted in the chair. "Now, tell me about you. Shall I call Dr. Garnier?"

"Please, no. He doesn't help me much, so I don't want to waste the money."

I considered. He'd cured Germaine the previous year when she was seriously ill with the croup, but, in truth, he'd done little for my mother.

"If you insist, I won't call him now," I said, "but don't let money be the reason."

My mother nodded, a wistful smile curling up her lips.

We visited for a while longer, then the time came for me to go. As I walked to the door, I glanced at the painting hanging opposite the window. Its subject was the park outside the apartment building where I'd grown up. I'd painted it as a teenager, and its bright-green foliage and red flowers were so vivid that they nearly burst from the canvas. It reminded me of a time in my life when colors had been richer and more alive. The colors in my world must have been fading for years, and I hadn't noticed.

My aunt joined me in front of the painting. "It's beautiful," she said. "By the way, our neighbor, Madame Corbin, came to see Claudia yesterday. She loved the painting and asked how much it would cost to purchase it. Claudia would never sell it, I know, but wasn't that a sweet offer?"

Warmth flowed up my neck and into my head. No one had ever asked to buy one of my paintings before.

Grinning, I turned to my aunt. "If she asks again, tell her the price is two hundred francs."

I winked, knowing it was an outrageous number, and we laughed. As I walked down the stairs, I reflected that I really might sell it for twenty francs. That would be nearly a week's income from a room at the inn. The thought of making my own money brought a spring to my step.

I headed to lunch with Hélène, who'd been my best friend since we were five. Hélène stayed busy with her husband, four children, and large apartment, so having her to myself for an entire meal was a delight. We met at my favorite bistro, and I ordered my regular meal of steak frites and salad. While we ate, we chatted about our lives and our children.

After the meal, as we settled in with wine, Hélène gave me a look I recognized, the one that said, *Time for truth telling.*

"Has Arthur hit you lately?"

I sucked in a breath at the rawness of the question. For an instant, I was beset with a jealousy so strong that I almost lashed out verbally at my friend. I didn't need to ask Hélène if Claude had hit her, because we both knew that was impossible. Her husband was a loving man who would never touch her in anger. And oh, I wanted so much for someone to love me as he did her.

But the moment passed, my breath returned, and I remembered this was the person who'd saved my life and had been there for me whenever I needed her. She was justly concerned, not simply throwing her good fortune in my face. She couldn't help that her life had gone in an easier direction than mine.

"No, but I avoid him as much as possible, especially when he's been drinking heavily. He loves his spirits, as you know." I tried to chuckle, but the sound emerged as more of a croak.

Hélène leveled a look at me. "Are you telling me the truth?"

I glanced at my arm to make sure my long sleeve covered the bruises. It did. "More or less." I managed a brave smile.

Hélène gave me an appraising stare then shrugged. "I don't know if I should tell you this. Before we met, I'd decided not to, but now I think I must."

"What is it? Are you sick? One of the children?"

Shaking her head, she said, "No. It's about Arthur." She placed her hand on top of mine. "I saw him walking down the Avenue Trudaine last week with his arm around a woman I didn't know. They stopped to kiss, and then they walked on. I don't think he saw me." She squeezed my hand. "I'm sorry to be the one to tell you."

I sat back, aghast. Arthur wouldn't have been walking down the street with a prostitute, so she must be someone he supported financially—a mistress, then. He had many faults, but I hadn't realized he was also a philanderer. I struggled to take in the implications.

"Give me a moment, please."

Things fell into place at the speed of a bird's flight: our constant lack of money, the lateness of his returns on Friday evenings, maybe even why he'd been so determined to move the family to Auvers the previous year. He wanted the freedom to spend nights with his mistress in Paris with no consequences.

When I could trust my voice, I said, "Thank you for telling me. It was the right thing to do." I hesitated, inching my way toward my feelings. "Frankly, I'm a little surprised Arthur could attract another woman. He's not handsome, and his manners are rough, and he's already married. Be that as it may, now that I know, I can... I don't know what I can do, but the knowledge is helpful." I pursed my lips to keep from crying.

Hélène nodded and patted my hand. "If you don't mind, I'd like to offer an observation. You used to be a bright star, shining forth in the heavens, but ever since you married Arthur, you've become a timid mouse." She grinned and shook her head. "Sorry for the bad metaphors. But you know what I mean. You had goals and dreams—more than most women—and you were willing to do whatever it took to make them happen. Being with Arthur has sapped your confidence." She thanked the waiter, who had come to ask if we needed anything else, then turned her attention back to me. "I know you've been through a lot, but I miss the spirited woman you used to be. If you can find her again, she'll know how to handle this situation."

I sighed. "I appreciate your support, and I'll think about what you've said."

Hélène was right. I had changed. Before my marriage, I'd been determined to make my living as a painter. I'd taken lessons and painted all the time, and my teachers had said I had a good chance at success. Denis was also a painter, and we were thinking of marrying.

Then, in the space of a few months, everything fell apart. My father became ill, and we ran out of money for art lessons. Denis had been called back to England by his family and hadn't asked me to accompany him. Suddenly, I was alone, without prospects and without a plan. I was so overwhelmed that I didn't argue when my father asked me to meet Arthur, who was the friend of a friend. Arthur seemed nice enough at first, and he promised to allow me to continue painting after we married. That was one of the many promises he'd broken.

I'd hoped to drink another glass of wine and enjoy my crème brûlée, but my stomach threatened to revolt if I swallowed another bite. The conversation foundered, and we soon parted.

I turned to my shopping in a fog, wondering if I should confront Arthur about his mistress. If nothing else, I could demand that he choose between us. He would undoubtedly choose his family because he would likely lose the inn's lease if I left him. Still, he would be angry about it, and I knew where his anger led. I shuddered at the thought.

Hélène hadn't recognized the woman, so I likely wouldn't know her. At some point, I might even thank her for taking my husband off my hands for part of the time.

That was my mind speaking. For long moments, I felt strong—clear and relatively composed about this abrupt change in my circumstances. But then my heart would take over and cry out with questions such as *What did I do wrong?* and *Why wasn't I enough?* Even though I'd never loved him, I'd done my best to make the marriage succeed, but apparently that wasn't adequate.

Then rage would fill my soul. The rat probably treated his new woman like gold whereas he treated me like yesterday's garbage. I'd put up with his abuse for years, and that hadn't even gained me his loyalty.

A few moments later, after the rage ebbed, my mind would take over again, and I'd think, *Who needs him? Not I.*

All afternoon, my thoughts tumbled together, one after the other, as I considered my options. More than once, I found myself standing in the middle of an aisle, staring into space with something in my hand—a cabbage, turnip, or cucumber—and no memory of having picked it up. Each time, I shook my head and moved on, eventually purchasing most of what I needed. I chose not to buy Arthur's favorite cheese, though, because I saw no reason to make his life any easier.

By the end of the afternoon, I decided to bide my time and keep the knowledge of his adultery to myself, at least for a while. I might need to trade that information for something important one day, so I shouldn't squander it.

After the long day, the flowers on my hat had wilted, as had their owner. Although I sat with Danielle on the train ride home, I couldn't bring myself to engage in pleasant conversation. My friend seemed to understand and retreated into her own thoughts, while I stared out the window, wondering what was to become of my life. I had no answers.

Fortunately, Arthur wasn't at home when I arrived. As expected, he'd taken an earlier train into Paris, so I would have a few days to recover from the terrible news before facing him. Despite my decision to keep the knowledge to myself, recriminations might have burst from my mouth if we'd come face-to-face. Instead, Germaine greeted me at the door and wrapped her little arms around my legs, hobbling me.

"Maman, Maman, me make tower. Blocks. Come see."

"Yes, darling, I will. Let me put these down first."

Without getting up, Adeline asked, "Maman, can I go to a party on Saturday afternoon for a girl in my school?"

Struggling to maintain my balance, I said, "I suppose so," as I attempted to untangle myself from Germaine.

"And can I go for a walk with the other girls on Friday night?"

My patience gone, I snapped at her. "Adeline, I could use some help here."

The girl slowly rose from the table and came toward me.

Before she got there, Monsieur Vincent was by my side. "Allow me to carry your packages, madame." He took the two large baskets and carried them into the kitchen, which enabled me to pick up Germaine and kiss her cheek. When I passed him in the kitchen, he gave a slight bow.

I was thankful that a few gallant men still existed.

When he sat down, one of the other artists must have made a rude comment, for Monsieur Vincent stood abruptly, and his chair crashed over backward as he shouted at the man. Two other artists led him outside, where they presumably calmed him, but none of them came back inside right away.

Shaking my head, I walked back into the kitchen. I'd had enough drama for the day.

I gathered my children and went to bed.

Chapter 4

A great fire burns within me, but no one stops to warm themselves at it, and passers-by only see a wisp of smoke.
—Vincent van Gogh

WITH ARTHUR AWAY, I was free for a few days and resolved not to spend the entire time brooding about my husband's unacceptable behavior. Maybe if my mind had a rest, it would come up with a solution to my problems. Instead, I daydreamed about how I would spend my time if I didn't have to clean people's rooms and run the inn. I would paint, certainly, if I could remember how to do it and could hide it from Arthur. Or I could put together a cookbook of all my family's recipes and sell it to our customers. Thinking about which recipes to include made the time pass relatively quickly.

But no matter how hard I tried to ignore Arthur's infidelity, it remained in the back of my mind, always pushing toward the front. By Friday morning, I'd grown tired of spending every minute trying not to think about my cheating husband. He simply wasn't worth it.

In the afternoon, I honored the decision I'd made in Paris to take a couple of hours when things were quiet to go for a walk. The maid could watch Germaine and wait on customers while I was gone. I would explore the village on my own and try to find peace within myself.

Although Auvers-sur-Oise was just thirty kilometers from Paris, it seemed an entirely different country. Instead of the hurry-hurry city, this was a small community of fewer than two thousand souls, most of them wheat farmers. Auvers sprawled along the banks of the Oise River, and our inn was in the middle of the town, across from the city hall.

Feeling like a child escaping from school, I headed east and walked past the train station and the church. Few people traveled on that winding road, so I didn't need to watch too carefully for horses and buggies. I strode as quickly as possible and breathed in the fresh spring air, which was wonderfully scented with fragrant violets and lilacs. I walked past homes and businesses, with their overflowing flower boxes, and eventually found myself in an area with thatched roof cottages. Idly, I wondered how the farmers kept the rain from trickling through the thatching. I was happy to have a solid roof over my head even if the inn wasn't as alluring as these cottages.

A few minutes later, I saw that an artist had set up his easel in the middle of the road. From that distance, I didn't recognize him. Several well-known artists had painted in Auvers in recent years. Daubigny had lived in the village until his death some years before, and his widow still lived down the street from the inn. I appreciated his paintings of the river Oise. The great Cézanne had worked there a few years back, too, while Pissarro had stayed in a nearby village. Compared to these great artists, few of our boarders were any good, in my opinion. In fact, I might have done better myself if I gave it some time and effort. Chuckling, I felt almost young again as I considered how I might paint the thatched cottages.

As I drew closer, I recognized Monsieur Vincent. He was sitting on a stool and would stare fixedly at the row of cottages for a few seconds then attack the canvas in a frenzy before doing it all again. Other artists painted carefully, covering the entire canvas with basic shapes before filling in the details, which was also how I'd been trained. Monsieur Vincent painted what appeared to be finished shapes with every quick brushstroke, and a version of the cottages appeared before my eyes.

I considered turning away and heading back the way I'd come, so as not to bother him. *But no.* If my presence annoyed him, he could tell me, and I would continue my walk. I tiptoed up to stand beside him. When he realized someone was watching, he started and glanced my way but didn't stop what he was doing. He merely nodded and kept on painting.

Taking that for permission to stay, I watched his paintbrush fly over the canvas. Every few minutes, he would stand back and glance between his canvas and the cottages then return to his work, changing or adding details.

I wasn't sure what to think about his painting. On the one hand, it astounded me. This row of ordinary cottages was nestled in a green field on a hill. In reality, the thatching was sweet, but the colors weren't particularly vibrant. Under Monsieur Vincent's brush, though, the cottages and the colors came alive, their brilliance announcing them to the world. I wanted to walk into the painting and live in its lushness.

I'd thought the colors in my Paris painting were bright, but they were dull compared to these.

On the other hand, I'd never encountered anything like this style of painting. It was in the Impressionism family but more intense than what others painted. And the shapes of the houses and the woman in the picture weren't quite realistic. The perspective was a little off, and the colors were almost too bright for my eyes to tolerate. The ground beneath the cottages gyrated as it never did in actual life. Surely, the man was a good enough artist to paint the scene accurately if he chose, so he must have wanted it to look like this.

I couldn't tear my eyes away.

Eventually, I began to comprehend his vision of texture and movement. As I stared at it, the picture spoke to my emotions and my senses, and I felt more alive than I had in a long time. After another few minutes, I decided I was in the presence of genius. His work was indeed unique but in a good way. I'd just needed to give it a chance.

We stood together for maybe an hour. He painted, and I watched, completely taken with this man who saw the world in such a fanciful, magical way.

After a while, I looked up at the poplar tree under which I was standing. Its new leaves were uncommonly green and glowed in the dappled sunlight. The branches were a deep brown, darker than I remembered ever seeing before, and contrasted beautifully with the leaves. Glancing around, I observed deep blue holes in the clouds, and the flowers growing around the houses were more effervescent than usual. In fact, everything within my vision seemed to shimmer.

I smiled, delighted. This had been an occasional aftereffect of an especially wonderful art class. The world would be brighter for a few hours, but eventually the colors would fade back to their ordinary drabness. I wondered if my vision would remain expanded after witnessing a master at work. The world I saw would probably never pulsate as Monsieur Vincent's did, but I would not soon forget this enchanted moment and my introduction to his unique painting style.

Finally, he stepped back. "Thank you, madame, for not interrupting my train of thought. At first, I thought you were one of the boys from the village, come to harass me. They bothered me yesterday when I was painting. I was pleased to see it was you, and then when you didn't speak but just watched, it spurred me to find more depth in the scene." When he smiled, I noticed that his teeth were covered with paint.

I made a face and gestured toward my mouth.

He understood immediately and turned away as he pulled his handkerchief from a pocket and rubbed his teeth. When he turned back, the paint was gone. "Please forgive me. I sometimes don't want to take the time to clean my brush when I change colors, so I run it through my teeth. Afterward, I must clean them. With your presence, I simply forgot. Is that better?" He smiled again.

"Yes, thank you. It was a bit unsettling to see your teeth all green and yellow."

We laughed.

A little shyly, he asked, "What do you think of the painting?"

"It's different from anything I've ever seen. Simple but evocative of the earth and the simplicity and contentment of the people who live in those little cottages."

He took a breath. "Thank you, madame. That is one of the most perceptive things anyone has said about my paintings."

I smiled. *Are we flirting?* That was possible, but I wasn't sure. I wouldn't mind rekindling my flirting skills with this man, especially since Arthur was in Paris and wouldn't see us. We chatted for a few minutes about his painting techniques until I realized I needed to get back.

I pulled myself out of my daze and said, "I must put together the evening meal. By the way, are you satisfied with your room and the food?"

"Oh, yes, they are beyond adequate. I feel at home at your little inn." He paused. "Thank you for watching me paint, and I appreciate your comments. Would you like to join me again tomorrow? I will probably be somewhere in the village. I like to paint the cottages that are all around."

"Oh." I was reasonably certain he was flirting with me then, which filled me with delight.

Apparently, Arthur wasn't the only one who could be attractive to the opposite sex.

I would've loved nothing more than to watch this painter create his works and flirt with him some more. But sadly, it was impossible. I had other things to do and couldn't spare the time. Also, tongues would wag in the village if someone saw me in his presence more than once, and I didn't want anything getting back to Arthur.

"No, I can't, but thank you."

Another thought occurred to me: a way to spend time with the painter that would be without reproach. Also, it would allow me to rediscover a part of myself that I'd long discarded. It would be a bold move, however, and the words to ask him struggled to form in my mouth. I hesitated so long that he gave me a quizzical look.

"Uh, I have taken art lessons in the past, but I wouldn't call myself a painter. More like a dabbler." My heart beat faster. *Should I continue? Yes.* He was not Arthur, so I didn't need to be a timid mouse. "I wonder if you would consider giving me lessons? I could bring my easel, and possibly, we could paint together?" My face grew warm at my impertinence, but I continued quickly so that I wouldn't be tempted to retract the words. "I can't pay you, but I could trade for some service. Maybe launder your clothes for an occasional lesson?"

I was sure my face had turned crimson, but I stood my ground as I took a deep breath and waited for his response.

He cast his eyes downward and seemed to shrink inside his skin. When he spoke, his tone was flat and the words brusque. "I'm sorry, madame. I don't take students anymore. When I've done so in the past, it hasn't worked out very well." He glanced at me then looked away as the silence drew out. Finally, he continued, "I would hate to ruin our lovely time together. I bid you good day, Madame Ravoux."

He turned back to his painting and picked up a brush.

Disconcerted at being dismissed so abruptly, I turned away. *Well.* That hadn't gone smoothly at all. Apparently, I held no interest for him if I wanted more than just to watch him paint and admire his technique. I could understand him not taking students, but a true gentleman would have been more understanding and gracious when refusing my request.

I must have completely misread the situation. He wasn't flirting at all, just being polite to an admirer. Feeling stupid and inadequate, I turned and almost ran back into town.

When Monsieur Vincent came in, just before dinner, he walked straight back to the Artists' Room and placed his equipment in a corner then carried his finished painting up the stairs to his room without giving me the opportunity to see it again.

All right. If that's the way he wants to be, so much for flirting. Besides, I had other concerns, such as what to say to Arthur when he returned from Paris in a few hours.

Chapter 5

ARTHUR DIDN'T ARRIVE until after ten that evening, which left me to deal with the customers on my own. That night was our busiest since we'd leased the inn, and whether or not I liked my husband, I definitely needed his assistance. Fortunately, the maid stayed to help serve, and—bless her—the cook had prepared extra meals in the afternoon, due to some sixth sense that they would be eaten.

When Arthur finally walked in, most of the customers had gone, and I'd found a moment to sit at an empty table and catch my breath. The girls were sitting on the porch, Adeline in one of the rocking chairs and Germaine on Monsieur Vincent's lap.

Arthur looked tired and irritable. Without even greeting me, he asked in a low, mean voice, "Why is Germaine still up? And did you know she's sitting on that painter's lap?"

I sighed, unwilling to be sucked into his anger. "Where have you been, Arthur? I needed you this evening. You know Fridays are our busiest evening, and this one was even busier than usual. You left me to handle it all on my own. Your daughters are both safe, so I don't know why you're upset."

He dropped into the empty chair beside me and spoke in a gentler tone. "There was a rush at the shop, and the new assistant didn't show up for work today. What can I do to help?"

So, "good Arthur" had replaced "bad Arthur" for the moment. His apology was a welcome surprise, but I'd heard it before and didn't trust it. His moods were too volatile for "good Arthur" to stay around for long.

I shrugged. "The worst is over now. We're closing in half an hour. Why don't you check to see if anyone wants more to drink? I want to sit on the porch for a while and cool off before I clean up."

The restaurant had been especially hot and stuffy that evening, and even the rain hadn't helped much.

"Please light the lamps too," I added.

Not waiting for his response, I wiped my face with a napkin and removed my apron before stepping outside. The only rocking chair available was beside Monsieur Vincent. I plopped down and glanced curiously at Germaine.

"Hi, Maman. I draw." She held out a slate on which she—or someone—had drawn a passable image of a horse.

Either she was a budding talent, or someone had helped her. I smiled and glanced at Monsieur Vincent. He winked. Apparently, he'd forgotten our unpleasant interchange from earlier in the afternoon. *All right.* I would do the same.

"Horse," Germaine said, clapping her hands. When she did, the slate and chalk fell to the floor, and Monsieur Vincent reached to pick them up.

"She likes to draw," he said in a pleasant tone.

The little girl turned to him and patted his chest. "Story," she demanded sleepily.

I sighed. There was to be no rest for me, at least not yet. *What is this child doing up so late?* I'd told Adeline to put her to bed at least an hour before.

"No story for you tonight," I said firmly as I plucked Germaine from his lap. "Thank the nice man for drawing with you. It's bedtime."

She made a face as though unsure whether to go along peacefully or scream.

Monsieur Vincent grinned at her. "Good night, *ma bichette*. I'll see you tomorrow. Have a good sleep."

She buried her face in my shoulder, which was my cue that she was ready for bed. "Good night, monsieur. Thank you for entertaining her."

"It was my pleasure. Besides, I saw you were busy." He stood and bowed stiffly. "Good night."

I carried Germaine into the inn and fortunately avoided a sleepy tantrum. After the little girl was in bed, I saw Adeline still sitting out on the porch, even though nearly everyone else had left and the restaurant was dark. *What now?*

I went out and sat beside my older daughter. "What's going on? I asked you to put Germaine to bed, but you didn't."

I didn't want to start a fight that late at night, but the girl needed to do what she was told. She'd turned thirteen a month before, and with the birthday had come a sharp, bitter tongue and a resistance to doing chores.

"Some girls in my class were meeting for a walk this evening, and they invited me to join them, but I had to take care of Germaine. I asked you about it the other night, remember?" Her body was tense and her face red.

I took a breath and tried to keep my voice level. "I don't remember it, so I must not have heard you. If I had, I'd have told you that I need you to help me on Fridays and Saturdays. I'm sorry things didn't turn out as you wished. You can spend Sunday afternoons with your friends, but that's all, for now."

Adeline stared at me in horror. "But I have a party to go to tomorrow. I asked you on Wednesday night, and you said I could go."

I stiffened, trying to remember if that was true. The trip to Paris might've driven Adeline's request from my mind.

Regardless, I couldn't back down. "You should have thought about that before you shirked your duty tonight. I need your help tomorrow."

The girl stormed off, and I exchanged a glance with Monsieur Vincent, who smiled and shook his head in sympathy. I appreciated the sentiment but flushed at the intimacy of the moment because I always tried to keep my family's problems from the guests. I returned his smile and walked inside, where I collapsed onto a chair.

As I replayed the scene in my mind, I was surprised Adeline had been invited to a party and even more surprised that she was so determined to go. My daughter frequently complained that the local girls were stupid provincials. Apparently, none of them liked her, and all she wanted was to move back to Paris. I understood that wish and shared it, but neither of us could do anything about it.

After a few moments, I admitted that I should've allowed Adeline to go to the party, which could be her opportunity to develop friendships. Even though I truly didn't remember her asking me, I'd been angry at Arthur and had taken it out on Adeline. After I rested a moment, I would go in and tell her of my change of heart.

Before I could put my plan into action, however, Arthur stomped into the dining room. "What did you tell Adeline?"

"What?" I'd been half-asleep, but when I heard his voice, I woke quickly, tense and on guard. "I don't understand."

"She wants to go with her friends tomorrow. I told her she could. Did you tell her something else?" His tone was harsh, far different from the conciliatory one with which he'd greeted me.

The realizations came quickly: Adeline must have appealed to her father behind my back, believing I wouldn't dare argue with

Arthur because of what he might do to me. She had to have heard our arguments and been aware of the violence, despite my attempts to spare her that knowledge. I hated to think the two of them were in league against me, but that seemed to be the truth of it.

I shook my head. "I was about to tell her she could go, just this once. But if she goes to that party, it will double my workload tomorrow. I had to let the second maid go, so I need Adeline to do more work around here." My voice sounded weary and weak to my ears, and I suspected Arthur heard it the same way.

"No. Hire someone to do that heavy work. She's a child, and I want her to have a good time here. We can't look like we're destitute and need her to work like a maid."

"But we don't have the money to hire someone. We *are* nearly destitute."

"And we'll get a terrible reputation if we don't allow her to be with her friends. She's going, and that's all there is to it." He turned and stomped back to the billiard room.

Sighing, I rose from my chair and began cleaning up after the evening's customers. At least we'd made a goodly amount of money that night. I stuffed all but a few francs into my pocket, and I would hide them in case Arthur decided he needed more money to spend on his whore.

When I finished cleaning, I went into the girls' room. Germaine was sleeping soundly, but Adeline was awake, and in the light of the hallway lamp, I saw the angry scowl on her face. I sat on the bed and reached for her hand, but she snatched it away.

"I was going to let you go anyway," I whispered. "You didn't have to go to your father."

I needed Adeline to understand I was on her side, even though it might not always seem that way.

She grunted and rolled over, away from me.

Overwhelmed and weary, I walked out of the room and closed the door. In our bedroom, I washed the stench of cooking off my body and pulled my nightgown over my shoulders. Arthur was still playing billiards. Relieved that he wouldn't be bothering me that night, I prepared for sleep.

But sleep wouldn't come. I couldn't stop thinking about Hélène's question: what I wanted in my life.

Marriage to Arthur was a trial, but I'd survived it for fourteen years. He was seven years older, so he would probably die first. That was a paltry thing to hang on to, but at the moment, it was all I had.

Being a mother wasn't open to negotiation. I loved my girls more than anything. This had been a bad day, but even on the best of days, that role wasn't enough to satisfy my soul's deepest longing. The girls would grow up and leave home. *And then what?*

After a few moments, I realized that, if I couldn't have love, I wanted to paint. Hearing that someone appreciated my art had re-opened the door to my earliest dreams, and the time had come to revive them. Maybe I could actually earn some money and eventually support myself. Even if that didn't happen, painting my emotions into pictures might be my salvation.

How can I manage it? That wasn't clear, but I would need to figure it out because I refused to lose myself again. Even if Monsieur Vincent didn't want to teach me, I would find a way.

Chapter 6

If you hear a voice within you say you cannot paint, then by all means paint and that voice will be silenced.
–Vincent van Gogh

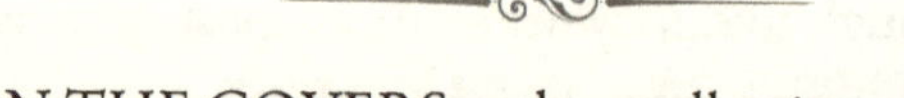

A TUG ON THE COVERS and a small voice awakened me before dawn, pulling me out of a dream of trying to straighten piles of francs to stop them from falling. Keeping them straight was critically important. I had that dream at least once a week, and usually the piles fell despite my best efforts.

"Maman, Maman, monster... monster." Tears, perhaps even screams, were just beneath the surface.

I struggled to understand what Germaine was telling me then realized the little girl must've had a bad dream. "Okay, *ma chérie*, crawl in with us." I picked her up and snuggled her to my chest.

Arthur groaned. "Too early. Go back to bed, Germaine."

I whispered to her, "Be still, or I'll have to take you to your own bed."

"Monster." The little girl's thumb went into her mouth.

"Did you have a bad dream?" I whispered.

The thumb popped out. "No. Monster."

I considered that for a moment. "Were you wandering around in the kitchen?"

Her head nodded. "Monster."

Finally, I understood. I'd set out Monsieur Vincent's breakfast the previous evening, since he'd said he would be leaving early in the morning. Germaine must have crawled out of the bed she shared with Adeline and seen him with his backpack and painting supplies in the dim light of the moon. With all that on his back, he probably seemed so big and bulky that she'd thought she was seeing a monster. Germaine had taken to wandering around the inn by herself too often lately. I would need to find a way to keep her in her room until morning because the little scamp got into trouble when she was unsupervised. I would speak with Arthur about building a gate to place in the children's doorway at night.

"No, not a monster. Just one of our guests. Did you speak to him?"

Germaine shook her head.

He must not have seen her, then. Well, that was one good thing. A second was that the little girl hadn't screamed. Germaine was one of those children with a voice so sharp it could wake a nearly deaf person from the soundest sleep. In the interest of not emptying the inn of its boarders, I did my best to keep my daughter quiet. Mostly, I was successful.

"That was good of you to come to Maman instead of screaming. Now, go back to sleep."

Germaine became still, and her little snores brought a smile to my lips. Although the girl was toilet-trained—except at night, when she sometimes had accidents—she still had that lovely baby scent of innocence and energy. But I would need to give her a bath that night.

Thinking about the day ahead made me realize the time had come to get started. The moon had set, and the sun had risen while I was lying abed. Time to get up and do the extra work that Adeline had shirked... again.

AT BREAKFAST, ARTHUR handed me a handful of francs. "Here. I took these from the butcher shop yesterday so you can hire another chambermaid. I don't want Adeline to have to work so hard. Let her have her youth."

I nodded, accepting his indirect apology. It was not his wife but his daughter he wanted to spare from hard work. Well, I would gladly rehire the young chambermaid whom I'd let go the week before. Maybe the girl could return soon. Unfortunately, that probably wouldn't be today, which meant I would need to clean the rooms and the entire inn by myself while Germaine toddled behind.

Despite my trepidation, the day went relatively well. Before Adeline dressed for the party, she carried in water from the well and helped clean the kitchen. She even played with her sister for a while, leaving me free to do other chores. When at last she left, she was wearing her prettiest blue frock and had a smile on her face, one of the few I'd seen in recent months.

Cleaning the inn wasn't as hard as I'd expected either. Arthur watched Germaine while I worked, which helped. Also, three of our artist boarders had gone to Paris to see some exhibit, so cleaning their empty rooms went quickly.

Monsieur Vincent was the only artist in residence at the moment, so I cleaned his room last. It was a mess. He'd hung Japanese prints all over his walls, leaving only a small space for his own paintings. He'd strewn papers around the room, along with tubes of paint and jars of turpentine that gave off a powerful scent. Several of his unfinished paintings leaned against the walls, drying. I wandered around the room and examined them. They were mostly scenes of village life, but each was filled with color and movement.

The man painted every day, and he either returned from his morning forays with a finished canvas or worked on it in the back room during the afternoons. Nobody else painted so much or so vigorously. He worked like a man possessed, as though someone or something was chasing him, and he was barely staying ahead of it.

In the five days he'd been with us, I had truly warmed to his painting style. His paintings were magnificent, unique, and distinctly better than those of the other boarders. But I'd heard the others laughing behind his back in the evenings as they made fun of his strong colors, which weren't even the actual colors of nature but ones he'd made up. I hoped Monsieur Vincent didn't hear their laughter, too, but nothing seemed to be wrong with his hearing, even though part of an ear was missing. Most nights, he kept his head down and ate by himself then went up to his room as soon as he finished.

Enough daydreaming. I had no time to waste. *How should I clean this messy room?*

I decided to sweep and mop the floor, make his bed, and empty his chamber pot. I would leave the rest alone. Well, I might tidy his papers just a little. Letters from a variety of people were there, but they were mostly from someone with the same last name. *His brother?* Monsieur Vincent sent out at least one letter each day and received just as many. I wondered where he found the time.

As I made his bed, I noticed a lump under his sheets. Pulling up the bedding, I saw a book of naughty pictures. Women had their legs spread, their bums in the air, or licked a finger with an expression of ecstasy on their faces. I laughed. That wasn't the first such book I'd seen. People did many surprising things in the privacy of their rooms. I shook my head and returned it to where I'd found it then made the bed around it.

Mon Dieu. Because of the smut, I would have to clean this room myself even after the maid returned. Her parents would definitely not approve of my allowing their young daughter to see such things. And if Adeline stayed home, she might've been the one to find the book. I shivered at the close call. Fortunately, most of our guests didn't read things like that, or I'd never be able to have any help.

ADELINE CAME HOME FROM the party with stars in her eyes. She grabbed my red, rough hands—chapped from cleaning the floors with lye soap—and swung me around.

"Thank you for letting me go, Maman. I had such fun. And I think the other girls accept me now."

I had to smile and hug her. As difficult as Adeline was sometimes, at other times, she returned to the cheerful, happy child she'd once been.

"I'm glad, *ma chérie*." Then another thought came to me. "Uh, were there boys?" Surely, my thirteen-year-old daughter wasn't old enough to be interested in boys. But that look on her face seemed to reflect more than just being accepted by the local girls.

Adeline looked away. "No. No boys." She skipped away to her room. "I'll change, and then I can help you with the cleaning."

My heart sank as she left. Sometime between the previous night and that afternoon, the child had changed into a young woman. It hadn't really occurred that quickly, of course, but I must've been so involved in my misery that I'd failed to notice. Adeline seemed to stand differently and walk differently, and she was sprouting breasts. *Too soon... Too soon.* I hadn't gotten to know the parents of her friends as I should. That would need to change, and I would have to keep a sharper eye on her. *As if I don't have enough to do already.*

I WAS WORKING IN THE kitchen when Monsieur Vincent appeared. He returned the dishes from the breakfast I'd packed for him.

"Thank you, madame. It was a tasty breakfast. Would it be possible to do this every day? I do my best work when I start early. My funds are limited, but I could pay you a few francs extra for this service."

I stopped peeling potatoes and wiped my hands. "I'll be happy to do that for you. No charge." I paused and pursed my lips, wondering how he would respond to my prepared speech. "Uh, monsieur, I cleaned your room this morning, and I noticed you've left paintings in there to dry. It occurred to me we have a room in the shed out back that isn't being used for anything just now. Would you like to store your paintings there and whatever else you choose? It's a dry space, so it might work for you." I didn't want to mention that one of the nonartist guests had complained about the pervasive smell of turpentine coming from his room. If he agreed, that would solve both problems.

He blushed, probably thinking about what else I might have found in his room. "Oh, yes, please, that would be helpful. May I look at it now?"

I led him out the back door and to the shed, which we'd furnished with a table and chair. I unlocked the door. "We sometimes allow writers to work in here, but you may use it while you're here."

He turned around, noting the good-sized window that allowed in northern light. "It is magnificent. Thank you so much. Most people are not so kind to me." He paused, blushing again. "Uh, madame, I was thinking about our conversation from the other day. I must apologize for being so brusque when you asked me to give you painting lessons. I have reconsidered and have a proposition for you." He took a breath then shrugged. "I'm afraid I'm too busy to teach you to paint, but I wonder if you would be interested in my helping you with your drawing skills. Drawing comes before painting, anyway, at least in my experience. We could do that in the afternoon or evenings as you wish."

Drawing. I hadn't drawn anything in so long—not since shortly after my wedding. I still had my sketchbook and charcoal around somewhere. The night before, painting had seemed to be the thing that would save me, but in the light of day, just the idea of dabbing a brush on canvas made my heart pound so hard that I feared I might faint. Thinking about drawing wasn't as scary. I might be able to draw something that looked vaguely like itself, especially under his tutelage.

Yes, drawing lessons were definitely better, at least for the time being. Arthur might object less to me drawing, as opposed to painting, because it seemed less time-consuming and needed fewer supplies. I had to think about how to broach the subject so he would agree to the lessons. His big objection, other than the cost, would be the time the lessons would take from my other duties. He definitely wouldn't be jealous of the scruffy painter, so that was a plus. Still, scheduling the lessons when Arthur wasn't around might be better.

On second thought, maybe I wouldn't even mention them to him, at least for a while.

"I would love that. Maybe next Thursday afternoon, then? Would that day work for you? Oh, and how shall I reimburse you for your time? Would laundering your clothes be adequate compensation?" In my excitement, I couldn't stop asking questions. Realizing I was badgering him, I stopped and took a breath.

He chuckled, shaking his head. "I wouldn't ask that of you. I'll be happy to exchange the lessons for your preparing my breakfast early. And Thursdays are fine. The early afternoon would be best, while we still have light."

"All right, then." I figured even Arthur wouldn't disapprove of that trade since I was already doing my part of it for free. I gave Monsieur Vincent a big smile, which he returned, a sparkle in his eyes. This was going to work out well—I could feel it. "Oh, monsieur, what would you like me to draw?"

He thought for a moment. "Do you have any flower arrangements? I've been enjoying painting flowers recently, and they're relatively easy to draw. We can put the arrangement on a table somewhere, and I could set up my easel and paint beside you." He paused.

"But forgive me—I presume. Do you like flowers, or would you rather draw something else? Your meals, possibly? They are always so beautifully presented."

I tried to sound casual as I replied, "Yes, I like flowers. I'll make a pleasant arrangement before we meet."

"Very well."

Without another word, he took the key and walked out of the shed, leaving me to wonder if his abruptness would be a part of every conversation we would have. That was a minor problem, though. He could be as abrasive as he wanted as long as he taught me to draw.

Drawing. Just thinking about making art made my heart sing. Thanks to Monsieur Vincent, I was going to return to my first love. I would need to locate my old art supplies wherever I'd stored them when we moved to Auvers. And when I went to Paris the next week, I might buy more. I did a few dance steps and twirled around, just as Germaine did when she was excited. My smile was uncontrollable.

Flowers were some of my favorite things. *Which should I choose—roses, maybe, or violets?* The countryside was filled with blooming flowers, and finding suitable ones during one of my strolls wouldn't be difficult.

Art called to me like a baby bird calling to its mother. If I could draw again, maybe I could find the meaning in my life that had eluded me for years.

But getting to reclaim my artistic side wasn't the only thing that excited me about working with Monsieur Vincent. I was aware that I perked up every time he walked into a room, and the magnetism between us drew me toward him. Even when he was abrasive, I couldn't help feeling that he saw me for who I was and appreciated what he saw. I would try to ignore the attraction, though, and treat him as merely my boarder and my art teacher.

All I had to do was make it to Thursday.

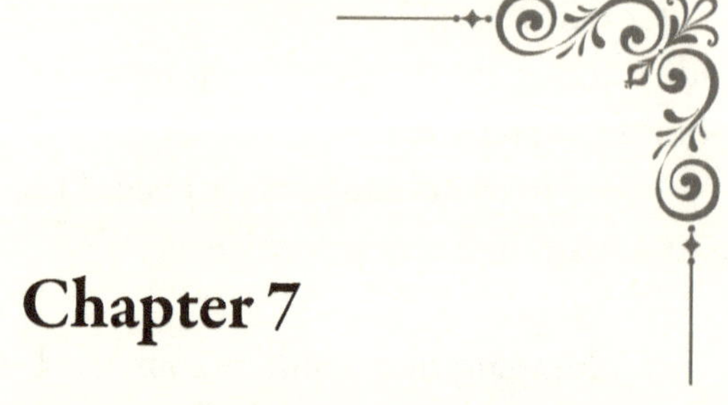

Chapter 7

THE DAYS CREPT BY. Instead of drawing, I focused my creative energy on planning beautiful, tasty meals, and I devised a new dessert made with fresh cherries and cream. The guests loved it. Edith, the cook I'd hired from the village to help with dinners, commented that I looked happier than I had in recent months. The comment was inappropriate, coming from a servant, but it was true. I hadn't realized how obvious my sadness had been to anyone who was looking.

I traced my new, more cheerful attitude to Monsieur Vincent's arrival. Perhaps he was my good luck charm. *No,* I chastised myself, art *is my good luck charm.* The painter would leave one day, and I didn't want his departure to push me back into a dark cave of despair. I could make art with or without him. But I had to admit that I looked forward to making it with him. Maybe I would even try flirting again.

Wednesday arrived, along with my trip to Paris. This time, I took Germaine so that my mother could visit with her younger granddaughter.

When I arrived at my aunt's apartment, I discovered Maman wasn't having a good day. Dr. Garnier was there, and I seemed to have interrupted an argument between him and my mother and aunt. They all turned to me with exasperation when I walked in.

"What's happening here?" I asked.

Maman was lying on the couch, and she looked like a pale, wilted lily. Her breathing was ragged, and she had recently vomited, judging by the foul aroma emanating from the bowl beside her. I set a sleepy Germaine on the floor and placed a doll into her hands, telling her to stay there for a moment. When the child was settled, I rushed to Maman's side.

"She had a spell," Aunt Ella whispered, "so I called the doctor. Fortunately, he came right away."

"How long has this spell been going on?" I asked.

"It started last night. I heard her coughing and struggling to breathe. This morning, against her wishes, I called the doctor." The two sisters exchanged glances, one angry, the other anguished.

Maman whispered, "I don't need him. He can do nothing for me because I'm dying. Please send him away."

For a long moment, Germaine's soothing song to her doll was the only sound in the room. I struggled to take in my mother's words.

Pulling the doctor to the far side of the room, I quietly asked him if what Maman said was true.

He shrugged. "Madame, most consumption patients die. You know that."

"You haven't answered my question. How long does she have, in your professional opinion?"

His face showed a pained expression. "Only God can answer that. But, in my experience, patients whose disease is this advanced may have only a few weeks or months left to live." He shook his head.

"You're saying that yes, she's dying."

He nodded.

Icy shock penetrated to the marrow of my being. Maman couldn't die—not so soon.

No, no, no. I wouldn't allow it. "I don't understand. She was only diagnosed a few months ago. How could the disease have spread so quickly?"

He started. "I diagnosed your mother about a year ago. I remember because it was just after Germaine was so sick. She asked me not to inform you of the situation, saying she would tell you herself. I respected my patient's wishes, but I gather she didn't do that."

I sank onto a chair as suddenly, many things made sense.

A year before was when Arthur had beaten me. Two days later, Maman visited me at Hélène's, and we had a conversation that continued to haunt me.

"I'm appalled by what he did," Maman whispered, horror showing in her eyes, "but I must ask you—did you do something to provoke him?"

I glanced at Hélène, who was sitting on the other side of the room, darning the children's socks, and her face reflected the shock she must've seen on mine. Speaking between lips so badly swollen that they would barely move, I said, "No, I didn't provoke my husband into beating me within an inch of my life. How could you side with him against your own daughter?" I burst into tears.

Still, a small voice inside my head wondered if I'd been partly responsible for what happened. If I hadn't flirted with that man, maybe everything would have been fine.

Maman immediately apologized, and the moment passed. Shortly after, she told me she'd decided to sell her apartment and move in with her sister Ella. My heart sank. Until then, I'd hoped that the girls and I could move back home with her. When I asked why she'd made this decision, she wouldn't meet my eyes.

"To save money," she said. Before I could open my mouth to say that I could get a job and share the costs, she continued, "Actually, this morning I accepted an offer to purchase the apartment. I'll be moving next week."

Oh. So that was that. My last hope for leaving my husband evaporated with her words.

Later in the conversation, Maman said she'd spoken with Arthur, and he'd told her about the opportunity to lease an inn in Auvers. After a long talk, during which she'd severely chastised him for beating me, she agreed to loan him enough money for the down payment if he promised to never hit me again. He promised. She grabbed my hand, one of the few places on my body that didn't hurt, and said she hoped Arthur and I could have a new start.

A new start. I could barely breathe, and she was asking me to make a new start with a man who could easily kill me if he broke that promise.

She'd stayed a few more moments and then left, and we'd never spoken of it again. That had been a difficult time, and none of us were at our best. I'd long forgiven her for accusing me of provoking the beating, so that wasn't an issue. But I finally understood what had been behind her hurtful words. She'd wanted to spare me the responsibility for her care, so she'd conspired with Arthur to give the two of us a second chance at happiness away from Paris.

I didn't know what to think about any of that at the moment.

I walked to my mother's side and sat on the bed. Speaking in the voice I used to comfort the children when they were ill, I said, "Maman, I don't think you're dying, at least not yet. Would you like to come to Auvers with me for a while, where I can nurse you myself and give Aunt Ella a rest?"

She stared at me with vacant eyes.

I glanced a question at the doctor.

"I gave her some laudanum. It will help her sleep, and that may restore her."

I picked up Germaine and handed her to Aunt Ella, who was sitting on a chair near the bed. The older woman held the child and sobbed as Germaine placed her tiny arms around her, saying, "There, there."

Those were the words I often said to her when she was ill or had hurt herself. *There, there.*

Dr. Garnier turned to leave. "I'll find you a good nurse. It will be costly but less than a hospital or sanitorium. And I'll be back later this afternoon to see how she's doing." He grasped my hand. "Stay strong, my dear. You can do this."

After a moment, I turned to see all three of them—Maman, Aunt Ella, and Germaine—sound asleep.

Sinking into a chair, I tried to sort out my next move. After some thought, I decided to leave Maman with Aunt Ella and hire a nurse, as Dr. Garnier suggested. Moving her might hasten her demise, and I didn't know how I could find the time to adequately care for her at the inn.

Losing my dear mother would hurt terribly, but I would survive. The doctor was right—I could do this. Meanwhile, I would do my best to respond appropriately to whatever the future brought.

AFTER A RESTLESS NIGHT, I awoke with a renewed sense of purpose. I needed to stop being so passive, allowing things to happen around me and reacting to them. The time had come for me to control what I could even if that wasn't as much as I would've liked.

First, I had to stop worrying about Arthur's philandering. Thinking about that was sapping the strength I needed for other, more pressing concerns. I would confront him about his behavior when I was prepared to face whatever consequences might transpire. Until then, I would squirrel away as much money as I could for the day when I could leave him behind.

Second, I would send a note to Hélène, asking her to gather information from Claude, her solicitor husband, about divorce laws. I didn't think divorce was the answer to my problems with Arthur, but knowing my legal options wouldn't hurt.

Third, I would send a telegram to Émile and tell him our mother was dying.

Finally, and best of all, I would prepare for my art lesson the next afternoon. Just thinking about it seemed to ease my burdens. Of late, nothing else did.

Chapter 8

AT LAST, THURSDAY AFTERNOON arrived. After searching for several hours, I'd discovered my art supplies stashed in a storeroom. But in the previous day's chaos, I'd forgotten to put together a flower arrangement. Unsure of how to proceed, I wandered outside and noticed that a small rosebush between the inn and the shed had bloomed. It was filled with light-pink flowers so fresh and fragrant that no arrangement of cut flowers could match them. Oddly, I'd never even noticed the bush before. It was a gift from heaven.

After I put Germaine down for her nap, I carried out my sketch pad and a table and chair and went in search of Monsieur Vincent. He'd just finished eating his lunch.

"Would you be willing to paint outside?" I asked.

He shrugged. "Any place is fine with me. I can find something to paint in the most modest of circumstances." After following me outside, he said, "This is perfect. I will set up my easel here."

When we were settled, he showed me how to find the best vantage point from which to draw, how to use a grid to draw out the flowers, and how to crosshatch around them. If I'd dug deeply into my memory, I might've recalled those instructions from the many art classes I'd taken. But nearly fifteen years had passed since I'd attempted to draw, so his instruction was welcome. And I was grateful to find him polite and easygoing. For the first time since I'd watched him painting a week before, he seemed almost happy.

I was so intrigued by being close to him that I struggled to concentrate on my work. Instead, I watched him paint. After a few moments, I realized that every one of his brushstrokes was deliberate. The process looked frenzied, but it wasn't at all. He did exactly what he meant to do with his brush, all in service of his vision for the painting. It—or maybe he—captivated me.

Within an hour, he sat down on his folding stool. "I'm finished, madame. How are you coming with yours?"

I was surprised that he'd finished already. I'd barely gotten my roses into the correct shapes. The paper was a gray mess because I'd erased them so many times.

"Uh, it's been a long time since I've drawn anything, and I'm struggling with the shapes."

He nodded and walked over to me, puffing on his pipe. After looking at my drawing with all its erasures, he said, "You don't have to get them perfect, you know. It's a drawing, not a photograph. Change it however you wish. And you don't need to draw the shed behind the flowers unless you want to. Let me show you what I did."

He carried over his painting, which was finished in shades of bright green and light pink. "You can see that I've placed the flowers on the grass, without the need to include the sky or the shed, or even much of the bush. In that way, they become the centerpieces of the painting. You might be trying too hard." He paused. "Is that kind of feedback helpful? I hope I haven't offended you."

I laughed. "It's very helpful. I see exactly what you mean. I'll try again. But your rendition is magnificent. You captured the essence of the roses. I'd be able to smell them even if it was darkest winter."

He blushed. "You are too kind." He sat back in his chair. "Madame, I have a favor to ask. You know I like to paint landscapes.

But I also love painting portraits, and I need to practice that skill because I think they will sell more easily than landscapes. I know so few people here that it's difficult to find subjects to sit for me. Would you allow me to paint your portrait? I believe I could do it in a single session although it might require two or three hours."

I immediately knew that was impossible. For one thing, I had no time to sit so still for hours at a time. For another, Arthur might become jealous if he saw that Monsieur Vincent had painted my portrait. I didn't need to give Arthur any reason to hit me even if the reason was only in his head. Besides, I hadn't told my husband I was working with the artist.

"No, monsieur. I'm sorry, but I cannot spare the time." I considered. "I wonder if you might want to paint Adeline? Germaine is too young to sit still long enough, but Adeline would much prefer to sit rather than do her chores. I could spare her for a few hours."

He smiled. "That would be most gracious of both of you. I will, of course, present you with the portrait when I finish it." He must have learned French during his school days, and he still spoke in the stilted manner of a nonresident.

I found his formal speech patterns to be endearing. "Uh, let me talk with my husband and daughter, and I'll let you know in a couple of days. Thank you again for the lesson. You don't need to stay around. I'll continue working on the drawing."

He nodded. "I've spent much of the past ten years 'working' on my craft, but it's only in the past year that I've allowed myself to bring joy to the process rather than work. Maybe that switch would be helpful for you as well." With a smile, he gathered his belongings and carried them into the shed.

He was right about everything. I would attempt to bring more joy to my art—and to my life, if such a thing was possible.

I turned to a different page in my sketchbook and started again, finishing the drawing just before Germaine shrieked awake. That time, instead of trying to draw the entire scene with the shed, the bush, and the grass surrounding it, I focused my gaze close to the flowers and drew them in a more free-flowing style. The new roses weren't exactly like the real ones before me. Instead, they showed a messy riot of flowers, some fully bloomed but others only recently budded out. Some were in focus, while others were smudged and only faintly suggestive of flowers.

Holding the sketchbook at arm's length, I decided I liked my new drawing. Also, I realized Monsieur Vincent's leaving had been a good thing, for I'd finally been able to concentrate.

Walking back into the inn to start the evening meal, I noticed an unusual spring in my step. I hadn't thought about my problems in more than an hour, and that alone was enough to make the lesson worthwhile. Also, I'd spent time with the best artist I'd ever met, and I couldn't help but be happy about that.

AT DINNER THAT EVENING, Monsieur Vincent seemed more ebullient than usual as he sat at the table with the other painters, who spoke excitedly about the exhibit they'd seen in Paris. I overheard them telling him he was being discussed in Paris as an up-and-coming artist whose works would soon sell. To celebrate, he treated them all to a round of Pernod after the meal. That was the first time I'd seen him drink alcohol. Until then, he'd held a hand over his glass when I came around with the evening's wine. I wondered what had changed, but it wasn't my place to ask.

Then I heard him brag that his brother, a Parisian art dealer, was coming to visit soon, and Monsieur Vincent hoped to convince him to move to Auvers. The group toasted the two brothers.

Later, though, an argument broke out between Monsieur Vincent and the other painters. As far as I could tell, it had to do with the colors he chose for his paintings.

"They're just not real. They make your work look like a school-child painted it," an Austrian artist said.

Monsieur Vincent replied with a curse, and the table lit up with raised voices. I hurried over and urged them to quieten themselves, as they were upsetting the other diners. After that, they were less raucous, but the other three artists soon pushed back their chairs and stormed out of the restaurant, anger etched on their faces.

Monsieur Vincent sat alone and drank three more glasses of Pernod before finally weaving his way up the stairs. I shook my head, reflecting sadly that the wonderful artist was sometimes overtaken by the not-so-wonderful man.

Chapter 9

I can't change the fact that my paintings don't sell. But the time will come when people will recognize that they are worth more than the value of the paints used in the picture.—Vincent van Gogh

THE NEXT DAY, I RECEIVED a telegram from my brother, saying he couldn't come to France until September at the earliest. He wondered if that would be all right with me. In his tactful way, he was really asking whether I thought Maman would still be alive in September.

I considered how to respond. I would've loved to hear his dear voice and to consult with him on what to do for our mother. I'd heard that telephones were common in America, but none existed in our area of France. Sadly, the written word would have to do.

After two days of working and reworking my response, I sent Émile a terse telegram: "Come sooner if you can." Since I couldn't predict the future, that was all I could offer. If Maman was still alive when he came, they could say their goodbyes. But as much as I hated to admit it, September might be too late.

Just thinking about what the next few months were likely to bring was enough to make me want to lie down and not get up again until everything was over. Maybe the doctor was wrong and Maman would live another two or three years. I decided to go to Mass and pray to have at least two more years with her.

THE CHILDREN AND I attended Mass every Sunday, which meant I had to prepare the midday meal early, and as soon as we arrived back home, I would set to work serving the tourists. Arthur sometimes joined us at church, but more often, he preferred to stay home and read the newspapers while he ate his breakfast. Most of the other inns closed all day on Sundays, but the Ravoux Inn stayed open until after the midday meal. Since June had finally arrived, tourists were plentiful, and they were willing to pay high prices for the excellent food I prepared. Things had been going so well that I'd even been increasing the quantities of my servings again.

As soon as the meal was over, Arthur locked the front door and pulled down the shades, which meant we had the afternoon to ourselves. Monsieur Vincent had arranged to paint Adeline's portrait that day. The timing worked well since she was still wearing the pretty blue frock she'd chosen for church.

When I'd mentioned to Arthur that Monsieur Vincent had offered to paint a portrait of our daughter as practice, he'd shrugged and said that was fine as long as he didn't have to pay for it. As soon as the artist got out his paints, Arthur took off to fish in the Oise River. I was relieved to see him go because I wanted to watch the painting develop instead of waiting on Arthur.

Monsieur Vincent asked Adeline to sit on a chair in the empty dining room, and he went to work. First, he arranged her with her face in profile and her hands in her lap. Adeline wasn't happy with the posture and moved slightly so she could stare at him out of the corners of her eyes. He laughed and allowed her to stay in that position. After that, he gently reproved her whenever she moved, and she would huff but resume the assigned position.

He started by drawing a few studies of her profile. They were small, fast sketches done with a charcoal pencil. When he was satisfied, he went to work with his brush. He surprised me by first painting a blue outline of Adeline's neck, bodice, head, and profile. In a short time, Adeline herself appeared on the canvas. From then on, he applied the paint thickly, with quick strokes.

I sat behind Monsieur Vincent with Germaine on my lap and watched the process. It was so fascinating I could've sat there all afternoon. Unfortunately, before long, Germaine began whining about being restrained. When I set her down, the little girl toddled over to her sister and lifted her arms to be picked up. Although Monsieur Vincent was gracious about the interruption, that clearly wouldn't work.

I had no choice but to take Germaine out of the room. As I reluctantly left, he turned to me and gave me a friendly wink. I grinned and nodded, pleased that he'd even noted my presence.

I packed some things and walked with Germaine down to the river, where I spread a quilt out on the grass so that we could have a good view of the boats going by. For a while, I held her hand to keep her from wandering off, but she was happy to pick wildflowers to make a posy. As I gradually relaxed, I daydreamed about scooping up both of my daughters and boarding a big boat, and the three of us would go out for adventure. Nothing horrible would befall us, and we'd happily live out our lives on the boat. Well, Monsieur Vincent could accompany us if he wished, and he would give me art lessons as we drifted down the river. And we would flirt if we wanted, without fear of reprisals.

I picked up my sketch pad and drew the river as well as I could. Afterward, I held it out and saw that the picture wasn't bad. The river flowed from one edge of the paper to the other, with boats placidly drifting by. I wondered how a placid life would look and feel. I hadn't known it since before I married Arthur, but I relaxed for a while in the memory of languid days, laughter, and hope.

When we returned to the inn a couple of hours later, I put Germaine down for a nap and went looking for Monsieur Vincent and

Adeline. Their painting session had ended and the room had been tidied, but Adeline was nowhere to be found. She'd probably gone out with her new friends. The school year was almost over, and Adeline would be much easier to be around if she had friends to spend time with during the summer.

Monsieur Vincent was working on the painting in the Artists' Room, but he refused to show it to me. The friendly artist I knew had disappeared, and he had been replaced by a grumbling man who grew irritated at my interruption. I sulked and took myself off to my bedroom for a nap, wondering why I'd bothered to offer my daughter as his subject. Just because his landscapes were beautiful didn't mean he could paint people well.

ON MONDAY AFTERNOON, Arthur and I sat together in the café to discuss the budget, and to my surprise, the discussion was relatively congenial. We'd made it through May—barely—and business was steadily increasing. Arthur had been much easier to get along with in recent weeks, and I wondered whether that was because of the financial situation or if his mistress was taking the edge off his temper. The bruises on my arms had healed, and I appreciated every day in which nothing bad happened. Still, I wasn't about to let down my guard. Arthur was nothing if not mercurial.

As I sipped my tea and listened to my husband drone on about liquor sales, I mused about the trials of life. *How is it that terrible things can happen, including violence and betrayal, yet a person can absorb them like a sponge and continue to move forward? And yet, what choice do I have?* I couldn't exactly return to my mother's home.

Thoughts of Maman's declining health made me lose track of what Arthur was saying. I didn't want to ask him to repeat himself, so Monsieur Vincent's intrusion was a welcome relief. The artist carried a medium-sized canvas into the café and leaned it against a table at eye level.

He was smiling as he asked, "What do you think?"

I leaned forward, eager to see what he had done with our daughter's likeness, but I bit my lip and sucked in my breath when I saw what he presented.

The painting was definitely of Adeline, with her dark-blue dress and ponytail tied with a blue ribbon. Although her face was mostly in profile, her eyes peered out the side toward the viewer. Her expression was solemn, which was appropriate for a portrait, but she looked almost angry, or at the very least, irritated. Adeline might have been preparing to scold the painter for taking so long to finish. She definitely wasn't the happy girl I'd experienced in recent days.

My stomach sank because I knew Arthur would hate the painting. I stared at it for several moments as I tried to think of something positive to say. Finally, I came out with, "My, it's really *blue*, with her dress and the background reflected in her eyes."

In an angry voice, Arthur burst out, "It doesn't look like her. Oh, maybe she'll look like that in ten years, but I don't see my little girl in the picture. What have you done to her, monsieur?"

Monsieur Vincent sucked on his pipe as he stared at the portrait. "Ah, I am trying to paint portraits which will appear as revelations to people in a hundred years' time. I'm not trying to create a photographic likeness but to use color to exalt character. Did I make a mistake with her character?"

Her *character*? Other artists spoke of likeness, not character. *Has Monsieur Vincent captured Adeline's true character instead of the part she shows us, her parents?*

As I tried to formulate my thoughts, Arthur slammed a hand down on the table. "Monsieur, I know you are doing this for the practice, but I don't think it looks like her. She is far sweeter than she's shown here." He shook his head. "I don't like it. At all."

Monsieur Vincent calmly nodded, sucking on his pipe. He turned to me. "And you, madame?"

Oh dear. What can I say that won't alienate either of these men? "You have captured her likeness, but not as she is today. Possibly as she will be as an adult." I bit my lip. "I'm sorry, monsieur. I wish I had something more positive to say."

After a long silence, the painter asked, "Shall I paint another one and see if you are more pleased with it?"

Arthur shook his head. "She's too busy to pose for you again. She's taking her exams this week, and I don't want her to be distracted."

"Very well. I shall paint a second one from the sketches I've already made, and then I will give you a choice about which one you would like, if either." He picked up the painting and headed toward the back room. "Good day, then."

I released my held breath and spoke before thinking about how to soften my words. "You might have been a little more encouraging, you know. He tried so hard, poor man."

I winced, wondering if I'd gone too far in criticizing Arthur. His reaction usually depended on his mood and how much he'd had to drink.

Thankfully, he just grunted. "It's a good thing he's not trying to earn his living by painting portraits. And that his brother pays his bills." He snorted. "His paintings won't last a hundred years. People will probably use them for kindling."

I wanted to speak up for Monsieur Vincent, who had clearly painted an accomplished portrait even if it didn't look like our thirteen-year-old daughter. But I dared not push Arthur further. "Maybe the next one will be better. His paintings are an acquired taste, I think. I wonder how Adeline will respond."

He exchanged his coffee for a beer and took a swallow. "Where were we?"

WHEN ADELINE RETURNED from school and saw the painting, she was furious. "I don't look like that. That girl doesn't resemble me at all!" She stamped her foot. "I can't believe I spent an entire afternoon sitting still for *that*. Can we ask him to paint over it or something?"

I shook my head. "No. It's his painting, and he's practicing doing portraits. He's going to do another one, though, and maybe you'll like it better. Now, if you don't mind, would you collect the eggs before you study? Oh, and play with Germaine for a while, will you? She's been missing you. Thanks, dear."

The girl stomped off in a huff.

That same evening, Monsieur Vincent presented us with a different painting. In the new one, he'd shown Adeline sitting at the same angle but with a more neutral expression.

"Maybe you like this one better?" he asked.

Arthur shrugged and said nothing.

The painting was definitely less objectionable, but it also made Adeline seem less interesting. "Her dress is still blue, but it's a lighter shade than in the other one," I said. "Thank you, monsieur. I *do* like it."

"Then it is yours." He placed it on a chair, nodded, and walked out.

Arthur turned to me. "He did it that fast? It's only been a few hours since he showed us the first one."

I smiled. "He's quick, I agree. But this one looks more like her, don't you think? Shall we hang it in the dining room?"

"No. I don't want to look at it. It's better, but still not good. Put it wherever I don't have to see it."

Chapter 10

The French air clears up the brain and does good—a world of good.
-Vincent van Gogh

AS PROMISED, THE JUNE days presented themselves gloriously, one after the other—sunshine, a few clouds, an occasional shower, warm temperatures, and plenty of tourists who entered the inn's small shop and ate at its restaurant.

Adeline finished her exams and, to everyone's relief, passed them. She would enter a private lycée for girls in the fall. Until then, school was out for the summer. In the afternoons, Adeline often shirked her chores and slipped out of the inn without permission for a few hours. When I asked her about her absences, she replied vaguely. I was too exhausted from struggling with my problems to pay much attention. After all, I had sneaked out when I was her age, and nothing terrible had happened. I promised myself, though, that I would look into what was going on with her as soon as things calmed down a little. Until then, I would give her a little leeway because the past year had been brutal for all of us.

My mother was failing far more rapidly than I'd believed possible. No matter how hard I prayed for a miracle, Maman would clearly not be making a full recovery. I started going to Paris twice weekly, on Mondays and Wednesdays, to give the nurse and my aunt a break from the sickroom. Arthur wasn't happy with the new arrangement,

70

but since we hadn't been able to repay the loan to my mother, he didn't try to keep me from her side.

During my visit on Wednesday, Maman grabbed my hands and repeated the words "Forgive me—please forgive me" over and over. She wouldn't turn her attention to anything else or tell me what she'd done that required forgiveness. When I said I forgave her, she wouldn't accept my words. Nothing made sense. Except for the difficult conversation we'd had after Arthur beat me, my mother had always been wonderful. Finally, I decided her mind must be failing, and the thought brought me to tears. I tried to hide them, but I was more than ready to leave when my aunt returned from shopping.

More than anything else, I looked forward to my Thursday-afternoon drawing lessons. I hoped the joy of losing myself in creativity and beauty with Monsieur Vincent for a few hours would compensate for the feeling of having my soul sucked from my body every time I saw my mother sliding toward death. The guilt for having those feelings often kept me from sleeping. I walked around the inn most days in an exhausted stupor.

The only thing that helped was drawing. I'd drawn something every day since my first lesson the week before—wine glasses, a loaf of bread, a stuffed animal. The act of moving my pencil soothed my nerves even though I hadn't improved much.

I still hadn't mentioned the lessons to Arthur, mostly because I wasn't sure what I would do if he refused to allow them. He was always gone on Thursdays, though, so I was safe for the time being.

Earlier in the week, Monsieur Vincent had asked me what I wanted to draw during our lesson, so I suggested we try flowers again. On Thursday morning, I went out early to pick wildflowers in the countryside and arranged them inside a red vase. It was striking, I thought, and would make a delightful picture. I had also purchased some of the new wax crayons in a Parisian art store, and I would use them to color my drawing once it was good enough.

When Thursday afternoon finally arrived, Monsieur Vincent and I settled in to draw and paint in a clearing between the inn and the river. That time, the drawing went much more easily. I made a decent likeness of the flowers and vase in less than an hour and set about adding color. I was so excited about my work that I even forgot about my tutor's presence.

At some point, I glanced up and saw him standing beside me, watching me work. I jumped. "Oh, monsieur, you startled me. Is everything all right?"

He looked at my sketchpad then frowned. In a gentle voice, he said, "I... I don't know how to ask this, madame, but I feel as though I must. The colors you are adding are appropriate and nicely enhance the drawing, it is true, but I notice that your flower arrangement is quite small, taking up only half of your page. Is there some reason you've made it so small? I hope I'm not being impertinent, but I wonder if you are trying to make yourself small, in addition to the flowers. Is all well in your life?"

Stunned by the accuracy of his observation, I sat completely still for several moments and did my best to hold back the tears that threatened to overflow. Despite my efforts, I ended up sobbing into my hands. I cried for my mother, certainly, but also for myself—a person who only felt large enough to fill up half of the page in her own life.

Monsieur Vincent handed me a clean handkerchief, which I gratefully held to my dripping nose. He placed a hand on my shoulder, and the warmth of it provided a grounding sensation that eventually helped me find my way back to a sense of calm. Gradually, the tears stopped.

He removed his hand and stepped back. When he spoke, his voice was tender but very sad. "I'm so sorry, madame. I've never been good at being tactful, and I fear I've put my foot in my mouth again.

Shall I get you some water or something to eat? Or call someone for you?"

I shook my head and looked down at my drawing, finally seeing what he saw. The flowers were tiny, just as he'd observed. It looked like the work of a person who was too frightened to express herself—in other words, me.

"I... I don't know what to say. You're exactly right." I wasn't willing to confide to this near stranger about my struggling marriage and my fear of my husband, but I could explain part of the problem. "My mother is quite ill in Paris and has not long to live, I fear. I don't know how I'll be able to go on without her." I dried my eyes, smoothed my skirt, and stared up at him. Not at all sure what I wanted from him, I waited to see what he would do.

He relit his pipe and puffed on it then nodded. "I've heard something of the sort, and you have my sympathy. I apologize for prying. This must be a very difficult time for you. Shall we stop our session now?"

My eyes widened, and I shook my head. "Please, no. This is my favorite time of the week. I'd like to try again, if you don't mind."

"Most certainly. While you're doing that, I will take a walk down to the river. I am planning to paint a picture of the boats one day soon, so I need to make some sketches. Please join me when you're ready."

"Oh, did you finish your painting?"

He nodded, and I rose to look at it. His painting took up the entire canvas, from bottom to top, and ran off both sides. The colors were lovely, and the painting was bold without being overly so. In fact, it gave me a feeling of peace.

"It's wonderful. I see what you mean about filling up the space." I hesitated. "I'll join you in a few moments, after I've outlined the flowers. If you're willing, maybe you would look at it again?"

"Certainly." He smiled and meandered down the path toward the river.

I took a breath and started again. That time, I outlined all the flowers and their vase as it sat on the table, taking the shapes to the edges of the page, then filled them in with charcoal. The crayons could wait until I had a good likeness.

After twenty minutes, I was reasonably pleased with the drawing. I carried it with me as I walked to the river and joined Monsieur Vincent, who was sketching pictures of the boats in a small book.

When I stood beside him, he glanced up and studied the drawing I held out. "Ah, yes, that is a much more commanding picture. It fills out the page nicely."

I let out the breath I'd been holding and smiled. "Thank you, monsieur, for your honesty. I can see that creating art requires one to delve deeply into one's... psyche, for want of a better word."

"Ah, so you are a purveyor of Greek mythology. Psyche, the beautiful princess who fell in love with Eros, god of love, and went through terrible trials before being allowed to marry him." He nodded and puffed on his pipe.

I wondered if he had willfully misunderstood my meaning or if I was being too vague. I cleared my throat and tried again. "Actually, I was using it to mean something like the soul. I suppose artists must be in touch with the depths of their souls in order to create honest art." Speaking of depths, I was out of mine and wished I could take back my pontification. I abruptly stopped speaking.

He laughed. "I don't think all artists are that deep or that honest. Look around you. Most of the art you see is pure garbage." He paused. "The road of art is difficult, I agree, but worthwhile, at least for me. I can't imagine what else I would do although my family would love for me to find something that would bring in more money. Or *some* money, even." He laughed again, and the somber mood broke.

We chatted about ordinary things for a few more moments until I needed to leave. I touched his arm and said, "Thank you again for pointing out what you saw. I want to learn, and I appreciate your willingness to help me even if it is uncomfortable for both of us."

He smiled, his eyes crinkling. "It is my pleasure, madame. Very much my pleasure." He hesitated then added, "My brother and his family are coming to Auvers to visit this Sunday afternoon. I hope you will have the opportunity to meet them."

"Why, yes, I look forward to it." I smiled and took my leave.

THAT NIGHT, MONSIEUR Vincent did not appear for dinner, and I wondered what had detained him. He hadn't spoken about having other plans, but I reminded myself that I wasn't his wife. Or his sister, I hastened to add to my thoughts.

After dinner, when the last guests were lingering over their desserts, Monsieur Vincent stumbled in the front door. He reeked of cheap perfume and was outstandingly drunk, very close to falling down. I realized he must've gone to one of the town's brothels. He wandered into the billiard room and challenged a player to a game. The other man politely demurred, and Monsieur Vincent roared his indignation.

Adeline and I exchanged horrified looks. *Can he be the same man who'd been so sensitive and thoughtful in our lesson just this afternoon?* Something must have led him to this excessive behavior. Whatever it was, I would need to intervene.

I took a breath and moved into the billiard room, where he was still shouting. If the confrontation went on much longer, a fight would likely ensue. As soon as I placed my hand on his arm, though, he stopped and looked down at me, grinning a little.

"Please, monsieur, you have had too much to drink. I must ask you to vacate these premises until you're under control."

He blanched and backed away from my hand. "Sorry. So sorry, madame. I'll go to my room." And he made his way up the stairs, holding onto the banister. In a short while, his door slammed.

The other man shook his head before returning to his game. On shaky legs, I walked back into the dining room and sat at an empty table. Adeline sat beside me.

"You know, Maman," she said, "he has a terrible reputation in town. He's always asking people to pose for him, but he does it in such an aggressive way that they're frightened of him. He's too intense. And the boys tease him all the time because he's so odd. It's not just the ear, though. So much of it is his manner. And I hear he gets drunk a lot in the poacher's bar at the edge of town. That may have been where he was tonight."

Oh, my. I didn't know how to respond to Adeline's words. The only good thing about her report was that she appeared to be unaware of the brothels on the other side of town.

"Uh, how do you know all this?" I asked. "Until now, he has seemed to be really nice."

Adeline shook her head. "Oh, Maman, it's common knowledge. If you ever got out of this place, you'd know too."

I shrugged and shook my head. "We'll wait to see how it goes. But I hope you're not spending time with the boys who tease him."

Adeline sniffed. "That's ridiculous." She stood and walked to her room.

Someone would surely tell Arthur about tonight's fracas, and I hoped he wouldn't ask the artist to leave when he found out what had happened. Monsieur Vincent was a complicated man with many faults, it was true, but he seemed the only person in my world who understood me and sympathized with my plight.

THE NEXT DAY, MONSIEUR Vincent found me in the kitchen and apologized for his behavior, saying he didn't know what had gotten into him, and he offered to compensate the inn for any damage. I assured him no damage had occurred, but I hoped it wouldn't happen again. Blushing, he nodded and quickly left the inn.

Adeline, the edges of her mouth turned down in a disapproving frown, was quick to tell her father about the incident as soon as he returned from Paris. I stood at the edge of their conversation, wringing my hands and wondering why she was being so vindictive and judgmental. The situation had nothing to do with her. Maybe she was angry at Monsieur Vincent for teaching me to draw. That was the only reason I could imagine. I would need to keep a sharper eye on her in the future and ensure that the painter and I didn't appear to be overly familiar. I didn't want her to go telling more tales to her father and cause my new friend to be evicted.

Arthur laughed and said Monsieur Vincent wasn't the first guest who'd had too much to drink and gotten rowdy. He pinched his daughter's cheek and told her not to worry then went on about his business.

A little while later, I saw the two men talking. I couldn't hear their words, but the conversation ended with a handshake. Thank goodness Arthur was being his best self—as, apparently, was Monsieur Vincent. The muscles in my chest relaxed just a little.

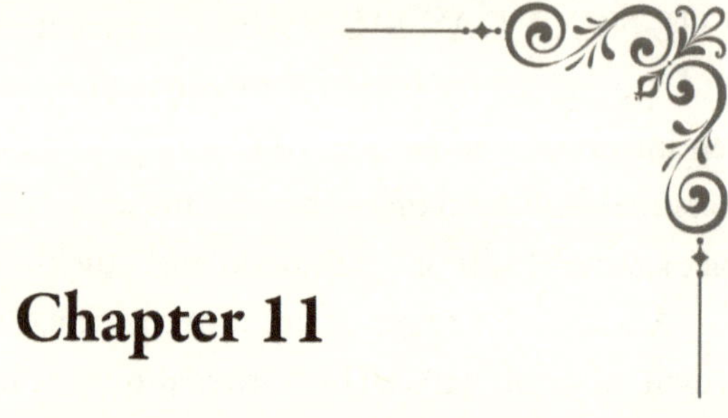

Chapter 11

The heart of man is very much like the sea. It has its storms, it has its tides, and in its depths, it has its pearls too.—Vincent van Gogh

ON SATURDAY MORNING, I received a letter from Hélène in response to my questions about divorce. With all the other chaos, I'd almost forgotten I'd written that letter. When Arthur was busy with something else, I took it into the bedroom and tore it open.

My Dear Louise,

As you requested, I asked Claude to educate me about the current divorce laws. At first, he thought I wanted to know for personal reasons, but I sweetly assured him I had no intention of divorcing him. He understood I was probably speaking of you, but he didn't ask directly. Here's what he told me.

The government changed the laws to allow divorce in 1886, but so far, it's exceedingly rare. You could apply for one, but unfortunately, Claude says it's unlikely to succeed. Divorce in the event of desertion, yes, that is possible, but for adultery, not as likely if Arthur still comes home to you.

Claude wasn't as sure about divorce in the case of violence, but he thought it would take a major beating—worse even than the last time—for the court to consider it. I hope, for your sake, that isn't happening.

I hate to say it, but your best option—legally—would be if he deserted you. It would be a difficult thing, but you could then divorce him and go about your life. Needless to say, the Church wouldn't recognize your divorce, so you might not be allowed to take Communion or remarry in the Church. But that would be the worst of it, I think.

I'm sorry to be the bearer of such bad news, my dear. We can talk more the next time we meet. I hope you're well.

Hélène

I sighed. I'd been correct that trying for a divorce wasn't the answer to my troubled marriage. Arthur might desert me, but that would be a mixed blessing. Maybe I would end up working in one of the new sewing factories, leaving my aunt to watch the children. Even worse, the court might award Arthur custody of the children. An icy chill ran through me. No, that couldn't happen. I would need to figure out something else.

After a moment, I realized that, if Arthur ever found Hélène's letter, he might do more than desert me. He might kill me. So after reading the letter twice and committing it to memory, I ran into the kitchen, fed the paper into the stove, and watched it slowly disintegrate into ash. The cook gave me a strange look, but she didn't say anything.

Afterward, feeling much better, I sat down to think. I could cope with the bruises on my arms as long as they got no worse. And I supposed I could ignore the mistress as long as Arthur continued to come home to me. As much as I loathed my husband, I didn't want to be known as a woman who couldn't keep her man.

Still, having the information was useful. I might need it someday.

AFTER SUNDAY'S MIDDAY meal, Monsieur Vincent wandered in, accompanied by a man and a woman carrying a small baby. Monsieur Vincent's excitement made him look like a different, happier man, and he walked as though his feet weren't touching the earth. He approached me as I stood beside Arthur.

"Ah, madame and monsieur, allow me to present my brother, Theo, and his wife, Jo, and their son, little Vincent." He beamed and turned to his brother. "These are the proprietors of my inn, Madame and Monsieur Ravoux and their daughters. I've painted a portrait of the older girl, along with many other scenes in this charming village."

The brothers looked very much alike except that Theo appeared to be sickly, as did the wife. Despite the mother's efforts to calm the baby, he wailed continuously while the brothers attempted to talk over the noise.

Monsieur Vincent remarked to Theo, "See how healthy the Ravoux family looks."

I inwardly groaned because he appeared to be praising Arthur and me the way he might praise a horse that was for sale: lavishly and inappropriately. He should've realized the impoliteness of mentioning other people's health status if they weren't close family. Maybe he was trying to convince his brother that his family would also look healthy if they moved to Auvers.

Then I remembered how unhealthy Germaine had been when we first moved from Paris, and how rarely she fell ill now. Maybe Monsieur Vincent had a point, and being here had some advantages, after all.

Ignoring the crass remark, I said, "Welcome to the Auberge Ravoux. We're happy you're here." I glanced at the wife, who looked increasingly uncomfortable at being unable to calm the screaming baby. "Uh, madame, would you like to go into the kitchen with the infant for some privacy? I have a chair in there where you and your child can be alone."

She nodded, looking grateful. After I showed her into the kitchen and began cleaning up the dishes, she held the baby to her breast. When he was suckling well, she said, "Thank you so much. I wasn't sure what to do. My husband means well, but he's hopeless when it comes to raising a child." She paused. "Not that I'm any more proficient, but I was leaking so much that I was about to stain my dress."

I smiled. "I remember those days. Here, let me get you some towels and a cup of tea."

When I gave them to her, she started to speak but then closed her mouth.

I squatted down so our faces were even. "Madame, was there something you wished to say?" I asked gently.

She took a breath and nodded, her eyes filled with tears. "I just wanted to know how my brother-in-law is doing. He's not an easy man, but my husband adores him."

I bit my lip. "Well, I can see what you mean about him, but I also see a big heart. Truthfully, he has been no trouble for us. But I won't mind if you and your husband want to take some of his paintings home with you. Our inn is slowly being overrun by them."

She laughed. "Oh, you don't know. Our entire apartment is overrun. Vincent's paintings cover the walls, and they're stacked under the bed, under the furniture, everywhere. Theo has tried to sell them, but no one wants to buy. Still, Theo believes in his brother, so he'll find someplace to store them until they sell. *If* they sell."

"Please don't worry. Everything will work out." With a smile, I left the mother and child to themselves.

When I returned to the restaurant, I discovered that Monsieur Vincent had taken his brother upstairs to see his room. I heard them clomping around for a few moments, then they clomped back down and out the back door to look at the paintings he'd stacked in the shed. I was relieved when their conversation turned to shipping some of the paintings to Paris. They were all wonderful, but it would be nice if some of them were elsewhere.

As soon as the wife returned with her sleeping infant, they all left. I hoped the day would continue well for Monsieur Vincent, since being with his family was obviously something he wanted very much. And now, I could close the inn for the afternoon.

WHEN ALL WAS QUIET, I decided to draw a picture of Germaine as she napped. I was in our bedroom gathering my art supplies when Arthur entered and walked to the wardrobe in the corner. I tensed, wondering if he would criticize me for trying to reclaim my interest in art. But he ignored me, for which I was thankful.

He pulled down a box, opened it, and took out a revolver. He rummaged around in the box for ammunition and finally pulled out a handful of bullets.

"What on earth is that?" I hadn't known he had a gun in his possession.

Guns were rare in our community. Occasionally, farmers would shoot at crows eating their crops, but they usually just set up scarecrows and assumed the birds would take what they needed and leave the rest. The crows weren't worth worrying about, I'd heard one say.

"It's the gun I was issued in the war. I conveniently 'lost' it when I was discharged." He turned his satisfied grin in my direction. He was speaking of the Franco-Prussian War of 1870, for which he'd been conscripted in the brutal and losing fight against Germany. He often spoke of his experiences, especially when he was drunk, and he loved to regale the bar customers with his bloody stories of stupidity and defeat. I'd stopped listening years before. He'd never mentioned, though, that he'd brought a gun home with him.

I froze. I'd never thought that Arthur might come at me with anything other than his fists. This was a new threat to my safety. Speaking carefully, I asked, "What are you planning to do with it?"

"Huh," he said, ignoring my question as he took the gun apart and checked it. After a few moments, he replied, "I talked with a farmer after Mass who's going hunting for pheasants this afternoon. He asked if I wanted to join him." He reassembled the gun. "I don't know if this relic can even shoot, but I'll try it. Maybe I'll bring back dinner."

I shuddered but had no intention of trying to talk him out of going hunting. Maybe he would shoot himself by accident, or someone would shoot him when they aimed at a pheasant. That wasn't likely, though. I wouldn't mind a plump pheasant to cook for dinner, but that was also unlikely. The gun looked old and poorly maintained, and I couldn't imagine Arthur would shoot well after so long.

I really didn't care what he did with his afternoon off. With him out of the house, I would have more time alone to indulge in my drawing project and possibly even take a nap.

Adeline went out with some girls from school to play lacrosse, a game that had recently been introduced from Scotland as an appropriate sport for females. I was glad she had something wholesome to occupy her time, and I was especially glad she was playing with girls and not boys. Maybe I would watch the game the next Sunday.

I gathered my sketchbook and went to check on Germaine. My little girl was curled up on her bed, thumb stuck in her mouth, her light-brown hair hanging in sweaty ringlets around her face. I spent half an hour quietly drawing her picture. When I finished, I thought

I'd captured the innocence of youth, as well as her charming beauty. My technique wasn't great yet, and I would ask Monsieur Vincent about the perspective, but overall, I was pleased with my rendition. For the first time, I'd drawn something I might keep and even frame.

Adeline and Arthur both returned home at dusk, tired and dusty from their time in the outdoors. Arthur hadn't killed a pheasant or any other bird, but he was happy to have made a friend and renewed an old interest in hunting.

A slow afternoon and a nap hadn't revitalized my energy. I still felt as though I was carrying the weight of the world on my shoulders. Another week lay before me, each day bringing me closer to the news I dreaded to hear about my dear mother.

Chapter 12

I TOOK ADELINE WITH me to Paris on Wednesday so she could visit her beloved grandmother, possibly for the last time. When we entered the apartment, Adeline scrunched up her nose against the smells of urine and old, unwashed body. I squeezed her hand, and she slowly walked over to the bed. In a weak voice, she said, "Hi, Mémé, it's me, Adeline."

Her grandmother gave her a wan smile. "Addie." She held Adeline's hands and told her she loved her, then she rolled over and went to sleep, her breathing as loud as a whistling teakettle. Adeline dropped her head into her hands and sobbed. I sobbed with her, but I couldn't ease her pain.

After a few moments, I realized nothing could be gained by my staying. Adeline had said her goodbyes, and Maman continued to sleep. I hoped to cheer Adeline by taking her shopping. She needed some new clothing, and since we didn't have the money to hire a dressmaker, we went to a department store. When the salesclerk fitted Adeline for her first corset, I feared I might burst into tears again. One day the horrible, confining things would surely go out of style, as bustles had, but that hadn't happened yet. Adeline agreed the tightness would take some getting used to, but it gave her the round-ed figure of a woman, for which she was thrilled.

Afterward, we went for tea and pastry. I'd prepared for this discussion because I didn't want Adeline to be as unaware of her body's functions as I had been at her age. My mother had told me very little, and I didn't want to follow in her footsteps.

Near the end of our meal, I cleared my throat. "Uh, now that you are officially a young woman, there are some things I need to tell you."

Adeline groaned. "What is it?"

I told her about getting her monthlies and that they should start soon and would continue for many years. Adeline said she'd suspected there was something she didn't know about, for the girls at school had hinted that "it" had happened to them. Now that she knew, she would be prepared, even though it sounded like no fun at all.

I agreed. "There's more." I paused. "It's about male-and-female relationships." I explained—vaguely and in a whisper so I wouldn't be overheard—the basics of how intimate relations occurred. She wouldn't need this information for years—not until she was married—but I wanted her to be prepared. I was tempted to add that I hoped she would find a man gentler and more loving than her father when the time came, but I kept that piece of advice to myself. Maybe I would work it into a conversation later, when she had a beau.

All that information seemed a bit much for Adeline to take in at once because she asked no questions and wouldn't meet my eyes. We quickly finished our tea and walked to the train station.

At home, Adeline donned one of her new dresses and wore it around the inn as she showed diners to their tables. They were mostly tourists who didn't realize the difference between that day and the day before, but Monsieur Vincent noticed the fresh new look and praised her beautiful dress.

He pulled me aside and said that, unfortunately, he would have to cancel our regular lesson that week because he'd agreed to help Dr. Gachet with a project.

Monsieur Vincent, of course, didn't know how much I needed our time together to maintain a semblance of a positive attitude. Even though I wanted to beg him to change his plans, I gave him my best smile and agreed to wait until the next week for my lesson. Without him, Thursday would just be another dull, sad day as I awaited the inevitable.

ON FRIDAY AFTERNOON, as I was showing the new cook's helper her duties, the front door burst open, and in walked the proprietor of the sidewalk farmer's market, Monsieur Masse. I'd bought many things at his stand and knew him to be a pleasant, easygoing man. But his face was bright red, and I imagined I could see steam rising from his head. He was holding Adeline and an unknown boy by their upper arms. Adeline was biting her lip and struggling to get out of the man's grip, but he held on tightly.

Something was terribly wrong. I gestured for the cook's helper to slip into the kitchen. Walking toward the group, I asked, "What has happened?" I pulled Adeline from his grip and clamped my hands onto her shoulders.

"Nothing, Maman." Adeline was trembling and breathing hard. "He's wrong. I didn't do anything."

Monsieur Masse shook his head. "I'll tell you what's wrong, young lady." To me, he said, "Look in her pocket."

Inside Adeline's skirt pocket, I found two tomatoes and held them up to him. "Are these what you're talking about?"

"Yes. She and this ruffian here"—he shook the boy, who stared at the floor—"were stealing my tomatoes. Potatoes too."

The boy focused an angry glare on me. He wasn't a local, or I'd have seen him before. About fifteen or sixteen years old, he wore a strange costume that made him look like an American cowboy: a buckskin tunic with a fringe that rippled when the farmer shook him, cowboy boots, and a rodeo hat. He also wore a gun holster with what looked like a toy gun in it.

I frowned at him. "Is that a real gun?"

The boy shook his head and, using his other hand, pulled it out. "No. A toy, madame."

Monsieur Masse shook him again. "You hush up, boy. I'll get to you in a minute." He turned to me. "What do you plan to do with her? It's the third time I've seen her steal from me, but this is the first time I've caught her red-handed."

Horrified, I took a breath and stared down at my daughter. "Is this true?"

Adeline looked at the floor and nodded, tears streaming from her eyes. "I'm sorry, Maman," she mumbled.

"All right." I took a breath and turned to the man. "I apologize for my daughter's actions. We didn't raise her to behave like this, and I assure you it won't happen again. How much do I owe you for the fruit she stole?"

He stood up taller. "I won't charge you for those, madame, if you keep her under control in the future."

"Oh, I definitely will do that. And she will work for me until she's earned enough to pay you back." I paused, staring at the boy, who continued squirming. "Now, who is this young man?"

"René Secrétan," the boy said, holding his head high and spitting out the words. "My family lives here in the summer."

I pursed my lips as I stared at him. "And how do you know my daughter?"

He glanced at Adeline then mumbled, "We met at a party a few weeks ago."

Ah. So this was why Adeline had been so happy after returning from that party. And I was willing to bet he was the reason my daughter had been regularly disappearing from the inn since then.

"What were you two planning to do with the tomatoes?"

They both stared at the floor and didn't answer.

Monsieur Masse harrumphed and said, "I've heard about a group of young people who throw tomatoes at boats as they float down the river. They hide in the bushes and dart out to throw the tomatoes then duck back in and laugh like crazy. I suspect these are the ones responsible—or at least some of them."

"Well." I took a moment to digest this information. When I was calmer, I turned toward the man. "Thank you, monsieur, for bringing her home and for letting me know what was happening. I will take care of the situation now. Adieu." I grabbed Adeline's arm and pulled her toward her bedroom.

Behind me, the man said, "Next, I will take him to his parents. *Parisians.*"

Adeline turned her head toward the young man and made a face as they were each hustled in different directions.

I pushed Adeline into her room. "Young lady, I'll need to think about what the appropriate punishment is. You will stay here until I come for you."

Adeline threw herself onto her bed, sobbing, and I marched out, slamming the door behind me.

I SAT ON MY BED AND considered what I should do. This was clearly a thing the young people did to create mischief, and no actual harm was done. I'd stolen fruit from outdoor stands myself when I was young. The difference was that I hadn't gotten caught. Adeline had. But that wasn't all. We were new in town and trying to establish a reputation as honorable people, so having a petty thief for a daughter was unacceptable.

I'd told the man that Adeline would work to earn enough money to reimburse him, and I would follow through with that. *But is that enough punishment? Probably not. What, then?*

The biggest issue was with Arthur. He would be home from Paris in a few hours, and I needed to decide what—or if—to tell him about the situation. No, I would have to tell him, for if he heard about it from someone else, that wouldn't be good.

I trembled. Arthur would likely be furious at Adeline, but the real question was what he would do about it. He hadn't hit the girl since she was small, and those were merely swats that all parents used to discipline their children. But he'd threatened twice in recent months, when he'd been drinking, to take a strap to her for being surly. I'd managed to distract him then, but I didn't think I could stand it if he beat our daughter. The girl deserved some punishment, but to receive a thrashing from her father at her age would've been unacceptable.

Maybe I should administer a switching to the girl myself and hope Arthur would accept that as enough punishment.

Just then, the cook came to my door and told me customers were waiting to be seated. "Should I do it, madame, or will you soon be out?"

Oh no. I'd wasted an hour thinking about the situation when I should've been preparing for the Friday-evening rush.

"Yes, thank you. I'll be right there."

I had only enough time to arrange my hair, smooth my skirt, and take a few breaths, then I was out the door, rushing as quickly as I could to prepare for the guests. When I had a minute, I went into Adeline's room, where my daughters were playing together with blocks.

"Adeline, I need you this evening. We'll discuss your punishment after the guests leave. I expect you to be on your best behavior."

She nodded and joined me, a sad look on her face.

ARTHUR ARRIVED AMIDST the busy evening and immediately began waiting on customers. When things had calmed down a little, he turned to me and asked, "What's wrong with Adeline? She's pouting."

"I'll tell you when it's quiet." I'd lost my chance to do anything about what had happened.

Adeline's punishment was up to Arthur now. I could only hope he would be reasonable.

When the dinner guests had left, and the only people remaining were the regulars at the bar, Arthur sat down at a table next to me.

"You can tell me now."

I related what had happened. When I finished, I asked what he thought Adeline's punishment should be, other than working at the inn until she'd earned the money to pay for what she stole.

He rubbed his face and looked around for Adeline. Huddled in the corner, she glanced from one of us to the other, an expression of terror on her face.

"Both of you, in our bedroom. Now," he said in a harsh whisper.

We all traipsed into the bedroom. I clenched my muscles, prepared to jump on him if he struck Adeline with his fist.

Inside, he closed the door. "Now, we shall deal with this."

He turned to Adeline. "You have brought shame on this family. You will not leave the inn for at least two weeks, and it will be longer if you don't wipe that pout off your face. And you will do what your mother says. Do you understand?"

She nodded, a look of surprise in her eyes at having received only a mild rebuke instead of a switching.

He dismissed Adeline, telling her to tend to the customers. When she was gone, he turned toward me. "I blame you for this. It's your job to watch over her, and you didn't do that, or else it wouldn't have happened."

My heart became a dead weight in my chest. He was blaming me for Adeline's misbehavior. I should've realized that would happen. Everything that went wrong was always my fault. I turned to leave the room, but he grabbed my arm and jerked me toward him. His grip was viselike, and pain coursed up my arm.

"You stay here. What has occupied you instead of looking after the children?"

"Worrying about my mother," I said, trying to speak assertively and not show fear. Cowering always made things worse. "Adeline disappears every day and won't tell me where she's been. I don't have time to follow her." I wanted to add that he could've watched her, too, but I didn't dare. I needed him calm, not angered further.

He pulled back a hand as though to strike my face, but he stopped and lowered his arm. Then, grabbing me by the shoulders, he shook me. My teeth rattled as I tried not to bite my tongue, and my head jerked back and forth until I feared it would fall off.

A few seconds after he started, he stopped and dropped his hands.

I could still see anger in his eyes, so I braced myself for what might follow. I wondered whether I could get out the door before he grabbed me—not likely, unless I could put some distance between us before I ran. I edged away.

"Do not sass me, woman," he said through gritted teeth. "Watching her is your job. If she gets in any more trouble, my promise will not stop me from administering your punishment." He turned and walked out of the room, slamming the door behind him.

I collapsed onto the bed and mentally scanned my body to see what might be damaged. My neck was sore, and I had a terrible headache, but that was all, other than a little dizziness. Fortunately, my teeth were all intact.

Slowly, I sat up, chastising myself for not thinking through the situation. I should've been prepared for him to blame me instead of Adeline. I wasn't sure what I might've done differently, but I should have known how Arthur would react. Obviously, I didn't.

When the dizziness abated, I walked back into the restaurant, holding myself carefully.

Adeline was sweeping the floor, her shoulders hunched and her eyes red. She must've heard what had gone on in the bedroom. I went to her and laid a hand on her shoulder, intending to speak words of comfort, but she jerked away and continued sweeping without looking at me. Apparently, I couldn't win with her, no matter what I did.

Monsieur Vincent glanced at me with concern several times, but he didn't speak. I averted my face and, as soon as I could, went into the kitchen to make myself some willow bark tea for the headache. I didn't need him to get involved in my family drama. No good could possibly come from that.

Chapter 13

AFTER A SLEEPLESS NIGHT, I woke Adeline early so that the two of us could go for a walk. She wasn't happy, but she went. Near the river, we found a bench from which we could watch the sun rise. I turned toward my daughter, who sat, sullen and tense, beside me.

"Please tell me the truth now. I won't punish you anymore, but I need to know the truth. Who else was throwing tomatoes?"

Adeline looked anywhere but at me for half a minute then mumbled, "Cécile."

"Danielle's daughter—that Cécile?"

Adeline nodded.

"But she's sixteen or seventeen. I didn't know you two were friends." I paused. "Who else?"

"She's sixteen. That's all, except for René's older brother, Gaston."

"Older brother. All these young people are at least three years older than you. What happened to the girls in your class?"

"They don't want to be friends with me anymore." Tears threatened to spill over, but Adeline brushed them away. "They think I'm stuck up since I came from Paris and I passed my exams. They didn't."

"Oh, *ma chérie*." I took her hand and held it. "It must be very lonely for you here. Whose idea was it to throw tomatoes at boats?"

After a long pause, Adeline said, "René's."

"And you all went along."

She nodded.

"All right, thank you for letting me know. But you need to realize this is a small community, and we're new here. People will judge us—all of us—for what you do. If they think we're bad people or we disrupt the community, the locals won't come to the inn, and we'll be bankrupt. I don't know what we'll do or where we'll go if that happens."

Adeline looked down at her hands as a tear splashed on them. In a small voice, she said, "I didn't think about that."

I hated having to be so firm with her, but she needed to understand our precarious situation. "I know you didn't, but in the future, I hope you will." After a short pause, I continued, "Now, let's figure out what to do from here. Cécile seems like a nice girl whom those boys also led astray. You can see her as long as you don't get into any more trouble, but you need to stay away from René and his brother. They aren't good for you." I thought for a moment. "Tell me more about René."

Adeline took a moment to answer. "He's kind of wild but fun. His brother is quiet, but René is loud and likes to play pranks on people." She hesitated. "He put a snake in Monsieur Vincent's paint box the other day, and he laughed really hard when Monsieur Vincent nearly fainted after opening the box."

"Huh." I couldn't tell if Adeline disapproved of or admired René for being wild and full of pranks. I remembered the wild boys from my childhood, who were always the most enticing. "Has he kissed you?"

The girl looked at the ground and wouldn't answer.

So he had. *Mon Dieu.* Arthur was right—I hadn't watched our daughter nearly well enough.

"Has he done anything else?"

Adeline shook her head.

I could be grateful for that, at least. Our talk the other day in Paris hadn't come a moment too soon. "All right. You know, you really should look for a more proper boy, someone your age who's been brought up well. Boys like René are fun, but they will get you into all kinds of trouble and ruin your reputation, and that's all you really have in this world. Besides, he will leave at the end of the summer."

Adeline jerked her hand from mine and stared at the ground, and I could sense the wall she was constructing around herself after hearing my unwelcome advice. Regardless, I needed to broach one more subject, and it was a tricky one.

I cleared my throat. "*Ma fille*, I know you think your father is always right about everything. But I want you to keep an open mind. We *both* love you and want the best for you."

"No." She stood and faced me. Her glare could have melted an iceberg. "You hate me. He's the only one who loves me." She turned and ran away, back toward the inn.

I shook my head. That hadn't gone well at all.

ADELINE AND I SERVED breakfast to the boarders, a heavy cloak of silence between us. Afterward, I sat alone in the restaurant with an empty teacup on the table in front of me. I wondered what I could do to fix the situation I'd inadvertently worsened.

Monsieur Vincent walked in the front door, carrying his painting kit, and came over to me. "Madame, you look like you've lost your last friend. Can I do something for you?"

I gave him a wan smile. "Thank you, monsieur. No, there's nothing. Just dealing with a family situation."

He set down his painting kit. "Would you like me to get you some more tea?"

No man had ever offered to get me tea. I couldn't possibly refuse to honor the sweet gesture. "Thank you. I would love that." I smiled up at him. "The kettle is on the stove."

"I'll be right back."

In a few moments, he placed a cup of steaming tea before me. "My mother used to say that tea works wonders for what ails you. And she wasn't even British." He laughed.

I chuckled. "Thank you. I agree with your mother."

He hesitated. "I came back to get another canvas. Is there any other way I can help you?"

"No, but thank you."

He bowed and walked up the stairs.

Adeline seemed to be attracted to men like her father instead of nice men like Monsieur Vincent. I wondered how I could help her learn from my mistake.

Sighing, I picked up my cup and took a sip.

ON SUNDAY EVENING, I set out a cold supper, and the family ate alone in the dining room. Life had regained a semblance of order after Friday night's emotional catastrophe. I'd avoided Arthur as much as possible, and Adeline had helped me with the chores, although she didn't speak unless spoken to. Of us all, Germaine was the only ray of sunshine, and her happy chatter somewhat brightened up the rest of the family.

Just as we finished our meal, someone knocked at the front door. I stared at Arthur in dismay. This had been a peaceful day, and I didn't want it ruined by having to take care of strangers.

When Arthur opened the door, a telegraph employee stood outside, an envelope in his hands. "Please give this to madame." After handing over the envelope, he held out his hand for a tip.

Arthur shook his head but reached into his pocket and gave the boy a small coin then closed the door. With a sinking feeling in my stomach, I understood that the telegram was probably bringing the bad news about my mother I'd been dreading for weeks. Arthur handed me the envelope, and I held it for a long moment, knowing my life might not be the same after I read its contents.

"I'll read it later. First, I want to enjoy a glass of wine." I placed the envelope beside my plate and picked up the glass of sparkling white wine I'd just poured.

"What is it, Maman?" asked Germaine.

That was one of her favorite sentences of late: *"What is that? What is it?"*

"Something about your grandmother, I think."

I sipped the wine slowly, wanting to draw out the time in which I didn't know the message and thus didn't have to do anything about it—five minutes, ten minutes, fifteen minutes. All eyes were on me. Adeline started to speak, but her father put a hand on her arm and shook his head.

Finally, I set down the empty glass, took a deep breath, and reached for the envelope.

Inside, the message read, "COME NOW. STOP. CLAUDIA IN COMA. STOP."

I inhaled deeply and stared at the words I'd predicted would alter my world. Wordlessly, I handed the paper to Arthur, and Adeline read it over his shoulder.

"Oh," breathed Adeline. "Does that mean she's dying?"

She placed a hand on my shoulder, and I could feel it tremble. Or maybe my shoulder was shaking instead. I wasn't sure.

"Probably." I stared at nothing while my mind moved as rapidly as an arrow flying through a forest.

It was too late to contact Émile. Even if he was en route, he wouldn't arrive in time. Also, I would need to stay in Paris for at least a few days, so I had to ask the cook to prepare the meals I'd planned. Without my guidance, she would not create the refined experience I usually offered our guests, but nothing could be done about that.

I shook my head, wondering why I was even thinking about those trivialities at such a time. Maybe more wine would help.

I forced my mind back to the issue at hand. I would need to stay with my aunt until my mother died. Then we would plan the funeral. *Funeral.* What a dreadful word. I should set out the children's clothes because I couldn't depend on Arthur to know what was appropriate. And I should pack my black wool dress, the one I saved for terrible occasions.

But what if Maman doesn't die quickly? I'd heard of people lingering in comas for months, and the thought caused me to shiver. Maybe she would awaken and be herself again. People could come out of comas and be well afterward, I thought.

Of its own accord, my hand reached for the glass. I brought it to my mouth but discovered it was empty. Just like my life—empty.

Suddenly, I returned to myself. No, my dear mother was not likely to awaken. *No use hoping for a miracle now.* I'd prayed and prayed, but God hadn't seen fit to grant me one. *I must prepare for the worst.*

I set down the glass and pushed back my chair. "If I hurry, I can catch the last train to Paris tonight. I'll pack for a few days. Adeline, will you clear the table and wash the dishes? Arthur, you'll need to take care of Germaine. Make sure she uses the privy before she goes to sleep, or you'll end up with wet sheets." My voice sounded hollow, detached from my body. I leaned over and kissed Germaine, who stared at me, clearly confused about what was happening.

I rushed to my bedroom and packed a valise. Before I left, I kissed everyone and assured them I would send letters or telegrams to keep them informed.

Exuberant tourists returning home to Paris from their Sunday outings filled the train. I found a seat and tried not to be annoyed by their happy tales of the weekend.

As I stared out the window at the night rushing by, memories of Maman flooded over me. When I was a tiny girl, she'd read me to sleep every night. And when I grew a little older, we would spend every Wednesday together, visiting the museums in Paris. I especially loved looking at paintings of Parisian street scenes, and she would patiently explain the artistic techniques as well as she could. Afterward, she took me to lunch, and we talked about whatever had interested me during the day. She'd instilled in me a love of art for which I had probably never adequately thanked her. Later, despite Papa's objections that girls couldn't paint, she'd hired an art tutor who came to the house and gave me lessons.

She'd been my model for how to be a good mother. That was why I'd been so shocked at her response to Arthur's beating. As far as I could remember, it had been her only lapse.

AUNT ELLA OPENED THE door, tears streaming down her cheeks. "Oh, my dear, you made it. I'm so glad you've come."

She led me into the salon where Maman, cheekbones jutting from her pale, drawn cheeks, was struggling to breathe. The nurse moved around her, tucking in the sheet and rubbing lotion on her dried hands.

"Please speak softly," she said to me, "because I'm told that hearing is the last sense to go. I do not want her to be upset when she breathes her last."

I pulled up a chair and held the hand that was cooler than it had been just a few days before. "Maman, I'm here. Please wake up."

No response—just continued raspy breathing. The breaths were uneven, often with long spaces in between. I glanced at the nurse questioningly.

"This is the way it is, at the end. She has never died before, so she doesn't know how to do it. But her body will show her the way, and after a bit of practice, her soul will fly away to heaven."

I rubbed my face with a hand that felt almost unbearably warm after the coldness of Maman's. "What can I do?"

"There's nothing, really. You might read to her from the Bible or her favorite book."

My mother's favorite book was—I didn't know. And I might never know. My tears fell onto the sheet. Then my aunt placed a book into my hands.

"Shakespeare's sonnets were some of her favorites. She turned down the pages of the ones she especially liked."

I nodded my thanks and opened the book, which fell open to "Sonnet 9." My voice broke, but I read aloud through that sonnet and on to the next. And the next. I lit a lamp and continued to read. At some point, I couldn't read any more, and the book dropped from my hands.

Suddenly, I jerked awake. Something was different. After a moment, I realized Maman had stopped breathing. What must have awakened me was the silence.

I waited, but there was no breath. Only silence.

I picked up her cold hand and kissed it then closed her eyes and mouth as I pictured her soul leaving her body, turning around to wave goodbye to those she loved, then flying up to heaven as the nurse had described. Then I leaned over the inert body and sobbed until no more tears were left.

When dawn came, I was under control again. I would see no more beautiful smiles from her when I walked in the door, hear no more eager questions about how my girls were doing, and share no more walks through the parks together. Also, I had no more need to worry about Maman's health—and no more berating myself for not paying enough attention to her.

No more. No more.

When my aunt awoke, exhaustion washed over me, and I went into Maman's room to take a nap. After a long, dreamless sleep, I awoke and discovered that in my absence, the nurse had packed her belongings and left, the doctor had certified the death, and Aunt Ella had sent a telegram to Émile, telling him the news. All that remained to be done was to prepare the body and plan the funeral.

I took a few moments to draw a rough sketch of my mother's face in death. We hadn't thought to hire a photographer, so this would be the last likeness of her ever to exist. My skills were not great, but the drawing looked a bit like her. The next week, I would show it to Monsieur Vincent and see how he might fix it.

Later, the priest came. The undertaker came. Neighbors came. The machinery of dealing with death took over.

AS EXPECTED, THE FUNERAL mass was long and grueling. The priest spoke, the choir sang, and music rang out from the pipe organ. Everyone cried. By the time it was over, I felt as if my soul had flown away to join my mother's. I wasn't used to having no feelings at all, but at that point, I was an empty vessel.

Back at the apartment, my aunt and I served visitors a variety of cakes and other treats that the patisserie around the corner had provided. One by one, the mourners left. Finally, finally, the only people remaining were Aunt Ella, Arthur, the children, and me. I collapsed onto a chair, so exhausted that I could barely force my eyelids to remain open.

"I need to help Aunt Ella clean out Maman's things," I told Arthur. "I'll be back tomorrow or the next day."

"Do you think you'll be home by Friday? People are asking for you, and I don't know what to tell them."

I nodded. "All right. That will give me two days to put things in order."

Two days probably wouldn't be nearly enough to do all that I needed to do, but my family needed me. On the other hand, since Maman was gone, I had no reason to rush.

I kissed the children goodbye. Adeline looked shaken and gave me a quick hug, but Germaine clung to me like she would never see me again. Reassuring her that I would be home soon took most of an hour.

After Arthur and the children left, Aunt Ella and I straightened the salon then stood, looking at each other.

"It seems woefully quiet in here without hearing her breathing," Ella said. The older woman cried as I took her in my arms. After we separated a long while later, she wiped her eyes. "I think I'll retire, if you don't mind."

"Not at all. I'll see you in the morning."

I went into my mother's bedroom and sat on the bed, my tired mind moving through the things that still needed to be done before I could return to my own room, my own bed, and my daughters.

I would start in the morning.

Chapter 14

In fighting the difficulties, the inmost strength of the heart is developed.
–Vincent van Gogh

AFTER BREAKFAST, I opened my mother's desk. In the top drawer, I found sealed envelopes—letters, I presumed—addressed to Émile and me. I set aside Émile's to mail to him and turned mine over in my hands, apprehensive that it, like the telegram I'd received a few days before, would change my life. Finally, I broke the seal and opened the letter, dated six weeks before.

> *My dear Louise,*
>
> *You have been the best daughter a mother could hope for, and I love you dearly. Please don't grieve for me, because I've had a good life and am ready to go.*
>
> *There is something I must confess to you before I die. Do you remember when Denis left for London and didn't contact you again? We didn't tell you, but he wrote to us, asking your papa's blessing to marry you. He said he would provide for you handsomely, but you would need to move to London to be with him. Your papa was inclined to accept the offer or at least discuss it with you, but I couldn't bear the thought of you being so far away. So, in the end, he told Denis you*

would soon be betrothed to another and advised him to let you go.

I watched you wait for many long months for a letter that never came, and I ached at seeing your long face and dejected attitude. I even wrote to Denis and told him we had reconsidered, but he was already betrothed to another. After you accepted that you wouldn't hear from him, you dutifully followed your papa's direction about marrying Arthur.

Unfortunately, I have seen that your marriage is loveless as well as violent. I'm so very sorry, my dearest one. Sorry doesn't begin to describe the daily anguish I have felt at seeing your unhappiness. I had hoped things would work out for you with Arthur, and I thought you would be happier if you stayed in France, but the choice should have been yours, not mine. I have regretted my decision every day since then. But that regret is useless to fix the situation. I know I should have confessed to you years ago and borne your justified anger, but sadly, I had not the courage.

When Germaine was so sick last year, Arthur came to me with a plan for your family to start anew as innkeepers in Auvers. The plan required that I sell our home and give him money for the down payment. My darling, I knew I was sick, and it seemed to be the only thing I could do for you. Now, I see how unhappy you are away from Paris and your friends, and I blame myself for that as well.

To partially atone for my sins, I have left you the money I received from the sale of our home and your father's business. You may share some with Émile if you choose, but I've told him you need it more than he does. I hope you do not tell

Arthur about it but instead use it to chart your life's course in whatever way you choose.

Know that I've always loved you even though I made a terrible mistake. I hope one day you will forgive me.

Your loving mother,

Claudia Touillet

I read the letter over several times before its horrible message settled deep into my bones. I'd thought reading the telegram was bad, but this was infinitely worse. *My beloved mother sabotaged my life to keep me in France? How selfish could one person be?*

A rage grew in my chest, so huge and hot that it threatened to subsume me. Wondering where Maman would have kept her money, I rushed to her bureau and jerked open the top drawer. Inside were stacks of francs, more than I'd ever seen before.

For a moment, my mind could not process what I was seeing. Something about the situation seemed awfully familiar, but I couldn't remember what. Finally, I recalled the recurring dream in which I reached out for a pile of money, only to find it slipping through my fingers. I must have somehow anticipated this exact moment.

Moving slowly and carefully, I touched a stack with the tip of a finger and started when it fell over, clanking on the drawer. I tried to determine the number of coins but quickly lost count—maybe hundreds of them: gold and silver twenty-franc and five-franc coins, single francs, and various amounts of centimes, as well as banknotes in denominations of twenty to two hundred. *This is a fortune.*

I wondered how my mother had saved up so much. I'd thought she had given most, if not all, of her money to Arthur so that we could lease the inn. Apparently, I'd been wrong.

I shook my head in dismay. So much money—mine now—and it didn't even begin to compensate for the terrible wrong my mother had done me.

I slammed the drawer shut and let rage fill me. Never in my life had I been so angry. Maman had been right to wait until she was dead to let me know the extent of her perfidy. Otherwise, I might not have been able to restrain myself from doing something equally dreadful in response.

Now, nothing was left to do but accept the truth. I lay on the bed, and my entire world filled with a bright-red haze—around me, inside me. Hours passed before the rage diminished. When I was calmer, I carried the letter out to my aunt and dropped it in her lap.

In a clipped voice, I asked, "Would you read this, please, and let me know what you think?"

Aunt Ella shook her head. "*Ma chérie*, I've already read it. Claudia showed it to me after she wrote it and asked me to look out for you when you read it. She knew you'd be upset—"

"Upset?" The rage came again, bigger and brighter, until I was a dragon with flames shooting from my mouth. I breathed deeply, in and out, until the flames died down enough for me to speak. "I passed upset a while ago. I'm livid. No, furious. No, devastated." I kicked an ottoman across the room then sat on a chair, dropped my head into my hands, and sobbed.

Aunt Ella knelt before me. "She didn't know how to tell you. She was so sick and so sorry, but she didn't know how to tell you."

"Telling me wasn't the big problem. Doing it was what was devastating. She ruined my life. I don't know how to go on from here." I lifted my haunted eyes to meet my aunt's. "What do I do now?"

Aunt Ella thought for a moment then patted my knee. "I know this sounds banal, given all you've been through, but I think you should go for a walk." A slight smile turned up the corners of her mouth. "You've always liked to walk. After that, go to a department store and buy yourself whatever you want. Maybe a grand lunch or a new dress. Something to reward yourself for being so dutiful all these years." She gave me a rueful smile.

"And when you're finished, come back here, and let everything settle in. Claudia was very frugal, wanting to leave you as much as she could. Your father's business sold for more than they expected, and she could've lived more lavishly, but saving was her penance for her mistake. It was all she could do for you, but she did it well. You're a wealthy woman now."

I sat back, shocked. "I thought she was poor."

Aunt Ella shook her head. "Not at all. She left you enough so you can make different choices if you wish. That was what she most wanted for you, to have choices of your own, after she'd taken them from you when you were younger."

"Well." I shook my head. "I... I think I'll do as you suggest. And then I'll make some changes, but I'm not sure what yet."

Aunt Ella pulled out a basket for me to carry so that I would appear to be doing my daily shopping. I kissed my aunt goodbye and headed out.

I revisited the places Denis and I had frequented. Those included his painting studio and the many places we'd set up our easels together. So much was changing in Paris—older buildings had been torn down to construct larger, fancier buildings. The charming city I'd grown up in was gone, and people were moving farther out to make way for the museums, department stores, and theatres being built. That wasn't a bad thing, but the new city felt unfamiliar to me, as I felt to myself.

I stopped at À la Méré de Famille for some chocolate then walked to the Square

d'Orléans to sit beside the fountain and eat. The small, historic park where Chopin had lived was only a block from my parents' old apartment, and it had always been my favorite place to sit and think.

That day, my thoughts were jumbled almost beyond repair. My custom was to push away difficult thoughts when I couldn't do anything about them, but I couldn't push these away. One by one, they came.

Denis had loved me enough to approach my father by letter. He'd probably been devastated when he received my father's response. But many years had passed, and he was surely married, with children of his own. I wanted to write to him immediately, but I wouldn't intrude upon his life. Besides, I was married, too, and I'd already discovered divorce wasn't an option.

The mother I'd loved wasn't the good person I'd always thought but someone whose selfishness had betrayed her own daughter.

I walked on, all the way to the Jardin des Tuileries, where I sat on a bench and watched lovers stroll, arm in arm, around the reflecting pool. I'd never felt more alone in my life.

Finally, exhausted, I backtracked to the Printemps Haussmann department store, where I ate a huge lunch served with several glasses of wine. Feeling slightly better, I bought myself a new pair of shoes. All my shoes were worn and no longer stylish. At least my feet would be happy while I considered what to do with my life and my new-found fortune. At long last, I hailed a cab to take me back to my aunt's apartment.

When I returned, the two of us talked again. "My mother wasn't a good person, was she?" I asked, granite in my voice. "I'd always thought she was, but now I see her differently."

Ella shook her head. "No, she was a wonderful person. She just made some mistakes—big ones, I agree, that changed the course of your life." She paused, looking sad, and took a moment to collect her thoughts. Eventually, she held my hands and searched my face for any softening, but finding none, she sighed and continued, "We all make mistakes, Louise. We regret them, we apologize, and we move on. Claudia should have apologized to you and allowed you to be angry to her face. I told her that many times, but she couldn't do it. That doesn't make her a bad person, merely a cowardly one."

I took a breath. "Thank you, Aunt. Thank you for your kindness and generosity to my mother and to my family and me. I will need to think about all of this before I decide whether I can ever forgive her. Until then, do you need some of the money she left me?"

"Oh, no, dear. I'm fine. But thank you. I have a suggestion, though. I keep my funds in a bank, and the manager there, Monsieur Lefèvre, is someone whom I trust to invest my money. He's done very well by me, and he's discreet. I don't know if you are aware of it, but the law won't allow you to have the money unless you're a widow. If your husband finds out about it, he will claim it as his own, and there will be nothing you can do. Monsieur Lefèvre won't question you if you tell him you're a widow. I'll give you his card, and you can visit him and see what you think."

I nodded. "I wondered about that. This is all a terrible shock, and I probably won't know for some time what I want to do with the money. I'd like to spend some of it to take care of the girls' dowry and maybe hire some more staff at the inn, but I don't know how to do that without Arthur getting suspicious. The most important thing is to keep it safe until I have a plan. Thank you, Aunt. I will contact Monsieur Lefèvre this afternoon."

I spent the rest of the day cleaning out my mother's things, boxing them up, and hiring a moving company to take most of them to Auvers. When that was finished, I walked to the bank. Monsieur Lefèvre asked no questions when I identified myself as a widow, so I placed most of the money under his management—except for a hundred francs that I would tell Arthur was the total sum of my inheritance. As Maman had suggested, he didn't need to know about the rest.

After that, I stood in my mother's bedroom and looked around. With all traces of her gone, it was just a generic room. Exhausted from all the emotions of the past week, I said goodbye to my aunt.

"Consider this your home in Paris," Aunt Ella said. "I hope you'll continue to visit me when you can, my dear."

"Thank you for everything. I'm sure I'll be back to finish dealing with her papers and such. And please visit me when you can too. The children will be thrilled to see you."

As I walked toward the train station, I wondered what would await me back at the inn. I steeled myself for the deception I was about to undertake and carried myself carefully, fearing I might break into a thousand pieces if anything else went wrong. I hoped nothing terrible would happen until I'd grieved my losses and grown a thicker skin.

Chapter 15

If I am worth anything later, I am worth something now.
–Vincent van Gogh

WHEN I RETURNED TO the inn, the dinner rush was in full sway. I hugged Arthur and Adeline, but Germaine was already asleep and didn't stir when I planted a kiss on her forehead. As everyone went about their duties, I felt like a ghost or a visitor from another continent. In only five days, I'd become a stranger, both to the inn and to myself.

I walked around the restaurant, touching tables, chairs, and the fresco of a country scene painted on one wall. I'd paid little attention to it in the past, but that day I realized it was beautiful.

The air in the kitchen was stifling. I stood in a corner and watched as the cook and her helper dashed around in a coordinated dance. After they ladled food onto the plates, Adeline picked them up and carried them out to the diners. The process worked exceptionally smoothly.

I didn't fit into the moving tableau, which was fine. Even though the food they prepared was from my personal recipes, it tasted slightly unfamiliar, perhaps because of different spices the cook had added. I preferred my version, but that didn't matter. The customers complimented me on the meal.

Arthur worked at the bar and served drinks to the diners. People filled every seat, both in the restaurant and the bar, so the staff was working hard, but they had everything under control.

Truly, I had nothing to do. I looked around for Monsieur Vincent, but he must've eaten somewhere else. A touch of disappointment penetrated my fog but only for an instant.

I wandered into our bedroom and sat on the bed, thinking I might never recognize the person I'd become—sadder, richer, wiser in the ways that even the people I loved could betray me. I unpacked my valise and lay on the bed. Even that, the bed I'd so longed for, felt uncomfortable and strange. My mother's boxes would arrive on Monday, and I would unpack them and find places for everything. For the moment, I stared at the ceiling, my mind a bleak desert.

Arthur woke me sometime later, speaking from the doorway. "Louise, are you able to help us clean up? Cook has gone home, and the rest of us are exhausted. I'm still serving drinks, so if you could help, we'd appreciate it."

His voice was oddly gentle, as it might be in a sweet dream. I wondered where I was. Unsure, I raised my head to see my husband, sweat pouring down his face, concern filling his features. Seeing concern rather than anger was such an unexpected treat that I wasn't sure what to think.

I shook my head and rubbed my face. "All right, I'll be there in a minute."

He left, and I was alone again.

What time is it? Does the time really matter? Does anything really matter—tonight, this summer, my life? I took a breath, willing myself to come out of my fog and focus on what needed to be done. But the fog was more welcome than the focus, so even though I sat up, I didn't stand. Unsure of how much time had passed but certain it was more than a minute, I sat, reveling in the fog. Eventually, I lay back down.

Some time later, Adeline shook my shoulders. "Maman, are you coming or not?"

Ah yes, that angry tone was familiar, and the sharp sound pierced through the fog. I shook my head and struggled to a seated position. "*Ma chérie*, you were doing such a good job that I thought I would rest a while."

"Yes, but we need you. I'm not sure where to put all the dishes and pots. And Germaine wet the bed again." Her face screwed up into an expression of disgust. "Papa got her a small bed of her own while you were gone, and now I don't have to sleep in her wet. But she needs the linens changed, and I'm too busy to do it." The girl stood beside the bed, hands on hips, glaring at me.

I rubbed my eyes, partially myself now. "Yes, I'll be right there."

That time, I stood, straightened my clothes, splashed water on my face, and went to care for Germaine. My younger daughter clung to me and cried for so long that I ignored the wet bedclothes and sank onto the rocking chair with the child in my arms. I hugged her and sang the lullabies my mother had sung to me when I was small. Finally, someone had missed me, not for what I could do for them but for who I was. My lips curled into a smile, the first in what seemed like years.

Eventually, I changed what needed to be changed and got Germaine back to sleep then went into the kitchen and saw that someone had put everything away, swept the floor, and tidied up the mess.

Well. I continued humming the lullabies as I wandered around, touching things that seemed as though they belonged to someone else.

After a while, Arthur led me to bed. I was asleep even before he finished pulling off my shoes.

THE NEXT MORNING, LIFE gave me no more respite from my responsibilities. I woke early and went about preparing breakfast for the boarders. A new one had arrived, a Monsieur Hirschig, a likeable young man who seemed to know Monsieur Vincent. My hands remembered what to do, even though my mind was at a loss much of the time. Both Arthur and Adeline slept until nearly noon, and I didn't wake them. They'd worked hard while I was gone and deserved their rest.

Slowly, slowly, I regained my composure. I served people, answered questions from tourists, and played with Germaine. My head ached, and my body felt so heavy that I could barely stand or lift my arms, but I persevered. Occasionally, brief thoughts penetrated the fog then darted away.

Maman is gone. Truly gone. Maybe it would've been better if she'd never told me what she'd done. In a way, telling me was another selfish act on her part. She could die with her conscience assuaged, while I have to deal with the emotional result.

I won't have to make that extra trip to Paris on Monday. But I will keep my Wednesday routine.

I have enough money to hire more help now if I can figure out how to keep it from Arthur. Who will I hire, if I can?

What would it have been like to live in London with a wealthy man? And would I have still had these children if I'd married Denis?

I can run away with the girls now and find somewhere to hide where Arthur won't find me. If I left, where would I go?

Maman is gone.

I am alone.

Occasionally, a twinge of anger, even fury, also penetrated the fog. When I allowed such emotions in for more than a few seconds, the same powerful rage from a few days before overtook me. Everyone wanted me to live the life *they* wanted for me: my parents and Arthur, especially. *How could they? How* could *they? And why had*

Denis let me go so easily? Why didn't he break off his betrothal when he got Maman's letter and fight for me? We could've eloped and been happy, regardless of what custom dictated.

Every time the rage-filled thoughts arose, I pushed them away and invited the fog to envelop me again. I couldn't permit the rage to inhabit the core of my being, at least not yet. Small bits of anger were all I could handle if I wanted to keep my sanity.

In the afternoon, I left Germaine with Adeline and went for a walk. Tourists and buggies packed the lanes in town, so I headed out into the wheat fields. Their emptiness reminded me of the emptiness inside myself, and they brought a sense of comfort.

I wasn't completely surprised when I rounded a curve and saw Monsieur Vincent painting a very wide canvas of the same scene I was admiring. We often seemed to show up in the same places. He hadn't been at dinner the night before or breakfast that morning, so I'd wondered what had happened to him, but I hadn't had the energy to ask anyone.

He saw me and nodded. "Madame, your husband shared the news with me. I am saddened by your great loss. Losing a parent is hard."

"Thank you. Yes, it is." I stepped closer. "Do you mind if I look at your painting?"

He stood back. "Please. Do that while I make sure my teeth are clean." He laughed.

I'd never noticed how appealing his laugh was. Maybe I hadn't heard it before. It was a rising inflection of "ha ha ha ha" and a merry sound to my ears, which had heard so many difficult things recently.

I was completely taken in by the painting and stared at it for so long that he must have felt slightly uncomfortable because he filled the silence.

"I'm trying my hand at larger paintings. What do you think?"

"It's magnificent. The yellow of the field shimmers off the canvas. Yes, the scene you are painting is beautiful, but the painting brings an extra dimension of... light. Yes, light. Happiness. Almost like the world itself is glowing."

He stood back and puffed on his pipe. "Ah, thank you. You know, you see things that others don't. I hope you continue your artistic endeavors. Perhaps it's time for you to take up your paints again. Yes, I think so."

From what I could tell, he was speaking of giving me lessons in painting rather than drawing. I considered the advantages of picking up my brush again. Fixing mistakes would be easier with paints, and using colors rather than pencil and crayons would give me more latitude to express my emotions. "That would be lovely. Will you help, or must I proceed on my own?"

He blushed, perhaps remembering how he had summarily rejected my first request. "I will be happy to help you find your own style." He bowed slightly and gave me a smile that reminded me less of Denis and more of himself, the gifted but difficult artist.

Another realization penetrated my fog: how much I appreciated Monsieur Vincent. He seemed to feel things more deeply than other people, and he showed his emotions on his face and through his paintings. He wasn't always likeable—that was true—but something about him appealed to me. Although he resembled Denis physically, the two weren't at all alike. Denis wasn't the type to challenge the status quo, which explained why he hadn't come after me. I felt sure that Vincent, if he loved me, would make different choices.

A wave of disorientation washed over me so strongly that I feared I might faint. "Oh," I said, leaning over to place my hands on his stool.

"Madame, please sit."

I sank onto the stool, but it wasn't sturdy enough, so I dropped to the ground, to the soft grass with its sweet summer scent. Suddenly, a profound insight penetrated through the fog, sounding almost like a voice speaking from on high: although my mother had described me as *dutiful*, that wasn't who I really was, at my core. For years, I'd done what others wanted me to do, but I possessed free will and could make different choices, regardless of the consequences. I couldn't say just yet what my true self was, but it definitely wasn't *dutiful*.

Slowly, slowly, the separated part of my soul reintegrated with my body, and I felt whole and complete, satisfied to be sitting on the grass while I talked with this attractive man who was neither Arthur nor Denis.

He stood, awkward, since I'd collapsed at his feet and showed no interest in rising. "Are you sure you wouldn't prefer to sit on the stool?"

"No, it's quite nice here. The grass is cool and soft. You might try it."

He grinned and sat, crossing his legs in front of him. "Yes, I see what you mean. When the wind is blowing strongly, I sometimes lie on my stomach and place my canvas on the ground so it doesn't blow away." He laughed again. "I often find insects in the painting."

We sat like that for a length of time, not speaking but comfortable in each other's company. I picked some blades of grass and began weaving them into a chain, something I hadn't done since I was a young child. The act was surprisingly soothing.

I felt him watching me—observing, really. His eyes seemed to see the essence of the things he painted. I wondered if he could see my essence, too, though I wasn't ready to know the answer.

After a while, I wanted to hear his scratchy voice again. "What brought you to Auvers, monsieur?"

Monsieur Vincent picked some blades of grass and blew them away. "My health has been fragile for some time now. I was in a hospital in the south and then an asylum. When I left, I wanted to be near my brother in Paris. But Paris jangles my nerves, so I came here, where I could be under the care of Dr. Gachet." His words were slow, halting. While he spoke, he didn't look at me but down at the ground. "I feel calmer here, and I hope to stay."

Such raw honesty must have cost him a great deal. Rarely did near strangers speak so baldly about their health struggles. His mangled ear was visible to everyone, all the time, despite the floppy hat he wore outdoors, and I'd seen how people recoiled from the sight.

"I'm glad you're here. It's a beautiful place, and it seems to have been good for your painting."

He nodded, a question in his eyes.

After a pause, I answered it. "I came here because my husband, without discussing it with me, signed a contract to lease the inn for two years. We moved from Paris, and here I am, whether or not I want to be." I heard the bitter edge to my voice and did nothing to reduce it. I would speak the truth as I experienced it, letting him respond as he chose.

"Oh. What a hard thing. But you've been here some months now, no? And you seem to enjoy at least some of it. I see the care you put into the meals you serve."

After considering his words for a long moment, I said, "Yes, you're right. I suppose I have been so upset about the lack of choice that I've not appreciated the opportunity to feed people. I do like that part."

He laughed, and I laughed with him. How wonderful that felt. We spent a pleasant half hour sharing details about our lives: his struggles, first to teach himself to paint and now to sell paintings—my struggles to keep my teenage daughter in line and to find enough time in the day for myself. Our sharing wasn't deep or searing, but we took another step toward connection. The first word that came to my mind was *intimacy*, but I shied away from that and settled for *connection*.

Much time passed before I realized how long I'd been there. *Oh, dear.* I'd kept Monsieur Vincent from finishing his painting, and I'd forgotten about my walk. Still, I felt greatly refreshed and ready to return to my life.

"Thank you for such a wonderful time, monsieur. I must go now." I rose and brushed off my skirt.

He licked his lips, seeming to struggle to find the proper words for something.

I waited.

Finally, he said, "Madame, please do not think me overly impertinent, and I will apologize if you think of me so. But I wonder if, in our private times together, you would call me by my name? Vincent. That's all. No *Monsieur.* And possibly, could you address me using *tu* instead of *vous?* It would be a special gift to hear my name and the familiar pronoun coming from the mouth of a friend."

I considered his request. Rarely did men and women call each other by their given names, unless they were related or had been friends for a long time. Or, I thought with a slight tightness in my chest, they were engaged or married. Oddly, his invitation made sense because it acknowledged the connection between us.

"Yes, I would be honored to do that. Vincent. And please call me Louise."

He bowed, smiling. We stood an arm's length apart, awkward in our new intimacy.

Finally, he said, "Louise, then. Thank you."

I said goodbye and walked away. The rage I'd been carrying with me for days had dissipated a little, although I wasn't sure it would remain that way. No, it would probably return with a vengeance if conditions warranted. But Vincent's smile had helped me move forward through the thicket of my life.

Chapter 16

In the end we shall have had enough of cynicism, skepticism and humbug, and we shall want to live more musically.
–Vincent van Gogh

ON MONDAY MORNING, I noticed Germaine playing with a doll I'd never seen. It had a porcelain head, a cloth body, blue glass eyes, and hair that felt realistically human. We'd never owned anything so expensive.

I picked it up and stared at it. After a moment, I returned the doll to my daughter, who was screaming for it. "Where did you get this?"

Germaine's face lit up. "Lady."

"What lady?"

"Lady and Papa."

My blood turned cold, and I wondered if the woman could possibly have been a customer. That wasn't likely because Arthur would've mentioned it. Besides, customers didn't hand out such expensive gifts to little girls they'd just met.

I called for Adeline to come into the room. When she arrived, I asked, "Where did Germaine get this doll?"

Adeline tensed. "Uh, from a lady at Papa's work."

"What lady?"

"I can't remember her name, but she's the new bookkeeper at the butcher shop." She wouldn't meet my eyes when she spoke. "Uh, we had dinner with her at a restaurant in Paris after the funeral." She shrugged.

I bit my lip. Ever since Arthur and I had been married, bookkeeping had been my job. The person who'd taken over for me when we moved to Auvers was a man we'd known for many years. Either this was someone new whom Arthur had not bothered to mention, or she was his mistress. Or both.

I struggled to breathe. So the mistress had met my children and given at least one of them an expensive gift. I looked at Adeline, who had paled and was wringing her hands. "Did she give anything to you?"

Adeline nodded.

"What was it?"

"A book."

"Let's not play twenty questions. Please, just bring me the book."

Adeline went to her room and brought back *Les Misérables*, by Victor Hugo. I'd read it, but its content seemed far too mature for my thirteen-year-old daughter. I frowned and handed it back to her.

"Have you read this?"

"No. I started it, but I have too many other things to do."

I needed to tread carefully because Adeline would quickly rebuild the wall between us if I made a misstep. "Have you met this lady before?"

Adeline shook her head. "May I go now?"

"In a minute. What did she look like?"

Adeline hesitated. "She was very fancy. Younger than you. She didn't know much about children. We didn't know what to say when she kept asking us questions." My daughter opened the book and flipped the pages, looking like she'd rather be anywhere but there.

"All right, you may go now. Keep the book if you like. But please let me know if you meet the lady again."

Adeline gave me a look of pity before running from the room.

I shook my head and tried to keep from screaming. *The bastard.* I had just buried my mother, and that same evening, Arthur was cavorting with his mistress, who never should have been allowed within a mile of my children. As I thought about it, I realized I shouldn't have been surprised, not really. Consideration and loyalty had never been my husband's strong suits.

I wanted to take that doll and smash it against the wall. But Germaine loved it, and I wouldn't punish my daughter when what I really wanted to do was throw Arthur against the wall. Needless to say, I wouldn't let my children out of my sight again. Arthur might leave me for that hussy, but he would never have the children. I would get back at him when the right time arose. I wasn't sure when that would be, but I would know it when I saw it.

FOR THE REST OF THE day, Adeline became the lovely girl she'd once been—no sulking, no outbursts of anger, and she helped with the chores without being reminded. She seemed to watch me more carefully than usual, as if bracing for something terrible to happen.

I had no intention of asking her what had changed, but I believed I knew: Adeline had finally grasped that the life she knew was tenuous and that maybe I wasn't a total villain, after all. Whatever my daughter's reasoning and however long it might last, I appreciated the turnaround.

My mother's boxes arrived, so I had to find places for everything. I spent much of the next day working on that project. Adeline would have some new dresses after the seamstress cut them down, and the prospect thrilled her. She wasn't so happy when she discovered that she couldn't wear the new clothing until her period of mourning ended. Tradition called for three months for her and six months for me.

As I was putting away the last of my mother's things, Arthur walked into the bedroom. He sat on the chair and watched for a few moments. I had an idea what was coming, but I wouldn't help him. This was his topic to broach.

Finally, he did. After clearing his throat several times, he said, "Uh, I see you took some of your mother's things. She must have gotten rid of much of it before she moved in with Ella."

I nodded but didn't speak.

Eventually, he continued. "Uh, did you find her bankbook? Did she leave you anything?"

There it was, the big question. I took a moment to relax my shoulders and take a breath before finding the envelope where I'd placed Maman's personal papers. Scrounging around inside, I pulled out five twenty-franc gold coins.

Turning to face him, I held them out. "This was all that was left after I paid the medical and funeral expenses and closed out her accounts. Almost nothing remained from her share of the apartment proceeds. She gave us nearly half and sent some to Émile, and she only kept a small bit for herself. I honestly don't know what she would have done if she'd lived a little longer."

As I spoke the lie, it became the truth for me, and I covered my face with my hands as the tears emerged for a mother who had given almost her last franc to her daughter and son-in-law and must have worried about money in her last days. I sobbed into my hands. "I didn't know all this until after she died."

Arthur walked to me and put his arms around me.

I did my best not to stiffen at his touch but instead forced myself to lean into him. He was trying to be sympathetic, which was unusual. Maybe something had happened with his mistress, I thought bitterly. Either the woman had rejected him, or else she'd convinced him he would achieve better results if he were gentler with his women.

After a while, I pulled away and dabbed at my face with my handkerchief. "I didn't mean to break down like that."

He patted my shoulder. "I understand. I miss her too. She was always a kind mother-in-law to me. When I asked her to help us lease this inn, I didn't realize she would give us almost all her money. I thought she had plenty."

I nodded. "So did I, or I else I wouldn't have taken it."

Inside, my thoughts went in a different direction: *I think you would've taken her last centime if it would've gotten you what you wanted.* But nothing would be gained by voicing those thoughts.

After a moment, I asked, "Should we do something with this money? It belongs to both of us, I suppose." I placed the coins on his dresser. "Maybe we could buy something we need—I don't know what, right now—or we could save it for Adeline's dowry." I paused. "What do you think?"

He shrugged. "You decide." After a moment, he spoke in a peculiar voice, with undertones of fear. "I need to tell you something else. While you were gone, Levert came to tell me he's decided to sell the inn. He wondered if we wanted to purchase it."

"Oh, no. What did you tell him?" My hand went to my mouth.

That was completely unexpected. Levert visited us every month to collect the rent, but he'd never hinted that he was interested in selling. So that was why Arthur hoped we'd inherited a pot of money. He could buy the inn rather than lease it.

I considered this bombshell from our landlord. With my inheritance, we—I—could purchase the place. I would have no more worries about being thrown out into the cold if we couldn't make the rent payments. And if things with Arthur didn't work out, I could ask him to leave and run it on my own, with hired help. Or I could sell it whenever I wanted.

For an instant, the idea seemed appealing. Then reality hit me like a brick to the head. If I told Arthur about the money, he wouldn't allow me to buy the property in my name. No, according to law, it would be his alone. Then he would have even more power over me. In that instance, if anyone were asked to leave, it would be me, and I wouldn't be able to do anything about it.

I shook my head. No matter what happened, we would not be buying the inn.

Arthur sat heavily on the bed. "I told him we couldn't afford to buy it right now, but we'd like to continue leasing." He frowned. "He said he'd received an offer, but he wanted to offer it to me first. Since I wasn't interested, he plans to complete the transaction with a local landowner—he didn't mention the name—in early July." Arthur turned a panicked face in my direction. "What if the new owner wants to run the place himself? What will we do?"

I tried to organize my thoughts. My friend Claude had looked over the lease as soon as Arthur had signed it the year before, and he'd explained the various clauses. I thought I still remembered what it said. "I don't think he can do that, at least not right away. Our lease is good for a little more than a year from now, so even if this new person owns the property, I don't think he can evict us until then."

Arthur grunted, sounding relieved. As he turned to leave, he said in a low voice, "I want to stay here even after the lease is up."

I nodded, but I wasn't sure about my own preferences. The banker had informed me I could afford to purchase a small apartment on the outskirts of Paris. But he recommended I take several months, preferably up to a year, to make such a momentous decision. That timing would likely coincide with the end of the lease. But I would share none of this information with Arthur. The nest egg was *mine*, not his.

Chapter 17

I have nature and art and poetry, and if that is not enough, what is enough?
–Vincent van Gogh

ANTICIPATING PUTTING brush to canvas brought me both joy and pain: joy because I could recover a part of myself I'd believed lost forever and pain because even the thought of painting reminded me of the hope for a bright future that my mother had squashed so many years ago.

Regardless of my confusing emotions, I purchased a few tubes of paint and gathered the rest of the supplies I would need. On Thursday afternoon, when Arthur was in Paris, I met Vincent behind the inn for my first lesson.

We walked to a small clearing behind the shed, where Germaine's new nanny could easily summon me if the little girl awoke during the lesson. I'd quietly used some of my inheritance to hire the woman, and since I did the bookkeeping for the inn, Arthur would never know. I felt great relief at having someone else whose entire job was to watch my daughter and keep her out of trouble so that I could do other things, the most important of which right now was painting.

An acacia tree was blooming, so it became my first subject.

"First, find your heart, and then paint what you feel when you see the tree." Vincent paused then added softly, timidly, "Louise."

My name, without the customary *Madame*, sounded delicious coming from his lips. I smiled and gave him the same gift: "Thank you, Vincent. I will." I didn't mention that I'd thought of him for weeks without the *Monsieur* attached, even though I'd not said it aloud before.

Turning my attention to my subject, I tried to understand what my heart was saying about the tree. It seemed as wide as it was tall, with lustrous yellow blossoms hanging like grapes on its slender branches—such a lovely vision. But I wondered if painting something so beautiful less than two weeks after my mother's death would be disloyal to her memory.

I sat on my chair and considered what I could paint that would do justice to both the beauty around me and the blackness in my heart. Bees tunneled inside the blossoms to suck up nectar then flew off to deposit it elsewhere. I'd never particularly noticed bees before, other than to worry about them stinging me or my children, but on that occasion, I was more taken by their industriousness than with the beautiful blossoms. They had such an important mission, to store food so that they could survive the winter. And if I were to step on one of them, it would immediately sting me.

In a sense, Maman had been like those bees, lovely and industrious, but she would sting anyone who impeded what she saw as her needs, such as keeping me close to her. I wondered what happened to a bee that had stung someone. I didn't know, so I asked Vincent, who was busily painting.

He stopped and laid down his brush, looking thoughtful. Turning to me with a pained expression, he said, "I'm afraid they die after they sting you. It's a hard thing, both for the person they sting and for them." He glanced around at the bees. "Has one stung you, Louise? Is that why you ask?"

I took a breath. "No, they haven't bothered me. I... was just struggling with what to paint. My heart is too heavy to paint the pretty flowers. But maybe the bees..." I drifted off.

"Oh, my dear lady, I'm so sorry. I shouldn't have brought you to something beautiful. I completely understand your problem." He paused for a moment. "Shall I kill a bee so you can study it?"

"No!" I exclaimed immediately. "No, I'm being silly. I'll paint the flowers."

He nodded. "All right, if not the bees, then what about one blossom only? I could bring one that already has a bee inside it, and you can paint the bee that way."

"Yes, that might work."

He picked a branch of flowers that held half a dozen bees and laid it on the grass in front of me. "All right?"

I nodded, my heart overflowing with gratitude that someone understood my pain and was taking it seriously.

I did my best to paint a bee inside a blossom. Unfortunately, my finished product resembled neither bee nor blossom. Frustrated, I painted over what I'd done but succeeded only in smudging the entire thing. It was a complete mess, and I finally gave up and set down my brush. Surprisingly, when I looked at my painting, I laughed. Instead of a branch of flowers with bees on them, it looked like the brown door of the shed.

"It's awful!" I said, overcome by laughter. Some painter I was. I'd clearly forgotten everything I'd ever known. I didn't understand why that was funny instead of tragic, but the laughter continued to burble out of me.

He walked over and looked at my easel. "Uh..."

"You can say it. It's awful, and I don't care. I'm painting again, and that's all that matters. I'll try again when it dries."

"Then I will agree. It's awful." He smiled. "But I have done worse myself. Your next attempt will be better."

When I continued to laugh, he joined me, and I was delighted to hear his "ha ha ha" in rising musical tones again.

At last, I caught my breath, wondering where that much laughter had come from. Maybe laughter was akin to tears. Or perhaps I was just a hysterical woman, as Arthur frequently threw at me when I was upset with something he did.

I wiped my eyes and walked over to Vincent's easel. "May I?"

"Of course."

He'd painted the blossoms on the branches in close-up. Yellows, browns, and beiges created a mood of seriousness I'd not seen before in his work. "This is beautiful, but it's so different from other paintings of yours I've seen."

He puffed on his pipe. "Yes, I admit to being distracted. It's not one of my best, I think. But I've learned to not overpaint and to put it aside, to move on. Someone somewhere might like it."

"I'll remember that. I think my first bee was better than what it became." Sighing, I looked around. "Still, it's a beautiful day, and I love the smell of turpentine and paint." After a moment, I said, "You said you're distracted. May I ask what it is about?"

"Yes, certainly. I like it here in Auvers, and I very much enjoy your company. I would love to found an artists' colony in the town and invite my brother and his family, among others, to live here and work together. It's all I can think about and all I've ever wanted. I hesitate to bring this up to you because it would mean that I would vacate your lovely inn, but I wonder if you know of any houses for rent in the area?"

I laughed again. "No, I don't keep up with that sort of thing. It sounds like a nice idea, though. Are you familiar with the family of American artists who live in the house just next door? Maybe you could talk to them."

He snorted then spoke sharply. "Those people are pigs. Their art is terrible, they're noisy, and they've made the place a pigsty."

Huh. He seemed angry all of a sudden, and I wondered what was going on.

"I'm sorry to hear that. My contacts with the family have been quite polite, and I hadn't noticed they had neglected the house maintenance."

Neither of us spoke for a moment as we studiously cleaned our brushes.

Sounding a little calmer, he spoke again. "I was thinking about leasing something on the edge of town—maybe one of those thatched cottages. But I don't know if my brother would go for that. They're probably colder in the winter, and that wouldn't be good for the baby." He paced back and forth as he packed more tobacco into his pipe, and his voice rose as he spoke. "Theo isn't happy in his job, and his little son is sickly, so I keep telling him, 'Come here, and all will be well.' But he continues to ignore me."

I didn't understand what was upsetting him, so I replied carefully, not wanting to inflame the situation. "I imagine it's difficult for an art dealer to live so far from Paris."

"That's what he says too. I don't believe it." He was nearly shouting. "Besides, he has an artistic temperament. He would do better living in a thatched cottage and painting until he regains his health instead of working for slave wages in Paris until it kills him."

His emotions seemed excessive for the situation. Unbidden, I found myself wondering if his agitation had something to do with his time in the asylum. *Should I be afraid?*

I grasped my skirts, thinking I would run back to the inn if his outrage worsened. Fortunately, he abruptly stopped speaking and shook his head. "I am sorry, Louise. I have frightened you." He sat again on his stool. "I assure you I am not dangerous—just passionate. I bring the same sort of passion from my art to my life, especially as it concerns my family. But it is not your concern."

"Yes, of course." I realized I'd been reacting to him as I reacted to Arthur when he was angry. But Vincent wasn't Arthur. Even though I couldn't say why, I believed I was safe with him.

Just then, Germaine screamed—her nap was over. The nanny could probably handle the situation, but I should be there to supervise. "Thank you for the lesson. Perhaps we could do this again next Thursday?"

"You would meet with me again, even though I cannot always contain my words or make them palatable? And I am such a terrible teacher?"

I chuckled. "You aren't a terrible teacher, but I am surely a terrible painter. Despite how poorly my painting turned out, I'm excited to be painting again, and I'm sure I'll improve under your tutelage. As for your passionate words, I imagine they're part and parcel of the artistic temperament."

He reached over and grabbed my hand. "Oh, thank you, Louise. You see me as I am, wholly. That means so much to me."

Smiling, I pulled my hand away. "And you, me. Now, my daughter needs me. I will clean up my mess later in the afternoon. Thank you again."

LATER, WHEN I RETURNED to my easel, I discovered that my canvas had been cleaned and was ready for a new painting. Bees were still buzzing around the blossom, so I picked up my brush, intending to try again.

Just then, Adeline walked into the clearing, startled to see me there. "Oh, Maman, I didn't know where you were."

"Do you need me?"

"Uh, Germaine is making a mess in our room, and I thought you should know."

I frowned. "Well, tell the nanny to make her clean it up. I'm busy just now."

"All right."

The girl disappeared. Shaking my head, I decided I deserved some time to myself after all the years of parenting. Having another adult around to deal with minor problems was a blessing.

A few minutes later, I heard a rustle in the bushes behind me. Thinking it might be Vincent, returning to watch me paint, I turned to look. No one was there, but the bushes were still moving. I walked over and saw a dead pigeon on the ground, its neck wrung, its body still twitching.

A chill ran down my spine. I spun around in a circle, but no one was there. Vincent wouldn't have done such a thing, so someone else must have been watching me as I painted. I wondered who it had been and what message I was supposed to take from the poor dead bird.

I raced inside and latched the back door.

Chapter 18

I DIDN'T MENTION THE bird to Arthur because he surely would've laughed and told me to prepare it for dinner. Within a few moments, I decided I'd overreacted in thinking it was some sort of sinister message. Possibly, one of the local cats had killed it, and I'd just thought its neck had been wrung. When I went back outside to check, only a few feathers were left. At least I wouldn't have to prepare it for dinner.

At last, Sunday arrived, and I could rest. Arthur went hunting again with his farmer friend. That evening, he talked about the other men who'd joined the hunting party. One addition was an odd young man, René Secrétan, whose father was a prominent pharmacist in Paris. The family also owned a second home in Auvers. Arthur hoped to entice the father to join them one day too.

I recognized the name immediately and opened my mouth to remind him that the boy had been involved with Adeline's vandalism, but I stopped when I caught Adeline's small shake of the head. Maybe she was right, and it was best not to bring it up again. The episode was over, and Adeline seemed to understand that her reputation would be ruined if she spent time with René, or any young man, unescorted.

Arthur didn't notice our nonverbal communication and continued talking. "My star is rising, my dear," he proclaimed as he chewed on the fricassee of rabbit with wine and herbs that I'd prepared for dinner.

I smiled but said nothing. For Arthur, the thrill of bringing home dinner was less exciting than becoming known in the village as a man of means. I didn't want to dim his excitement. If going hunting with the boy made him happy, so be it.

THE DAYS SPED BY, AND I stayed busy supervising all the new staff I'd hired: cook's helper, scullery maid, chambermaid, and of course, Germaine's nanny. Business was good. All seven of our rooms were continuously rented, either by artists or by tourists staying in town for the summer, and our restaurant tables were nearly always filled.

The only flaw in the summer days was that, several weeks after my mother's death, I still had to force myself to get out of bed every morning. I was exhausted no matter how long I slept, and I wasn't up to taking the long walks I'd previously enjoyed. When I complained about my fatigue to Danielle, she reminded me that grieving required an enormous amount of energy. She'd been exhausted for most of a year after her own mother's death. That made sense, but understanding it didn't revive my energy.

By July, our family's fortunes had vastly improved from what they'd been in May. The inn was doing so well, even without my inheritance, that I could pay all the bills on time and even pay ahead on the rent. Still, I constantly mulled over ideas of what to do with my newfound personal wealth. One thing that made me happy was knowing I would be able to provide substantial dowries for both girls when the time came. Also, I could send Adeline to a better school, where she wouldn't be shunned by the other, less motivated girls. I could easily persuade Arthur we'd made enough to pay those expenses out of our earnings.

Anger and grief continued to overwhelm me at unexpected moments. Surely, I would soon reach a point when I could forgive Maman for being human, for loving me so much that she couldn't let go, and for acting from selfishness instead of motherly love. Oh, I knew she'd had many wonderful qualities, but all I could remember was her single act of duplicity, which had caused my life to veer from its positive trajectory onto one with major bumps, disappointments, and pain.

The only thing that kept me going was routine, putting one foot in front of the other. I was so demoralized that I couldn't even bring myself to paint. Although Vincent invited me to paint with him at our usual time the following Thursday, I wasn't able to muster enough enthusiasm to pull out my easel or consider what scene I might paint.

I gave him a sad smile and shook my head. "Maybe next week."

A line appeared between his eyes. He seemed to be working out words he didn't want to get wrong, so I waited. Finally, he cleared his throat.

"Uh, may I make an observation?"

I shrugged. "I suppose."

"Whenever I feel particularly blue, I find it helps me to paint even if I don't want to do it at the start. Afterward, I always feel much better. Are you sure you won't try it?"

I considered. After sighing, I said, "All right. If you insist."

He beamed. "I will find us something to paint. Give me two hours, and then I'll come and get you. All right?"

"Yes."

Truthfully, just being around his enthusiasm made me feel slightly better. When he turned to leave, his fingers gently trailed across my back. *Oh.* He'd never touched me before, and it was inappropriate for an unmarried man to touch a married woman. Instead of being offended, my heart gave a little trill.

RAIN HAD THREATENED all day, and by the time of the lesson, the heavens were unleashing torrents of water. Vincent and I ran to the shed, laughing through the raindrops as we tried to keep our blank canvases from being drenched. Inside, we used the towels I'd brought to dry ourselves. Vincent's hair stood on end, and without thinking, I reached over and patted it down. He grinned at me, and I grinned back. Being with him was the only time I felt like grinning, so I didn't question my motivations for being alone with the man.

He'd provided a vase filled with poppies and daisies that he must have picked in a field somewhere, and he placed it on a table. We set up our easels. The poppies were bursting with light even in the dim shed, and I filled my canvas with them. After a while, I realized my scene looked more like the fires of hell than poppies, so I added a few white daisies and a hint of lavender. Yes, that was slightly better but not very much. Sighing, I considered what to do.

Vincent glanced at me but said nothing as we continued to paint.

After a while, he talked about his efforts to create an artists' colony in Auvers. In short, they weren't working. All his friends were either happily living in Paris or they were thinking of moving somewhere else, and Auvers wasn't on their list of possibilities. He'd found a house on the edge of town that would be perfect, but he had no money to lease it, so the landlord would hold it only for another two weeks before offering it to other prospective tenants. Vincent hoped to find two interested artists who wanted to live there with him, but he wasn't optimistic.

I gave up on my painting and reached for another canvas. Since money was no longer an issue, I didn't need to scrimp. I began again, painting the flowers differently.

Vincent's raspy voice, along with the rain pelting on the metal roof, put me in a state of such tranquility that I barely remembered where I was or even who I was. My mother's pale, expressionless face as I'd last seen it vanished from my mind.

Within a few moments, my new canvas was abloom with flowers. Rich, vivid poppies and perfectly formed daisies nearly burst from the canvas. I did not paint them deliberately or even consciously, but they emerged instead from the deep state of serenity that had settled on me. Nothing like that had ever happened before, and I felt a great joy building as I realized I was connecting with some aspect of the infinite.

After a few moments, I sensed my mother's spirit nearby. She was watching me paint and flooding me with love. It occurred to me that, if I reached out, I might touch her. I did reach out once but felt only a slight warmth and a minor heaviness in the air where she stood. I returned my hand to my side and clasped the feelings into a loose fist. Under her doting presence, all the anger I'd felt toward her disappeared, leaving only tenderness in its wake. She'd made a mistake, true, but her belief in me had been a steadying influence in my life, and that gift was stronger than any mistake.

She'd always supported my interest in art, and I believed her spirit was blessing my return to it. I'd heard about people seeing or sensing their loved ones who had passed away, but this was my first experience of it. Nothing of the sort had happened when my father died. I could've been shocked or at least surprised, but in the state I was in, the experience felt completely natural and healing.

Time slowed as I completed the painting under my mother's benevolent presence. Suddenly, I realized that Vincent had stopped talking and was looking at me with a warm expression in his eyes.

When I smiled at him, he said, "I've been watching you. Where have you been?"

My smile widened. *Dare I tell him the truth? Yes.* "Visiting with my mother. She's been with me for the past hour, out of my sight but so very near." I glanced around the room and saw nothing unusual, only wooden walls draped with spiderwebs. The spirit hadn't lingered, but the love had remained.

"I'm sorry, Vincent. I was so involved in my own world that I might've missed some of what you said. The last I heard, you were talking about the house you wanted to rent. Was there more?"

"Nothing worth hearing, my dear." He chuckled as he ambled over to look at my canvas. After staring at it for a long moment, he said, "It is the best thing you've done. It's even better than the paintings you did when you were younger. One is hanging in the billiard room, no?"

I hadn't realized he'd noticed that painting.

When I nodded, he continued, "This is a more mature painting. The artist who painted this has been stricken by tragedy but has survived it, has laughed with abandon but not been overtaken by it, and sees the flowers as brothers and sisters rather than separate entities. I think your painting is finished. You are indeed a painter. Never doubt it."

I sat on my chair, completely overwhelmed by his words. I hadn't known he was a poet as well as an artist, but those were the observations of someone so sensitive to me that he could've been an extension of my own self. The magic of the day was continuing. Tears sprang to my eyes, but they were tears of deep gratitude rather than the grief that had consumed me for weeks.

After a moment, I found my voice. "Oh, my. Thank you. I'm speechless. I wonder if you might write down those thoughts so I won't forget them? They were the most beautiful words I've ever heard."

He hesitated. "I cannot promise to get them all correct, but I will try to recreate them. Thank you for the compliment of wishing to see my words on paper."

We sat in silence for a moment. Finally, I walked over to his easel. He'd painted the red flowers in front of a green background, and the colors leapt off the canvas. Bits of white and purple accentuated the red. Joy was the emotion I felt when I looked at this painting.

"Were you happy when you painted this? I notice that all your paintings seem to evoke some kind of emotion. Is this one meant to bring joy to the beholder? You were talking about how disappointed you were about your artist colony, so I would have expected something more somber."

His lips turned up contentedly. He tamped down the tobacco in his pipe and lit it, smiling all the time. When he puffed, the aroma of his cherry-scented tobacco filled the shed.

He turned to me and said, "Sometimes, I think you must be an angel who is hearing and reflecting my thoughts."

The heat rose in my face, and I wasn't sure how to respond upon hearing my own sentiments spoken aloud. I considered smiling and thanking him, but that response seemed far too superficial for the moment. *And yet, what else is there?*

Suddenly, I knew what I wanted to do. For once, I didn't question myself but merely set down my brush and wiped my hands on a towel. Slowly, deliberately, I moved closer to him. Vincent turned to face me, a question in his eyes. I placed my hands on his shoulders and stared up at him. Without saying a word, I pulled the pipe from his mouth and raised my lips to his. He leaned down to meet me.

His lips were cool and dry at first, but they quickly became heated and moist as he responded to my kiss. He wrapped his arms around my waist and pulled me toward him. A second went by, then two, then five, and I lost all sense of time as our mouths molded to each other.

Finally, panting, I pulled away. I had been kissed before but nothing like that. If I had thought before I acted, I probably would have only brushed his lips with mine for an instant. The kiss would acknowledge our connection in the flesh as well as the spirit.

But the strength of his reaction made me recognize that there before me was a man, not just a friend or a compatible spirit but a flesh-and-blood man who wanted me with a passion I'd never experienced. And I felt an answering response within myself.

With Denis, I'd been young and inexperienced, and I now understood my love for him had been that of a naïve girl. And with Arthur, well, the man was not very interested in kissing. He had kissed me when we were courting because I had denied him the rest of my body. But his kisses were only a prelude to the main event, for which I'd forced him to wait until our wedding night. Since then, he rarely kissed me. When he did, that was his version of foreplay, and the kissing progressed quickly into physical intimacy, if that was even the correct word for what we did together.

But with Vincent, I was in entirely unfamiliar territory. While he might or might not have been the most experienced of lovers—I didn't have enough information to know one way or the other—he was certainly the most passionate. Yes, he was my painting teacher, but our sensitivity to each other went far beyond the realm of painting.

When I pulled away, he stared down at me with such eagerness that I suddenly felt naked, exposed in a way I'd never known. To hide my response, I turned again to his painting. Suddenly, I understood it was his way of expressing his affection for me.

"Oh." As I tried to summon words to speak of what I saw, I heard a sound coming from behind the shed, possibly an animal walking toward the river—or not. In a flash, I remembered that the shed's door was standing open, and anyone could walk in.

Just like that, the magic disappeared.

This is wrong. I'm married. I'm just as bad as Arthur.

Germaine will call out for me soon, and I should go.

When can we do it again?

We can never do it again.

Then we were two separate people, artists who'd had an intense but brief connection. I pulled away from him then handed him his pipe and rubbed my hands on my skirt. I walked back to my easel and stared at my painting, seeing only odd shapes and colors.

He cleared his throat and sucked on his pipe, saying nothing.

My face was hot with embarrassment, and I couldn't look at him. Instead, I directed my words toward my painting. "Oh, monsieur, I'm sorry. I was too forward. I should never have done that."

He was silent for a long moment. Finally, in a voice filled with tenderness, he said, "I am so happy you did. I have been wanting to kiss you ever since we met that first day in the café, when you looked so enticing. But I didn't dare think it would ever come to pass, so I've forced myself to be content with the time we've spent painting together." He paused then exclaimed, "Oh, Louise, you are magnificent!"

I bit my lip, tasting his tobacco and his passion.

No, this can't be happening.

"Again, I apologize. I'm a married woman, so that can never happen again. Please accept my apologies." Leaving my painting on the easel, I fled from the shed.

VINCENT DIDN'T APPEAR for dinner that night, and I was grateful I didn't have to treat him as just another diner. After the children were asleep, I carried a lantern back to the shed to clean up my painting mess. Inside, I found that Vincent had cleaned my palette, tidied my paints, and cleaned my brushes. He'd also left me a tube of his paint because I'd used all mine. It was bright red, the color of poppies.

I'd seen etchings of poppies on headstones in the cemetery, symbolizing eternal sleep. It seemed an appropriate flower to paint at present, given my recent loss, and I was deeply touched that he'd thought of it. He'd seen what I needed and had given it, generously and with unselfish kindness. My heart beat steadily, filled with gratitude for his warmth and understanding.

I took my things back to the inn and prepared for bed. After settling in for the evening, I allowed myself to think about the day. So many wonderful things had happened. For one, I had visited with my mother's spirit and knew, without a doubt, she wished me to move forward with my life. Gratitude and forgiveness had largely replaced my anger toward her.

If that wasn't enough, I'd painted the best picture of my life.

The kiss with Vincent had merely added to the glory of the afternoon.

After a moment of reflection, I admitted that, no, I was deceiving myself. The kiss had been a major event, not an addition. To feel his passion focused completely in my direction was almost enough to last me through years of emotional drought with Arthur. *Almost. Maybe.*

I touched my lips with one finger, reliving the feel of his bristly beard as it rubbed on my face and the way his tongue reached out to meet mine, a little hesitant at first then with more confidence. And how my breasts had tingled as they pressed against his chest.

I wouldn't do it again—didn't dare. But I didn't need to do it again to luxuriate in the memory.

When I finally slept, I dreamed of walking inside a world of paint that had been spread on a canvas, where every squishy step resulted in something beautiful appearing: poppies, bees, people carrying umbrellas, and lovers kissing under an acacia tree.

Sometime during the night, I realized that I'd given up many things in my life, but I didn't want to give up Vincent. I didn't care that I was married or that he was a penniless artist. He was precious to me. I had no idea how a relationship with him would work out or even if it *could* work out, but I was going to do whatever I could to keep him in my life—for a while, at least.

Chapter 19

I AWOKE ON FRIDAY MORNING with a melody in my head. I wasn't sure if I'd heard it before or if I'd made it up, but it was light and lilting, and I started my morning duties humming along with the song. When I caught Adeline looking at me curiously, the melody abruptly stopped. We were in mourning, so singing was inappropriate. Nevertheless, the song burst forth again of its own accord a few moments later. I grinned when I saw my daughter glaring at me, her face a study in disapproval. I shrugged. "I guess I can't be sad forever."

I sent Adeline to the boulangerie to get some fresh bread and pastries. When she was safely out of sight, I did a few twirls around the kitchen as the song burst forth again. Such a difference a day made.

Around nine, Vincent came downstairs and joined me in the kitchen. He glanced around to make sure we were alone then gave me a bashful smile. I couldn't keep the answering smile from my face, so it was good that Adeline wasn't there. She would surely have picked up on the spark between us. I would need to be more careful about showing my feelings for the man when others were around.

As long as Vincent stayed at the inn, I wanted to share everything I could with him. After all, he would surely move on before long, and

I would be alone again, with only memories to sustain me. I hoped we could make a few more memories before that happened.

Vincent had taken pains with his toilette, and his freshly scrubbed face gleamed. He wore a clean shirt, and his trousers weren't spattered with paint. He joined Hirschig at the breakfast table, and the two men talked quietly until they finished their coffee. Vincent followed me into the kitchen when I went to brew a new pot.

"How are you?" he asked quietly. "You seem rested."

"Yes, I'm fine. And you?" Again, I couldn't keep the smile from my face. "Thank you for cleaning up after me last night. Again."

"You're welcome. Again." He cleared his throat. "I just want you to know that I will be in and out this weekend. I'm painting a portrait of Gachet's daughter Marguerite, and it might take all day today and tomorrow. Uh, this is awkward, but I wanted to ask if you would assign someone else to clean my room? I would rather not ask it of you." Blushing, he added, "And I have made sure that your maid will find nothing embarrassing there."

Relieved, I nodded. "Yes, I'm sure it will be more comfortable for both of us if someone else cleans your room. Thank you for thinking of it."

"Also, is there a place in town where I can have a bath and get my clothes laundered?"

I told him about the bathhouse and promised to send his clothing to my laundress if he left it just inside his door.

"Thank you," he said. "I am embarrassed that I have let myself go so much. I believe it was because, for the past several years, no one cared how I looked, so I stopped caring too. Now I want to improve my appearance, at least a little, so I won't embarrass you and your lovely inn."

I insisted I liked him just the way he was, but he threw me a cryptic smile and left.

The next time we spoke privately, I would need to request that he be a little more discreet about his attraction to me. Although I appreciated his attention, I didn't want anyone else to see it, especially Arthur. My husband would be unrestrainable if he noticed the ember glowing between Vincent and me.

ON SATURDAY MORNING, I was serving customers who had stopped in for pastry and coffee when I turned around and saw a face I recognized. Gérard Dubois, my old friend from the neighborhood where I grew up, was standing in the doorway. We both beamed when our eyes met.

Gérard. I'd been hugely infatuated with him when I was twelve or thirteen. He was two years older and a friend of my brother's. The two boys tolerated my presence but just barely. I remembered how studious Gérard had been, always carrying a book around. I couldn't remember when I'd last seen him—possibly when I was fifteen or sixteen, before Denis took over my world.

He stood in the doorway and smiled, and I rushed to greet him with a kiss on both cheeks. Afterward, I stepped back and searched his face, which was lined and worn but achingly familiar.

"Gérard, it's wonderful to see you, but what are you doing here?"

He smiled and shook his head. "I heard about your mother's passing from Madame Chastain. You remember her, the upstairs neighbor your mother hated?" When I nodded, he continued, "She and Claudia became close friends after your father died. Did you know that?"

The things I didn't know about my mother would have filled an encyclopedia. "No. But Maman was full of surprises."

"Anyway, I rent a home in Auvers for the summer every year. Madame Chastain told me you were here, so I came to visit."

Seeing him lifted a weight from my shoulders. Until that day, everything and everyone in Auvers had been new. But a sweet part of my past was standing before me, and I felt more whole than I had since we'd left Paris.

"I'm delighted to see you. As you can see, I'm a proprietor of this inn. Please sit, and I'll bring you some coffee. Or would you prefer wine or beer?"

He laughed. "Coffee would be fine." When he saw only one table was vacant, he asked, "Is this a good time? Should I come back later? I'd love to catch up with you when it's convenient."

"This is fine." I caught the maid's eye and signaled for her to take over serving the other customers. "Please, sit. I'll bring you coffee. A pastry?"

"Yes, certainly. But will you join me?"

"Thank you—I'd love to." I brought his order and sat down with my own. "I can't believe it's you. You've grown up," I said with a smile.

"As have you." He sipped his coffee. "I'm sorry to hear about your mother's passing." He paused for a moment. "She was a lovely woman. I'm sure you miss her terribly."

I took a breath and nodded. "Her last month was a nightmare, so in one small way, her passing offered us all relief."

He nodded. "I lost my wife two years ago. She died in childbirth, along with our daughter."

"Oh, Gérard, I'm sorry." I touched his hand. "Do you have other children?"

He shook his head. "No, it's just me now. If you're like me, it'll take a while, but you'll gradually come to terms with the loss and move on." His eyes slid to look out the window, where a family with three small children was walking by. "I don't mean to imply it's been easy, because it hasn't. I loved Denise and our life together, but she's gone and I'm still here. Being alive makes every day special because I can live for her as well as myself." He blushed. "Sorry for the lecture.

I'm not telling you what you should do, just recounting the process I've gone through for the past two years." Grief explained the tired lines on his face.

"Thank you for telling me. It means so much that you would share your experience with me." I wiped away the tears that had formed as I listened.

Hearing Gérard's tale of woe put my loss into its proper perspective. Other people had survived worse tragedies than losing a beloved mother who was ready to release life. Yes, only a short time had passed since Maman's death, but I might soon be willing to look forward instead of back.

We sat in silence for a moment.

"What are you doing now?" I asked, changing the subject. "Let me guess. You're a teacher or a doctor, am I right? You were always so focused on your studies."

He laughed. "Yes, I'm a teacher. I teach French literature at the Lycée Henri-IV. Have for fifteen years now."

"Oh my goodness, the most prestigious school in Paris. I'm impressed. But not surprised. And now you have the summer off, and you've come to Auvers. What are you doing with your time?"

He smiled. "I'm trying to write a novel. It's about a man who loses his wife and meets a widow, falls in love, and marries again." Color rose up his neck. "I'm having a hard time with it, though. Instead of writing, I wander around and drink coffee with pretty ladies."

"But I'm not a widow," I said, laughing. I told him about Arthur and the children.

Just then, Germaine wandered into the café and said, "Maman, I hungry."

"Speaking of." I laughed as I set my daughter on my lap and gave her the last of my pastry. "I must tend to her. We usually have a snack and do our lessons now." I smiled, and as I did, the tension in my face relaxed. "I'm so happy to see you. Please come again, any time. And best of luck with your novel."

I picked up Germaine and headed toward our family rooms then halted. Arthur stood in the doorway of the billiard room, glaring at me.

"Arthur, what's wrong? Did something happen?"

"Who is that man you were flirting with?"

"What? Oh, that's Gérard. We grew up together. He's spending the summer in Auvers, so he came in to say hello. You should have stopped by so I could introduce you." I shook my head, my good mood instantly plummeting. "But I wasn't flirting with him—just catching up with an old friend. Why would you think I was flirting?"

He grabbed my arm and pulled me into our bedroom. I tensed, wondering what was to come. I decided I would scream if he hit me.

Germaine tightened her arms around my neck and made the initial sounds that would soon lead to a screech. That sound would surely stop him. But no, I wouldn't use my daughter for my own protection.

I kissed her cheek. "Shh, little one. Maman and Papa are having a discussion. Why don't you go to your room and pick out a book you'd like us to read? I'll be there in a minute."

Germaine scampered off, and I turned to Arthur, who continued to scowl. "He's an old friend. What is the problem? I speak with many customers over the course of a day."

He shook his head. "Not like that, you don't. I haven't seen you smile since your mother got so sick, and there you were, laughing and chatting with him like you were lovers. And you touched him as though you were single. You were flirting."

I thought back to my conversation with Danielle about flirting. I enjoyed flirting with Vincent, so my skills might have returned without my even noticing it.

No, I hadn't been flirting with Gérard. I'd been genuinely pleased to see an old friend who happened to be male—nothing else. "But... it felt good to smile a little. Gérard told me about his life, and it made my heart a little lighter to know an old friend was nearby. What could be wrong with that?"

Talking back to him could be dangerous, but I was tired of having my joy crushed by my loathsome husband. I stood as tall as I could and gave him a steely look.

"I'm watching you," he said, sneering. "Know that. Think about how people might construe your behavior." He stalked off.

I rubbed my arm. Gérard had brightened my day, and that was all. The problem was with Arthur, not me. What a boor he could be.

"Maman!" came the screech from Germaine's bedroom.

"Yes, I'm coming."

As I read to Germaine, I thought of the response I wished I'd given. If I'd been able to think clearly in the moment, I would've said something about the pot calling the kettle black. I'd known about his philandering for nearly two months, but I hadn't said a word to him about it. That would have been a perfect moment to let him know he wasn't fooling me.

But that comment would've started a fight. Getting Arthur riled up was always tricky and sometimes dangerous. Since we moved from Paris, I'd had no place to go for safety that was easy and quick. Maybe Danielle would help if it came to that. Or Gérard.

A warm place opened in my chest from knowing I wasn't alone. Every time I entertained the idea that Arthur might've changed, he did something to remind me he hadn't. He was still a bully, wanting to have his way in everything. I would need to watch my back because I definitely would talk with Gérard again if he returned to the café, or to anyone I pleased.

That included Vincent.

ON MONDAY, I TOOK GERMAINE with me to Paris while I completed the last of the paperwork relating to Maman's death. Afterward, I visited with Aunt Ella, who looked at least ten years younger than she had the month before. Life moved only forward, I reflected, regardless of how much one grieved, and I needed to move with it. I couldn't deny that the afternoon I'd shared with Vincent had helped to decrease my grief and anger. I smiled whenever I remembered our kiss, but I tried to hide the smiles from my aunt. We shared a long hug at the end of the visit.

With a question in her voice, Aunt Ella said, "I'm glad you're beginning to shed the grief."

I told her about sensing that my mother was near when I painted and how I'd felt her love and approval. Aunt Ella had also sensed my mother's presence, which comforted us both. We fell into each other's arms and cried.

Back at home, I put Germaine to bed and wished Adeline goodnight. In his most polite tone, Arthur requested I join him in the café for a cordial.

Oh no. What have I done wrong this time? My mind raced through some possibilities. Maybe he'd found my hiding place for the money I no longer placed in the strongbox. Or maybe Adeline had told him about my painting lessons. I'd intended to tell him about them but had never found the right time. I braced myself for something difficult and possibly dangerous. Rather than showing my nervousness, I attempted to project an air of ease.

"The trip to Paris went well," I told Arthur as he poured me a drink. "I think I'm done with everything I need to do about Maman."

He grinned at me in his most disgusting, leering style. "I'm glad to hear it. You're looking better too." He took a drink and then waggled his eyebrows in my direction. "Now, shall we make another child? I'd like to try for a son this time."

I started, so taken aback that I couldn't respond.

He laughed at my discomfiture but waited for my response.

I wanted to gag at the thought of intimacy with him. But he was being polite, so I tried to be the same and not anger him with my rejection. After a long pause, I said, "I think it's too late for more children. It took years to get pregnant with Germaine."

He raised his eyebrows. "Doesn't mean we can't try." He reached over and took my drink from my hand, set it down, and led me to the bedroom.

Several weeks had passed since he'd asked me for marital relations, and I couldn't think of a way out of it. So I allowed him his due. I lay under him as he pumped away and wondered what it would be like if Vincent was making love to me. It couldn't help but be better.

Chapter 20

ON TUESDAY, A LETTER arrived from Émile. My brother was sorry he hadn't been able to see Maman before she died. He thanked me for caring for her and again invited me to come to America. "It's exciting here, and they need wonderful chefs like you. If you want to run an inn, there are several within a mile of where I live." Also, he told me he'd recently married the woman he'd mentioned before, a widow with a son about Adeline's age. "I'd love for the two of you to meet. Please come."

I'd never understood his attraction to America. To my mind, it was a lawless frontier filled with cowboys and Indians like the ones I'd seen the year before at Buffalo Bill's Wild West show. While I'd enjoyed watching them whoop and holler as they performed bareback tricks on their horses, the wildness didn't attract me. Rather, I loved the sophistication of the Old World, with its long history and beautiful architecture. I resigned myself to never seeing my brother again. Sighing, I put the letter away and went on with my day.

That afternoon, I finally saw Vincent, who'd been away for a few days. He tromped through the back door and dumped his easel and paint box on the floor in the Artists' Room. Arthur was serving customers in the café, so I walked into the back room to say hello.

Vincent scowled as he paced up and down the small room. After making sure no one else was around, I placed my hand on his sleeve and smiled up at him. "How are you?"

"Fine," he said, his voice clipped. He continued pacing. Clearly, he was not fine.

"What happened?"

He took a breath and turned to me. "I'm sorry. It has nothing to do with you. I went to Paris on Sunday and visited with my brother and his family, and things didn't go well. The three of us ended up yelling at each other about money. Theo and Jo are struggling to pay their bills because my brother's employer pays him next to nothing, so Jo suggested I stop painting and get some kind of job. 'Anything,' she said." He snorted. "If not, she wants Theo to stop sending me money or at least cut down on the amount he sends." He took a breath and exhaled loudly. "And he had the nerve to say that if I ever had a wife, I'd understand how he had to put his wife and son before me."

His voice had risen as he talked, and I wasn't sure what to do. If Arthur heard this diatribe, he'd know immediately the two of us were more than mere landlady and boarder. No boarder would speak so personally to a landlady who was not also a friend—or a lover. Arthur already didn't trust me, and that would make things infinitely worse.

"Come outside and tell me there."

He started as if he'd suddenly come back to himself and recognized the impropriety of his words. "Oh. Certainly, madame."

He followed me out to what I now thought of as "Vincent's shed," the little room where we'd kissed five days before. I left the door open and hoped Arthur wouldn't come looking for me.

"All right, now tell me what happened."

"Agony. That's all I can say. They don't understand that I'm doing the best I can. I can't help it if Theo isn't doing enough to sell my paintings. He's too busy with his job and his family to exhibit my paintings, and then he blames *me* for using all his money that he needs to support Jo and the baby." His face was crimson, his breathing heavy, and his tone bitter.

I wanted to go to Paris and tell Theo how hard Vincent worked day after day and that his paintings were masterpieces that would surely sell soon. But of course, that wasn't my prerogative. I was only the landlady, and as long as he paid his rent, I had no right to an opinion. Tentatively, I placed a hand on his arm again and, pitching my voice low and gentle, said, "I'm so sorry. How did it end?"

"Huh. I stormed out." He stopped pacing then turned to me and placed his hand over mine, curling his fingers around it. After a long pause, he said, "Theo was right about one thing. I would love to have a wife." He gazed into my eyes, his anger dissipating. Quietly, he added, "I would love to have *you* for a wife."

Oh no. He shouldn't have said those words, not after only one kiss—not ever, really. I closed my eyes, aghast that he had spoken so optimistically about something that was clearly impossible.

He must've seen the terrified expression on my face, because he hastened to add, "Sorry. It was just a thought at the moment. You are already Arthur's wife, so obviously you can't be mine."

When he smiled, I saw the pain in his eyes.

"Oh, Vincent." I wanted to hug him and brush his lips again with mine, but I didn't dare. Instead, I ignored his personal words and turned the conversation back to his brother. "I'm sorry you had such a terrible time."

He nodded and pulled an envelope from his pocket. "I received this from Theo just now, but I'm afraid to open it."

I understood his fear. Receiving a letter after such a painful altercation would certainly be frightening.

"You and Theo are brothers, and brothers don't always agree. Surely, this isn't the first argument you've had."

He shook his head, shoulders slumped, eyes on the floor.

"Would you like me to read it and tell you if he's still angry?"

He bit his lip then said, "No. Thank you for your kind offer, but I'll read it."

Vincent opened the letter, only a single page, and skimmed it. "Theo says he's taking his family to Holland for his holidays because he wants our mother to meet her grandson. He won't be stopping by here either on the way there or back."

He sat on the stool and buried his face in his hands for a moment. When he raised his head, his expression was bereft. In a jagged voice, he said, "I had so hoped they would come here and we could rent the little house and paint together. That won't happen now. I'll have to tell the owner I won't be renting it." He spoke in a flat tone, one that spoke of deflated hope. Possibly, it was even worse, an echo of devastation.

"Did he say anything about the money?"

I hated to be so pragmatic, but I would need to know if he couldn't pay his rent anymore. Arthur would surely evict him, which would change everything between us. Anxiety rose in my chest, and I struggled to catch my breath.

"Yes, he said he would continue to send my allowance for the time being. He'll reassess the situation after he returns from his holiday." Vincent said something in Dutch that might have been cursing.

I didn't understand the words and didn't ask. Vincent's French was perfect, but nothing was like one's own language for expressing deep emotion. I exhaled forcefully.

"I'm glad there's at least some good news." I paused. "I'm sorry, but I need to go before Arthur becomes suspicious. Is there anything I can do for you?"

He shook his head then looked at me with soft eyes. "You've given me a gift that no one else ever has, and that was listening without judgment. Thank you, dear Louise. I'm better now."

I wanted to kiss him again—wanted it in the worst way—but I dared not. Even if no one saw us, Vincent might have thought I did it because I wanted to marry him. As sweet as he was, nothing could be further from the truth. I already had one husband, and I didn't need another. Even though I might daydream about someday marrying Vincent, that was only a daydream, not reality. I wasn't sure if Vincent understood it the same way.

"I'll see you for dinner, then." Reluctantly, I left him there and walked back into my own life.

That night, when I served Vincent his Pernod, he asked in a soft voice, "Will you meet me tomorrow in the field where we last met? Midafternoon?"

I considered. That would be Wednesday, my typical day to go to Paris. Since I'd been there just the day before, I didn't need to go again, but Arthur would notice if I disappeared after lunch, and I wasn't sure he would believe I'd merely been out for a walk, especially if I returned with chapped lips and disheveled hair.

Shaking my head, I said, "I can't tomorrow. But I could on Thursday. Will that work?"

He nodded, but his eyes were sad. "Whatever your schedule permits. Thank you for seeing me." He looked down at his drink, and I turned around to see Arthur watching me.

The next time I went to the bar, Arthur asked, "What was that about with Monsieur Vincent?"

"Oh, he wants us to do his laundry. But I told him he'd have to wait until Thursday." I shrugged. "He smells like a skunk from that cheap tobacco he's always puffing on. I'm happy he wants his clothes laundered."

He laughed and patted my behind. "Good one, *ma belle*. It's nice to see your sense of humor returning."

With an effort of will, I kept myself from cringing at his touch and also from glancing at Vincent to see if he'd heard our interchange. I felt as though I'd been unfaithful to one of the two men but not the one to whom I was married.

ON WEDNESDAY AFTERNOON, Arthur finally left for Paris for a few days, and I could breathe more easily. I went about my duties with a song on my lips, knowing I would see Vincent the next day.

On Thursday morning, Adeline asked to go out with her friends for a while. Her two-week period of forced servitude had passed, so her request wasn't unreasonable.

I placed my hands on my hips and gave her a hard look. "Who else will be with you?"

"Uh, Cécile is one of them. I'm not sure who else. Just girls, though."

I considered. Adeline had been polite and helpful ever since the vandalism incident, and she'd even paid back the cost of the tomatoes she'd stolen. She deserved some leniency.

"Where are you going?"

"Cécile's maman said we could sit on the picnic table behind their inn and talk."

That seemed perfectly appropriate. "All right, then. I expect there won't be any boys in the group unless Danielle is around to chaperone. Is that understood?"

"Yes."

"Be back by lunchtime."

Adeline nodded and quickly left. I stood outside and watched her walk down the road. She didn't turn around to see if she was be-

ing observed, so I shrugged and stepped back inside. Maybe I was being too suspicious. But I knew whom Arthur would blame if Adeline
got into more trouble, and it wouldn't be Adeline.

A few moments later, Gérard entered with Danielle on his arm.
She grinned when she saw my mouth hanging open. They took a
table by the window. "I told you she'd be surprised," she said to
Gérard, speaking loudly enough that I could hear.

He laughed. "Indeed you did, my dear." He reached over and patted her hand then clasped it.

I came to take their order, a delighted smile on my face.

Gérard appeared to be years younger than he had the last time I'd
seen him, and much happier. He said to me, "I told you I was writing
a book about a man whose wife had died and his attraction to a widow. This is my widow. You two know each other, I take it."

I squeezed their hands. "That comment was too subtle for me,
I suppose. Arthur thought you were interested in me, but I assured
him it wasn't so. And now I know why." I laughed.

"But you are married, my dear Louise. I would never try to steal
you from your husband. Besides, I met Danielle in early June, when I
first arrived, and it was love at first sight."

Danielle nodded, her face alight with joy.

"Coffee and pastry are on the house. Best wishes to you both."

I decided not to tell Arthur about my friends' romance, to let
him think what he wanted because that would turn his attention
away from what was happening in his own home between Vincent
and me.

I also didn't ask Danielle whether Adeline was with Cécile that
morning. I didn't think I could cope with one more thing if her answer was negative. I would just have to trust that Adeline could stay
out of trouble for a while.

THAT EVENING, AFTER I cleaned the kitchen and put the girls to bed, I finally had some time to myself. I sat on the porch and again considered Vincent's words about how he would love for me to be his wife. They'd been resonating in my soul ever since he said them.

His wife. I was powerfully attracted to him—that was true. But he was the proverbial starving artist, and from what I'd heard, they made terrible marriage partners. Besides, we barely knew each other. Even if I could, I would never marry someone unless I'd known him for a long time.

Getting left by my first love had made me jaded about love, as had living with someone I loathed. I didn't know if I would be interested in marrying again, even if that was possible. So many of my friends in Paris described their marriages as difficult after the first bloom of love wore off. They joked about their desire to live separate lives and see their husbands only occasionally while enjoying lovers. But only the rich could afford that.

I sat up straighter as a thought came to me: I *was* rich, so maybe Arthur and I could live separately. That luscious idea tasted like the richest chocolate cake I could imagine. I could move back to Paris, and Arthur could stay at the inn if he wanted or go wherever he liked. And I could see whether a relationship with Vincent would be possible.

After only a moment's consideration, I knew it wouldn't work. As soon as Arthur discovered I had enough money to move away from him, he would claim my inheritance, and I would be without options.

Mon Dieu. Will this be my life until I die, even with the money? I wasn't sure I could bear that.

Unbidden, another thought arose. If Arthur died, I would be a widow and could control my money and live my own life—and possibly marry again if I chose. I brightened at the thought.

After a moment, reality set in. Arthur was only forty and in relatively good health. Of course, he drank heavily. Still, he might trip as he went down the stairs, hit his head, and die.

But no, I wouldn't allow myself to think that way. If he died, I would be relieved—I could admit that much. But wishing him dead could lead me to think about how to help his death along—pushing him down the stairs, for example. I refused to imperil my mortal soul in that way, and I wasn't sure I could live with the consequences even if I made it appear to be an accident and the police didn't arrest me. If my children lost their father, they would need their mother even more.

If Arthur died, it would not be by my hand.

Before I married him, I'd thought everything would be sunshine and roses, but instead I'd gotten thistles and rain. Wishing for life to be different didn't make it so.

Marriage to Vincent was out of the question for many reasons, but spending time with him made my spirit much, much lighter. I would enjoy our flirtation—and even our kisses—as long as Arthur didn't find out. I would have to be very careful, though, because I didn't want to consider what might happen if he did.

Chapter 21

Success is sometimes the outcome of a whole string of failures.
–Vincent van Gogh

ON THURSDAY AFTERNOON, I waited to meet Vincent until Germaine was napping and Adeline had gone out with Cécile. I wore my nicest black dress—I was still in mourning, unfortunately—but added a bit of perfume behind my ears and just the slightest bit of color to my cheeks. I probably didn't need it, since anticipation of another kiss would have brightened them anyway.

Vincent was just where I expected him to be, standing back from a rarely used path through the wheat fields. The wheat was higher than it had been when we met there before—it was taller than Germaine now—and it swayed in the slight breeze. The air was oppressive, as though a heavy blanket lay on the day. A storm might hit later in the evening, which would be a welcome relief, but for the moment, the July heat threatened to overtake me. Fortunately, I'd brought a bottle of wine in a hamper, as well as a hunk of cheese and a loaf of bread.

Vincent had painted another picture of the wheat fields, depicting them under a threatening sky. He'd increased the menace of the coming storm, making the sky a dark, ominous blue. That shade of blue hadn't yet arrived in the real afternoon, but it would be exactly right in a few hours. If I hadn't already felt the humidity, I could've done so by looking at that painting. It perfectly depicted summer—lush growth, hot days, and cooling storms.

He watched me examine the painting, a glint in his eyes. "What do you think? I did this one quickly. Maybe I should go back and re-touch it."

I shook my head. "Please don't. It isn't as elaborate as many of your others, but I can almost feel the promised raindrops." I laughed and glanced up at the sky, which at that moment was still a lighter, happier shade of blue.

"Then I shall leave it this way and give it to you when it dries."

He gestured toward a blanket he'd spread on the grass under the only stand of trees anywhere around. I recognized the blanket as the one from his bed. That seemed an appropriate use for it since his room was so hot that he surely wouldn't have slept under its weight for some time. I dropped onto it, straightening my legs and arranging my skirt so my ankles could peek out.

Just once, I would have loved to remove some of my hot clothes and let the breeze dry the sweat that dampened my entire front and puddled under my arms. But that wasn't possible—only a daydream.

I pulled out the food I'd brought.

"A jug of wine, a loaf of bread, and thou," he said, musingly.

"*The Rubaiyat of Omar Khayyam.* I love that poem. I've thought seriously of stitching it onto a cushion or hanging it on the wall of the café."

He nodded. "But only if lovers frequent your restaurant."

The thought of Gérard and Danielle made me smile. "Two of my friends are just getting to know each other, and they like to meet at our restaurant in the mornings. I don't know if they're lovers, but if not now, then soon."

He smiled and poured the wine into the small glasses I'd taken from the hamper. We ate and drank in silence for a few moments.

I wasn't sure what to say next, and he didn't give any indication of wanting to break the silence.

After a while, I couldn't wait any longer to hear his voice. "Uh, you asked me to come here today. Is everything okay? What about with your brother? I saw you received a couple of letters yesterday."

He sighed and said, "It gives every sign of working out, only not as I'd wished. My sister-in-law wrote to apologize for her 'tantrum,' as she called it. And she will go to Holland without Theo, at least for the first part of his holiday. He should be able to visit me here, he says, but only for a few days."

He drank a sip of wine and stared at me, the sides of his eyes crinkling with his smile. "Nothing is wrong. I just wanted to spend an afternoon with you, without rush, without fear of being interrupted, and without thinking about painting." He laughed. "At least as much as that is possible. I think about painting every moment of the day when I'm alone, so being in your presence should give my mind something else to do."

"I always look forward to painting with you, but this is nice too." I hesitated. "I'm glad the crisis has resolved itself somewhat. And I'm also glad you'll be staying on with us for a while longer, even if it's not your first choice." I smiled and patted his hand.

He didn't speak, so I changed the subject. "If you will, tell me about your early life. I know you're Dutch, but that's all I know about you."

"Ha." He told me about being the oldest of six children and growing up as a Protestant pastor's son in Zundert. "I was always different, as you can see. I wasn't an easy child, I'm told, and I left school before finishing. I knew I had to work to earn my keep, but I couldn't settle on a profession. Following in the family tradition, I started out as an art dealer, but my employer didn't approve of my penchant for telling people the truth, and we parted ways."

He laughed, shaking his head, then went on with his story. He'd tried to become a minister like his father, but that hadn't worked either.

"And now, I have no connection with organized religion. That led to many bitter arguments with my father. He never accepted me as I am, and then he died, so we will never reconcile." He pulled off a hunk of bread and chewed it slowly.

I opened my mouth to speak words of consolation, but he didn't seem to be finished, so I closed it and waited.

After a moment, he continued, "I know now that all the changes in profession were only to prepare me for my true destiny: to paint." He told me about how he taught himself to draw and paint, along with enduring many struggles to finally end up in the place where he'd mastered his craft well enough that he could communicate emotion through his paintings.

"And so, dear Louise, that's all there is to tell. Oh, well, there are a few other things, but we shall get to them at a later time. Tell me about you."

I described my early life in Paris and how much I loved my family and my city, and how I'd yearned to be a painter when I was younger. "I know it's hard for anyone to succeed as an artist—and even harder for a woman—but it was what I wanted."

I paused, wondering whether to tell him any more about my life. To my ears, I sounded boring, like every other dull housewife in the country. I decided to risk it, to dive beneath the surface and talk about some things that mattered to me.

"When I was very young, I fell in love with a young man named Denis, who looked a bit like you." I described our time together, how we'd planned to marry, and how it had ended. Finally, I told him about my mother's letter and how I was struggling to forgive her.

He sat in silence for a long time after I finished talking. Finally, he cleared his throat. "I am so sorry. You have been unfairly treated.

I can tell how much you loved your Denis. And so, your family arranged for you to marry Arthur, even though you didn't love him?"

I nodded, surprised as always at the speed of his connections. I looked away, at the wheat fields and the sky, but realized I didn't want to spend our time together in tears and recriminations. I could do that later, when I was alone. Right then, I wanted to be in the moment with this intriguing man.

"Isn't it interesting how life leads us on such uneven paths?" I asked. "With all that behind us, here we are, sitting beneath this lovely tree, enjoying the beautiful view, and having this delightful conversation."

He lay on his back and stared at the sky. "Yes, that is so," he said in an odd tone.

After a moment, he sat up, looking as serious as I'd ever seen him. "I need to tell you one more thing, and after that, you may not wish to spend any more time with me. But tell you I must if I am to be an honorable man." He stuck his pipe, unlit, between his teeth, as a child might grasp a favorite stuffed animal or blanket.

He sat up and stared into my eyes. "You see, I'm afraid I have a disease." He drew a breath. "For the past two years, at least every three months, I have been afflicted by some sort of seizures of the mind and body that have led me to do damage to myself—only to myself, not to others, in case you are inclined to worry."

I shook my head and made an attempt to smile, but it was a paltry one.

"Although I don't remember the incident, this was why I mangled my ear." He reached up to feel his left earlobe—all that was left of the ear. "I ended up admitting myself to an asylum in Saint-Rémy de Provence and stayed there for a year. The doctors believe I have some kind of epilepsy, although they aren't sure. There isn't any effective treatment, apparently, other than long baths and a peaceful atmosphere, so I have continued to have attacks every few months."

He paused and rubbed his eyes. "Finally, although the doctors were kind and the place was peaceful, I grew weary of being locked up. My brother asked me to come to Auvers so I could be under the care of Dr. Gachet. Truthfully, I don't know what he can do for me if I have another attack. Anyway, here I am." He stopped, watching me closely.

Most of what he said was news to me. Danielle had mentioned the asylum, but I'd assumed he was healed. His confession revealed that he was far sicker than I'd realized. How terrible for him.

My heart melting, I gestured for him to continue.

"That's the big thing about me," he said, trying to laugh but managing only a sad chuckle. "You deserve to know, if you're to have anything further to do with me. But I've dreaded telling you. In fact, I would rather have pulled out my tongue than tell you."

When he saw the horrified expression on my face, he shook his head and covered my hand with his. "No, I'm not about to do that. It was a poor joke to cover my embarrassment."

He paused and took a breath. "I may be due for another attack in a month or two. I don't know if it will happen, though. I feel much better than I have in a long time. And now that I know you, Louise, I feel like a new man. I have had some experience with women, as you must expect, but I have never known a gentlewoman like you who gave me a second glance."

He gripped my hand. "Even if we never speak again, know that you have made my grim days so much brighter, and I cannot thank you enough for that."

His eyes slid away from mine and stared down into the valley.

No words came to me. In fact, I could hardly draw a breath. This situation was much, much worse than I'd expected. Other than being abrupt and sometimes anxious, he'd appeared to be relatively normal—as normal as any other painter of my acquaintance, anyway. They were all unusual and eccentric, in my experience.

But this... This was in an entirely different league, far beyond eccentric.

I could sense him awaiting my response, but at the moment, I had none. I had to think about his words and speak to someone, to Danielle or Hélène, at least—possibly Dr. Gachet too.

I measured my words carefully. "Thank you for sharing this with me, Vincent. It must have been difficult to do so and even more difficult to live with the potential health threat hanging over your head all the time. I can't even imagine how hard this has been for you. I suppose that explains why you rush to paint, because you don't know how much longer you'll have."

He nodded, and his shoulders relaxed a bit. He let go of my hand, but he did not meet my eyes.

"I apologize for being unable to respond appropriately right now, but I need to think about what you've told me. What you've described is a serious malady, and I am so very sorry it afflicts you." I paused, feeling my way toward what I wanted to say. Finally, I continued, "You spoke of wishing I was your wife. I know it was just a passing thought, and you immediately withdrew your words and apologized. Even though I am strongly attracted to you, divorce is impossible, so there is no use speaking any further of that. But we enjoy each other's company, and the time I've spent with you has already enriched my life."

I took a breath. "Please give me some time to think about what we might mean to each other in light of your health situation."

He spent a moment lighting his pipe and inhaling before speaking. Finally, when all was set, he pulled it out of his mouth and said, "Thank you for your honesty, dear Louise. I did not expect you to be as open as you clearly are to even hearing about my condition. Your response is far beyond what I could have expected."

I placed the rest of our meal into my hamper, and we stood awkwardly a few feet away from each other. Before I left, though, he stepped toward me and wrapped me in his arms, and I reciprocated. We stood entwined for a long moment before I pulled away.

In a different, less serious tone, he said, "I am sorry to have used our usual painting time for this talk. If you would still like to continue painting with me, would tomorrow work?"

Relieved at hearing his lighter tone and knowing we could continue painting together, I said, "No. Not tomorrow. But what about Saturday?"

"Yes. I can manage that."

"Au revoir."

"Au revoir."

MY MIND WAS ABLAZE as I walked back to town. *The poor, poor man. How he must have suffered.* To have come out of all that misery with his mind still intact must have been a miracle.

I stopped at the local church to pray for him. Despite my turmoil, I smiled as I walked into the small building, which Vincent had painted as looking grander. He undeniably saw the world through eyes that differed from anyone else's. Maybe his illness had led him to see in that fashion, and if so, I was thankful for it, for I believed his art would outlast him even if he lived to be very old.

Sitting alone in a pew, I prayed that I would be led to do the right thing and that Vincent would live to paint for many more years. My prayer completed, I waited for a response. Long moments passed, but I received no clear direction, either from above or from within myself.

After a while, a thought came to me. *Vincent clearly longs for me, but do I need him? What can he offer me?* I was the one with the inn, the children, the respect of others, and—dare I think it?—the money. If we were lovers, I could give him a stability he'd apparently never known within his own family except with his brother, Theo. That kind of stability could doubtless be good for his health, and it might allow him to create his art without feeling such time pressure. *But what about me? What would I get from loving him?*

The answer came slowly. I loved so many things about him. First, he noticed me—all of me—and showed his caring in a way I'd never known. I loved painting with him and learning from him. Also, I loved the way he treated my children, so kindly and with the same level of attention he gave me. Of course, I loved his passion, both for his art and for me. And I loved that he was his true self all the time, showing both the good and the bad, and that he'd told me the truth about himself early so that I could make my own decision about any potential relationship. The integrity of that action warmed my heart.

Yes, I could love the man, and if I weren't married, I might have considered him as a potential marriage partner. But aside from the impossibility of our being together, I didn't know how much I would be willing to change my life for him, especially if I would be required to watch him descend into madness over and over for the rest of his life.

I needed to speak with someone about this right away. The urge to sit with a female friend, pour my heart out, then receive some objective advice nearly overwhelmed me. Hélène was my first choice, but I couldn't go to Paris right away, and this couldn't wait. Danielle was next since we'd already spoken about my attraction to Vincent. She had encouraged me to flirt with him, but I didn't know what she would say about the current situation. Vincent and I were far beyond the flirting stage.

When I returned home, I sent a message to Danielle, asking to speak with her confidentially as soon as possible. The reply came immediately: I was invited to her inn at ten the next morning, and we could speak privately for as long as I needed.

I sighed as I fed the paper to the stove. The next day, I would unburden my heart and hope to receive some answers.

Chapter 22

*Be clearly aware of the stars and infinity on high. Then life seems al-
most enchanted after all.*
–Vincent van Gogh

IN THE MIDDLE OF THE night, the sound of the shutters banging on the front of the building awakened me. The expected storm
had arrived. I rushed to close them, and then, wearing only my nightgown, I walked into the backyard and watched the show. Lightning
lit up the sky as if someone was turning on and off a magnificent electrical lamp: first, the shocking light was almost too strong for my eyes
to tolerate, then the night was completely black, leaving spots floating around the periphery of my vision. The thunderclaps might've
been a train wreck on the other side of the valley except they went on
and on. Faster, faster, the sound and light came, first a few seconds
apart then in unison. As I watched the squall, I wasn't sure which
emotion was stronger: fear or elation.

I stood, mesmerized, until the first raindrop plopped to the
ground in front of me. Suddenly, the rain was falling in buckets,
so I ran back into the building and watched the storm through the
screened door.

I wondered if Vincent was in his room, safe from the rain. I
hadn't seen him since I'd walked away from him that afternoon. I
hoped he wasn't sleeping outdoors, as he sometimes did. If that was

the case, he was already soaked through. I feared he'd stayed away because he couldn't face me.

Suddenly, I heard footsteps behind me—a boarder, most likely needing to use the privy. *Oh no.* I was in my nightgown. Before I could turn and rush to my room, hands rested lightly on my shoulders. I would know the feel of those hands anywhere—Vincent. With anyone else, I would've been embarrassed to be caught in a state of undress, but not with Vincent. He moved his hands to encircle my waist as I leaned back into his chest.

"I came down to enjoy the storm," he whispered close to my ear. "I didn't know you were here. It's a double delight."

"I didn't see you this evening, so I thought you hadn't returned," I whispered back.

"And yet, here I am. Here *we* are."

The wind shifted, driving raindrops through the screen. I closed the main door and

turned toward him. Forgetting my vows to never kiss him again, I welcomed his lips on mine. After a few seconds, though, I pulled away.

"We can't do this," I whispered, suddenly terrified. "Someone might come. The girls..."

"Yes." He stepped back, away from me. "I bid you good night." He brushed my face with his hand, then he was gone.

I tiptoed back into my bedroom, shivering from the sudden drop in temperature when he wasn't holding me. I lay awake and thought about the unexpected encounter. We were lucky Arthur was in Paris and neither of my daughters—nor any of the boarders—had gotten up to see the storm. Our delicious time together would've been ruined, and something terrible could have been the result.

I would need to be more careful in the future. Nothing like that could ever happen again, at least at the inn.

Still, I smiled and hugged myself the way he had hugged me.

ON MY WAY TO THE PRIVY the next morning, I heard a sound coming from the clearing where I'd seen the dead pigeon. Hoping to solve the mystery, I tiptoed to the bushes and, with a quick movement, pushed them out of the way. What I saw astounded me. Adeline and René were locked in each other's arms, kissing as though they were lovers or soon to be. They were so involved that they didn't see or hear me until I cleared my throat.

"Ahem."

Instantly, they broke apart, looking chagrined as they stared, horrified, at me.

I tried to calm my voice enough that I would sound stern instead of hysterical, but that was difficult when every ounce of my being wanted to scream and shout at this outrage. "All right, enough of that. Young man, despite her behavior, my daughter is still a child. I don't want to see you with her again. Do you hear me?"

He nodded but didn't move.

I turned to Adeline, who had wiped her mouth and was glaring in my direction. Drawing myself up to my full height, I straightened my spine. Regardless of what might happen later, I was the adult, and I would not back down, nor would I overlook my daughter's outrageous behavior.

"And you, young lady, you've been lying to me. Have you ever gone to Cécile's house?"

Adeline pursed her lips and held her head high, fury emanating from her eyes. She shook her head.

I could hardly comprehend what was happening. My daughter was openly defying me. *What now?* All I could think to say was, "Wait until your father finds out. At the very least, you will have to stay at home until school starts." I paused and stamped my foot. "Now, go to your room."

Adeline held her ground. "You know who Papa will blame if you tell him about this? You. Not me." Her voice quavered, but she continued as though giving a speech she'd thoroughly rehearsed. "I'll make a deal with you. I won't mention anything about this to Papa if you don't. But I *will* continue to see René whenever I want. I won't steal any more tomatoes, though, so Papa need not find out. Besides, he likes René."

René moved up to stand beside Adeline and held her hand as they both glared at me.

I stood like a statue, not believing what I was hearing, wondering what had happened to my sweet girl. My heart pounded so hard that I feared I might faint. I didn't know how to respond.

After a moment, the answer came to me.

I turned to René. "This was your idea, was it not? My daughter would never have defied me like this before you came around."

He didn't answer, but I thought I detected the beginning of a smirk on his face.

Something else became clear to me. "You killed the pigeon that day. You were waiting in the bushes for Adeline to come. When my presence kept her from joining you, you killed the pigeon to show your anger."

The smirk deepened. He shrugged.

I gave Adeline a grim look. "This is the boy you defy me for? He's dangerous, Adeline."

Adeline paled and dropped his hand, suddenly turning back into the scared child who must've been hiding behind the defiant young woman all along.

I spoke to René again, my voice icy. "I suggest, for your own welfare, that you leave this house and never return. I will chance a beating just to keep my daughter away from you. Now, *leave*. If I see you again, I will inform your parents and my husband that you're trying to seduce a thirteen-year-old girl, and we'll see who is blamed."

He glanced at Adeline and quickly shuffled backward until he was out of sight.

Adeline stared at the ground as tears fell from her eyes. "I'm sorry, Maman. I didn't mean to be so horrible to you." She thrust herself into my arms. "Please don't hate me."

I shook my head and held her as she cried. *What just happened?* Clearly, that young man was a bad influence on my extremely vulnerable daughter. Still, I didn't trust this turnaround to sweetness and tears any more than I trusted the anger and defiance. She seemed to be an actress who could change personas on a whim in order to get what she wanted from people. I would need to do something drastic to keep her away from René. But right then, I had to deal with the sobbing child in my arms.

"I don't hate you, *ma chérie*. But I have to be somewhere shortly, so we'll talk about this later. Go to your room now. And stay there until I get back."

Adeline ran into the inn, and I sank onto a chair, trembling. I had no idea how to address this mercurial child. But I would look further into the situation as soon as I returned from speaking to Danielle. By then, I might have developed or discovered some source of wisdom.

AT DANIELLE'S INN, a plate of pastries and a pot of tea awaited us in the sitting room.

After pouring our tea, Danielle said, "I can see how upset you are. I'm honored you've come to me, and I'll try to give you my best advice if that is what you want. Or I'll help in any other way I can."

On the way to Danielle's inn, I'd decided to focus on the situation with Vincent and leave Adeline out of it. I could expect a woman friend to help resolve only so many problems at any one time. I would ask Hélène later for advice about Adeline.

"Thank you. I have something to consult with you about. I know you're the soul of discretion and wisdom, but I need you to promise that you won't share what I'm about to say with anyone."

Danielle said, "Of course. You may wonder, given that I talk so easily about my personal affairs. But I can keep a secret, I assure you, so please do not fear on that account."

I nodded and smiled. That assurance was good enough for me. I sipped my tea and struggled to find appropriate words. Eventually, I started at the beginning, describing the physical abuse by Arthur, Germaine's illnesses, and how we'd ended up in Auvers to start a new life. Danielle knew most of the story already, but she listened carefully.

When my words came to a stop, Danielle's response held no trace of the frequent laughter with which she met the world. "My dear, I'm so sorry for you. My husband was not a brute like yours, but he wasn't an easy man. I tell you truthfully, I'm not sorry he's gone. But is there something more you wanted to speak about?"

"Ah, yes, there is." My neck heated up. "Ah, do you remember when I told you about the red-headed painter who is staying at our inn? Vincent van Gogh?"

Danielle's face lit up with an enormous smile. "I do. Is there more to say on this subject?"

"Well, yes." I told her about my attraction to him and what had led to his words about how he would love for me to be his wife. At that point, the smile on Danielle's face faded.

"Oh no. Things have become more complicated than a simple act of flirting or sexual enjoyment."

I took a breath. "There's been no sexual enjoyment yet, but the situation is even more complex than that." I told Danielle about yesterday's conversation in the wheat field. "The poor man—I feel so terrible for him, with all he's suffered. But what am I to do?"

Danielle was silent for a long while as we finished our tea. As I waited for my friend to respond, the dreadful anxiety that had beset me for most of a day lifted, and my shoulders relaxed. I hadn't known Danielle very long, but she was already a dear friend, and I hoped we would maintain our friendship for the rest of our lives.

Finally, Danielle set down her cup. "I see the problem, and it's a very real one. Being a woman and a mother, you don't have the luxury of dropping everything and running off with this man, as wonderful as he must be, even if he were healthy. Your responsibility is to your children first and then to yourself. Am I right?"

I nodded.

"You may or may not spend the rest of your life with Arthur. He's a bully, and you've suffered more than enough from his fists. But that isn't why you're here today. You want to know how to respond to Vincent's confession about his condition. Am I correct?"

"Exactly."

"Then let me say that I don't think you have enough information to decide whether to leave the life you've made here and try to make one with him. You don't know if he'll stay healthy, and you also don't know him nearly well enough to make that decision. Over the years that I've been a widow, I've learned to enjoy the affections of men from time to time, with no expectations of making a lifetime commitment." She blushed and smiled. "Gérard is different in that regard. After I've known him for a while, I may very well consider making a life with him."

She paused. "But we aren't here to talk about me. In terms of your situation, I suggest you spend more time with Vincent before you make any major changes. You're still grieving for your mother, and you might be tempted to find someone else to care for who will take her place in your heart. But your loss is still too raw for you to be certain of any decisions you make now. The world won't end if you have an affair with this man. Times are changing, and women will soon be granted the same rights to adultery or anything else that men have always enjoyed. Many women enjoy those things now, but they take their pleasure in secret and don't flaunt it." She beamed at me.

"But..."

"If he remains healthy while you're learning about each other, so much the better. If not, you've not made a lifetime commitment, and you can say goodbye and allow his brother to care for him."

Danielle took a bite of biscuit and chewed slowly. "I have an idea for you," she said after she swallowed. "As you know, Gérard has rented a house in town for the summer, but he is spending several days each week in Paris as he prepares to teach. So, his house here is available for the occasional tryst. I feel sure he wouldn't mind if you and Monsieur Vincent took some time to get to know each other there while he's away—maybe for an hour or two on days when you can get away from Arthur? I often go to Paris when Gérard is there, so we would be changing places. Isn't it delicious that I'll be in Paris with my lover while you're here with yours? You can get to know each other in private, and after a few months of this, you'll be in a better position to decide whether he's someone you will want to change everything for."

She paused. "What do you think?"

I grabbed my friend's hand and squeezed it. "I love it. You have perfectly described the issue. But would Gérard be willing to let us use his house for... whatever we wanted to do?"

Danielle laughed, long and loud. "I can't imagine he'd be anything but pleased to see you happy. He's told me several times how downcast you look when your husband is around. He will do whatever he can for you, I'm sure. I'll ask him, though, and let you know. My only concern is that he'll be leaving Auvers in mid-August to return to his teaching, so at that point, you'll need to make other arrangements. But we'll take it a day at a time and see what happens, no?"

"Oh, yes. Thank you, Danielle."

"And come to me with the children if your husband beats you again. You will be safe here for as long as you like."

We stood and embraced for a long moment.

"I will let Vincent know about this possibility when I see him," I said, the words burbling from a font of joy deep inside me, "and we can decide on a schedule. But I'll wait until I hear from you before I do anything. I hope it will be soon?"

"I'll get back to you by this evening."

We parted, and I nearly skipped down the road to our inn.

I FELT LIGHTER AND more confident when I went into Adeline's room and sat on her bed. My daughter laid down the book she'd been reading and looked at me, her eyes large and frightened.

While I was trying to decide how to start the conversation, Adeline began crying again. "I'm sorry, Maman. It sounded so reasonable when René told me what to say, but I didn't realize how the words would hurt you. I've been thinking about it, and I hate him now. He's a horrible boy and mean. I don't know how he convinced me to do the things I did."

I took a deep breath and blew it out. *Is that true? Maybe and maybe not.* Before that summer, I hadn't considered Adeline to be a particularly devious child, but her tears seemed altogether too perfectly timed to be believable. Someday, she might be a famous actress, but that was in the future. At present, I wouldn't be able to trust her again for quite a while. Words of regret weren't going to be nearly enough. Even so, I was happy to hear them.

I tipped Adeline's face up to mine and kissed her on the nose. "Men can be very convincing when they want something from you. But you need to think for yourself, especially in situations where you've met a persuasive talker." I kissed her again. "Now, let that be the end of it. I expect you to not see René again. In fact, I'll be watching you very closely from now on. I hope you've learned your lesson. And we won't mention anything about this to Papa."

Adeline nodded. "Thank you, Maman. *Je t'aime.*"

"I love you too."

As I was leaving the room, I noticed something different on Adeline's dresser. Walking closer, I saw a new pair of women's dress gloves. They were of fine quality and white rather than black.

"What are these?"

Adeline's face immediately assumed a guilty look, and her eyes darted back and forth. "Gloves. Papa brought them for me." She paused. After a moment, she said, in a small voice, "I didn't know what to do with them."

I sighed. "Put them away. You can't wear them until you're out of mourning, anyway."

I left the room, wondering if I had any idea what was really going on in my home. I'd always purchased Adeline's clothes and couldn't imagine why Arthur had bought her those fancy, grown-up gloves.

VINCENT DIDN'T RETURN for the midday meal, but he sat at his regular table for dinner. I could see that he welcomed the secret smile I gave him, for he grinned in my direction, his eyes soft.

Arthur had arrived home from Paris in time to help with the dinner rush. Afterward, when he was drinking with friends in the billiard room, I sat down with Vincent. Quickly, in hushed tones, I told him of Danielle's solution to our problem. I'd received a note from my friend that afternoon, in which she offered Gérard's house to us on Tuesday afternoons and Friday mornings, if that would work for us.

"Yes" was Vincent's answer. "I'll arrange my painting schedule so no one sees me arrive at the house—or leave it."

"I'll do my best. Fridays are easiest since Arthur is in Paris. I'll see about Tuesday afternoons. Maybe I can get away for an hour but not every week." I paused. "Will you do me a favor, though? Would you keep our friendship a secret between the two of us and our two friends who are lending us the house? Please don't share this with your brother or anyone else, at least for now."

"Certainly, my dear lady. You do not need to ask. As a gentleman, I would have done this anyway. I've painted a portrait of Dr. Gachet's daughter, and I believe she has taken a fancy to me. If anyone asks why I'm in such a good mood, I will allow them to think this young woman is the cause."

I laughed and rose to serve a customer who was calling for more beer. "Tomorrow is Saturday. I'll see you then for our lesson."

"It cannot come too soon, madame," he said, rising and bowing.

As I walked into the kitchen, I nearly collided with Arthur, who stared at me with a question in his eyes. "What were you talking about with that man?"

"What man?" I was startled, but I'd prepared for the eventuality of being caught speaking with Vincent. "Oh, Monsieur Vincent? Just that I'd like to take painting lessons from him. He agreed, and we'll start tomorrow. I've arranged to trade making his breakfasts early in exchange for the lessons." My heart pounded, but I tried to act casual. "Why do you ask?"

Arthur stared at me for a long moment. "No reason," he finally said. "You just looked different when you were talking to him." He paused. "You can take lessons, but you must not fall behind in your chores. Understood?"

I nodded and walked off. In the kitchen, I took a breath and leaned against the counter, panting. That had been close. I would need to be extremely careful as we undertook our plan.

When I went back out to the café, I told Vincent we should stick with our public schedule for painting lessons. I hoped we could meet on Tuesday for our private time, but I could make no promises.

"Certainly," he said, understanding my meaning. "Shall we paint in the town square tomorrow so that everyone will see us?"

I laughed. "Of course, if you like." Since it was across the street, Arthur could look out the window and see that nothing was going on besides a painting lesson.

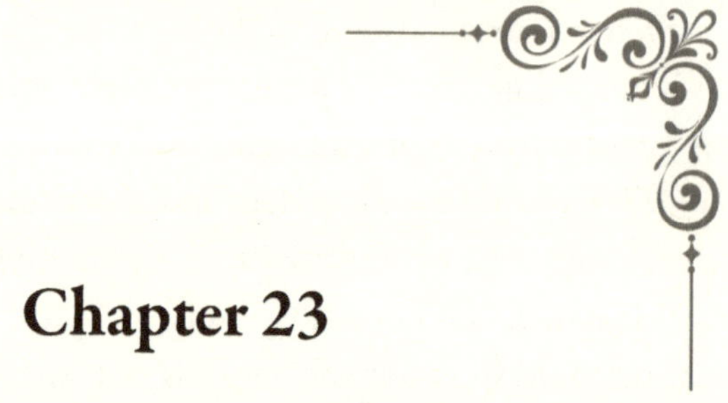

Chapter 23

WHEN I WENT OUTSIDE for my lesson the next day, I found Vincent pacing up and down in front of the inn.

"I know we planned to paint here, but how would you like to paint at Daubigny's garden? His wife is waiting for us now."

Daubigny. The famous painter had lived and worked in Auvers, and although he'd died some years before, his widow still lived in the same house. I'd heard the garden was marvelous, but I'd never seen it and had never spoken to Madame Daubigny. I grabbed my painting kit, and we walked down the street together as a painter and his student. I looked back and was surprised to see Adeline trailing behind us.

Turning to my daughter, I said, "Would you like to join us? I'm sure it would be fine. I even have a sketch pad, if you'd like to draw while we're there."

Adeline blushed but shook her head. "No. I just wondered where you were going."

I suspected she was spying for Arthur. Maybe he paid her in gloves or other trinkets. If so, I would make sure she had nothing to report, at least not today.

"Well, come and walk with us," I said. "Would you mind carrying my easel?"

The three of us spoke of inconsequential topics as we walked toward Daubigny's house. It was only half a mile down the main road, so we arrived promptly. Madame Daubigny met us at the door and ushered us around to the garden then retreated into the house. She'd been polite but distant, and I decided to write a note to the older woman when I returned home, to thank her for allowing us to paint in her garden. I would also invite her to dine at our restaurant as my guest.

The beautifully landscaped garden was enclosed by a wall and contained many flower beds as well as a table, bench, and chairs so that the occupants could enjoy meals outside. I set down my painting kit and took it all in. I hadn't known something so beautiful was so close to our house. Perhaps I could do something similar at the inn on a smaller scale. I'd never been interested in gardening before, but upon seeing the potential, I realized it might be worth the effort.

Vincent had already painted in the garden twice during his months in Auvers. This time, he planned on setting his easel in the back and directing his focus toward the house. I chose to paint a close-up view of the rose garden. As we chatted about how to create perspective and what colors to choose, I could tell Adeline was growing bored. She played with a cat for a few moments then announced she was going home.

I grinned, pleased that we'd allayed her suspicions. I encouraged her to stay for a while and either watch me paint, or draw something herself, but she shook her head.

"I see a gate, and I'll just creep out. This whole thing is tedious."

"All right. When you get home, would you check to see that Germaine is sleeping soundly? Her naps haven't been long enough recently, and she's cranky by dinnertime."

Adeline nodded and walked through the gate, carefully latching it behind herself. When she was gone, Vincent and I shared a smug smile. But we were twenty feet apart, so conversation wasn't possible, and soon we both became engrossed in our paintings.

A few moments later, I walked over to where he was working and asked what he would recommend as a background color for my painting—the blue of the sky, the green of the leaves, or some other color.

As usual, he had no definitive answer. "Green would be the closest complement to pink, but a light blue would work well too. Why don't you try each and see what effect you want?"

I'd known he wouldn't tell me what to do, but I wanted to see what he was painting on his canvas. While I was working close-in, he'd included everything, from the trees to the flower beds to the house behind it. His painting beckoned the viewer into the fairyland he'd created, and I had to restrain myself from crying out in delight. Everything in the painting was in motion, as though a wave of colors rippled across the canvas.

"Oh, it's amazing," I whispered, feeling like I was in church.

He'd painted something holy, in contrast to my ordinary flower garden.

"You know, your company improves my painting. I'm grateful." When he set down his brush and smiled at me, his teeth were stained again, as they'd been the first time I watched him paint.

"Vincent, you must stop cleaning your brush that way. Not only does it stain your teeth, but those paints can't be good for you."

He turned away and wiped his teeth then turned back to me. "You're right. It's a bad habit I got into when I first started painting outdoors. I'll stop." He beamed at me. "See how good you are for me? Already, I feel healthier."

I chuckled, shaking my head at his antics. I'd heard that painters could get poisoned by ingesting paint, and maybe that had happened to him. I led him over to my painting so that he could offer pointers.

After staring at it for a long moment, he asked, "What emotion do you want to convey in this painting?"

I was familiar with his approach by then, so I was prepared to answer. "I think I'm trying to show that it's a glorious summer day, and I want people to feel happy when they look at it."

"Yes, that's obvious. But you have no layers to this emotion right now. Try using some other colors to bring out something deeper than just enjoyment of a summer day. Maybe a deep red or teal or even brown. Life is more than just one color. But keep going." He walked back to his easel, leaving me to figure out my next step.

I bit my lip. *Deeper?* A dark brown would work, or maybe even the first yellow leaf of autumn that had floated down, showing that summer was a fleeting experience. I got to work.

By late afternoon, the light was leaning toward orange, and I needed to stop. "I have to get ready for a lot of diners tonight. We've started taking reservations, and every table is filled, beginning at six and going through ten." I laid the painting on the grass and folded my easel then noticed he was still absorbed in his work.

He glanced my way and smiled but didn't stop. "I'll be there for dinner. Can't leave now."

I didn't need to disturb the master at work, so I quickly gathered my materials and left.

AT HOME, I FOUND GERMAINE listless and crying, with the nanny hovering around her, ineffectually trying to soothe the little girl. Also, Adeline hadn't done her chores: the eggs hadn't been gathered, water hadn't been carried from the pump, and the tables weren't set for dinner. Even worse, Arthur had come home early from doing errands and was in a rage.

"Where have you been?" he roared at me after he pulled me into the kitchen and asked the cook to wait outside for a moment.

"Painting," I said, meekly. "Do you want to see my painting? It's in the Artists' Room."

He shook his head then slapped me on one cheek with his open palm. I was more shocked than injured. My mouth fell open, and I couldn't move. He'd broken his promise not to hit me. Even a mild slap was still hitting, and I was sure he knew that as well as I did.

"No more painting!" he shouted. "I gave you a chance, but you're done with that, since you can't manage your children or your chores. That was our agreement, and you've already broken it."

His hands were balled into fists. I backed away and felt my cheek. It was warm to the touch, which meant it would probably bruise. *Mon Dieu, what am I to do now?* I would not put up with his abuse again—that much I knew.

After taking a deep breath, I pitched my voice low so that it wouldn't reach to the dining room. "I took longer than I should have this afternoon, and I'll make sure I'm back earlier in the future. But you may not hit me, and you can't tell me what I can and cannot do. I will not tolerate it." I pulled myself up to my full height of five feet two inches and glared at him.

We backed away from each other, scowling.

"Now, I must see to Germaine," I continued as calmly as I could manage. "We can speak about this later if you wish."

I walked out of the kitchen, head held high, and nodded to the cook that she could return. Rubbing my sore cheek, I made my way to my daughters' room.

Adeline was sitting on her bed, reading a book, and I turned to her in a fury. "See to your chores. Now."

Adeline rushed out of the room, and I sat with my younger daughter. The little girl was warmer than usual but not burning hot. She clearly had a fever but not a high one. Germaine put her arms around my neck and sobbed into my shoulder.

"There, there, little one. Maman's here."

"Where were you?"

I sighed and said, "Out painting. I'm here now."

As I held her, I thought through the sequence of events. Arthur had had no business hitting me, but he must've been terribly upset at finding me gone with everything in such disarray. Guilt rolled over me like the thunderstorm I'd witnessed a few nights before.

Maybe I should stop seeing Vincent or, more accurately, never start. Perhaps I should even stop painting, as Arthur insisted. Despite my best efforts, my paintings were merely ordinary. Oh, I would certainly improve with time, but I would clearly never be a master, never be a Vincent van Gogh. More importantly, I shouldn't abandon my children in order to meet my own needs. I would have time to paint when my daughters were adults.

What to do? Just as I'd struggled to find the right colors for my painting, I would need to come up with the correct answer on my own. No one could do it for me.

Feeling emotionally depleted and still in shock from Arthur's assault, I walked into the Artists' Room and looked at my painting of Daubigny's garden. *Flowers again. Always flowers, always looking at the positive side of life, always forgiving.* Vincent had been right to say I was missing depth.

Without warning, a fury rose from deep inside me and welled out through my arms and hands.

I will give my life depth.

Without a moment's hesitation, I grabbed a kitchen knife and slashed the picture from top to bottom then from side to side. I slashed until I couldn't see the roses anymore. If I ever painted again,

I would choose the darkest, ugliest subject I could find. Vincent had painted tree roots and other gnarly things. I would do the same and unearth the depths of my being that I had submerged for as long as I could remember.

I stood as straight as I could and held my head high. No one—*no one*—was going to hit me again, ever. I should've left Arthur the first time he did it. But Maman's question about whether I had provoked him had haunted me and wrecked my confidence. I'd wanted to believe he would keep his promise never to do it again. But now he had. Maman and I had both been soft and forgiving, and I saw where that had led.

The building blocks of my history fell into place, and I knew—*knew*—my new self was not the demure woman I'd always been, the one who put everyone else's welfare ahead of her own. That woman had died the moment Arthur slapped me.

The new Louise was Athena, goddess of war who never lost a battle and goddess of wisdom. I imagined how I would feel with a helmet on my head and a sword in my hands. I was ready to change my life.

I left Germaine with the nanny and walked out into the wheat fields, telling no one I was going. My resolve strengthened with every step. Eventually, I turned back toward the inn and, for the moment, behaved like the Louise everyone knew—smiling, gracious, thoughtful. I told no one what was happening within me. They would know soon enough, when I was ready to show them.

NO MATTER WHAT ELSE was happening, people still needed to be fed. Arthur, Adeline, and I worked together to manage the evening rush, and I looked in on Germaine frequently. As the hours rolled by, the little girl's symptoms didn't worsen.

Probably a summer cold.

I noticed Vincent watching me as I moved around the restaurant. His eyes frequently focused on my cheek, which meant the bruise must've been noticeable. I hadn't taken the time to examine my face in a mirror before starting to work, but I hoped it looked more like I'd bumped into a wall instead of being struck. If anyone asked, that would be what I would say.

At the end of the evening, I considered where I would sleep. All our rooms were filled, and we had no extra beds. I might be forced, as usual, to sleep in the same bed as Arthur. Even thinking about that gave me a headache. Sighing, I walked into the bedroom.

After putting on my nightgown, I checked on Germaine one more time. Her forehead was the normal temperature, and she had scooted to the edge of her narrow bed, leaving room for another person. I stood there, considering what to do. I'd never slept apart from Arthur when he was in town, not in all our years of marriage. But that night, I had no patience for being pawed or further maligned by him.

I snuggled in beside Germaine and was asleep almost immediately.

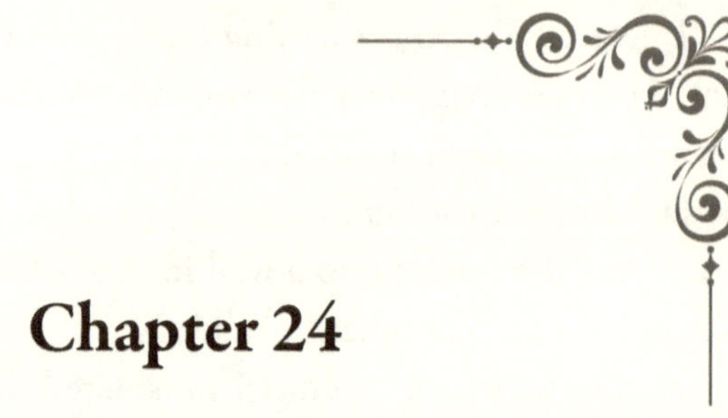

Chapter 24

*I try more and more to be myself, caring relatively little whether people
approve or disapprove.*
–Vincent van Gogh

SUNDAY WAS TENSE, BUT I carried on as usual. Arthur went
out hunting early with his friends, so we didn't interact. Just before
dusk, he returned to the inn, carrying two rabbits in one hand and
his gun in the other. René was with him, and the two were laughing
and joking. I glared at the boy and opened my mouth to speak
sharply to him but then thought it best not to fan the flames of
Arthur's anger, especially when he was holding a gun. Instead, I gathered my children and moved them into our bedroom.

After the boy left, I allowed the children back into the restaurant.
Arthur poured himself a drink and ignored us.

I slept in Germaine's bed again that night.

MONDAY WAS JULY 14—BASTILLE Day, or *la fête nationale*.
The celebration in Auvers would be considerably smaller than the
one in Paris, but it would still be the largest event of the year. Plans
for the day included a military parade in the morning, speeches in
the afternoon, music and dancing in the evening, and finally, a fire-

works display. The events would take place on the grounds of the town hall, directly across the street from the Auberge Ravoux.

We were going to be especially busy, so I rose earlier than usual and began my preparations. Just after sunrise, I glanced out the front window and saw Vincent standing outside with his easel and paint kit. He appeared to be painting a picture of the empty square decorated with flags. I chuckled. Most artists would wait to paint until the square was teeming with people, but not Vincent. He eschewed anything ordinary or predictable. That was one of many things I appreciated about him.

Tourists began arriving early, preparing to spend the day in the village then watch the fireworks later that night. They spread their blankets on the grass beside the town hall and came to the inn to purchase wine or beer, food, and the souvenirs I'd been stockpiling for the past month. By ten in the morning, all the reservations for both the midday meal and dinner had been taken.

I'd asked the whole staff to be available that day, and they bustled about, taking care of customers. Adeline's job was to watch Germaine, who seemed to be feeling better. I allowed the girls to wander around the festivities as long as Adeline kept her eyes on her sister.

Everyone worked steadily, and the day went smoothly. I was sorry I had to miss the parade and the speeches, but we were making a large profit, so I was willing to give up my own celebration. I took breaks when I could and went outside to make sure I could see the children. They were always visible somewhere in the crowd. Once, I saw Adeline speaking to a boy. I was about to charge over there and pull her out of René's clutches, but when he turned around, it was someone else. I breathed a sigh of relief.

Arthur and I went about our duties and rarely spoke, although I made sure I knew where he was at all times. I didn't want to be surprised by the back of his hand. When we spoke, our conversation was limited to polite requests to bring up more wine or beer from the cellar. We could've been strangers hired by the inn for a day of work. I would deal with him at the time I chose, and that day was not it.

I walked outside for a while in the evening to watch the dancers twirl to waltzes and polkas. Arthur and I had danced together only a few times, and I hoped never to dance with him again, but oh, I would've loved to dance with *somebody*. I did a few twirls by myself, but dancing alone felt silly, so I went back to my duties.

We closed the inn just before the fireworks show started, and everyone trooped outside to watch. I sat on a rocking chair with Germaine on my lap and watched the sky light up. She squealed, "Ooh, ooh," every time a firework shot into the sky. At one point, the little girl stood on the ground and twirled around and around with joy. My heart cracked open from the beauty of the event and the uninhibited emotions she was exhibiting. I would've liked to do the same, but of course, I didn't.

Afterward, Adeline and Arthur came back from wherever they'd been, and I let all the staff go home. We did the minimum of cleanup. The rest could wait until morning.

After I hid most of the day's income in my secret place, I fell into bed beside Germaine and slept better than I had in years. I didn't need the money now, but I most certainly would not let Arthur get his hands on it.

THE CLEANUP TOOK ALL of Tuesday. I continued to think of myself as Athena and went about my work with a straight back and an attitude of calm confidence. Arthur realized something was different right away. He tried to put his arms around me, but I moved away from him. When he smiled at me, I looked elsewhere. He tried to carry a tray of dirty dishes for me, but I pushed past him.

"Away, away" was becoming my motto. I needed to get away so that I could feel and experience this new person I was becoming.

I was eager to spend time with Vincent, though. He would appreciate my new self more than anyone else. I'd arranged to meet him at Gérard's house at midafternoon. In the past, fear of what trouble I might unleash would've led me to make an excuse and not show up—but not that day. As Athena, I would not be kept from meeting with him by anything on earth.

At the designated time, I made sure Germaine felt well and was engrossed in a game with her nanny. Arthur was building some new shelves in the basement, so he was unlikely to know I was gone. Even if he found out, I didn't care. I removed my apron and dropped it onto the counter.

"I'm going for a walk," I told the cook. "Back in a while."

Walking directly to Gérard's house wouldn't have been wise. I wanted to avoid being seen by gossipy neighbors. Arthur might even have asked someone to follow me. Adeline was the most likely person since she'd done it before. I needed to be extremely careful, but I would not be intimidated into missing this appointment.

After a few moments' thought, I walked to Danielle's inn, where my friend was busily checking out overnight guests. Danielle looked puzzled when I showed up and sat on a chair in the lobby. Then an expression of understanding crossed her face, and she excused herself from her guest and came over to me.

"There's a back door and an alley," she whispered. "Turn right, and his house is the fourth one on the right. No one will see you."

I smiled and nodded to my friend. "Thank you. I'll let you know how it goes." Then I was out the door and hurtling toward Vincent.

I LET MYSELF INTO THE house, praying it was the correct one, and walked through to the salon.

Vincent had been pacing up and down the room, but he bowed to me as soon as I entered. "I was worried you wouldn't come," he said, giving me a relieved smile.

"I was too. To be honest, in the past, I probably wouldn't have. But from now on, I'm going to make my own choices in life. And, right now, I choose you." I walked to him and lifted my face for his kiss.

He took my head in his hands and kissed my forehead, my eyes, the tip of my nose, each cheek—but lightly on the side that was bruised—my chin, and finally, my mouth. His lips were every bit as soft and warm as I remembered. He pulled me close, and we kissed for a long time. Tongues touched, pulled away, touched again, and finally made love to each other. Never had I had a kiss like this one.

Eventually, we pulled apart and sat together on the divan, fingers intertwined. I took a moment to calm my breathing and look around the room. The owner had furnished his rental house nicely. Long velvet draperies hung at the windows, a nice rug lay on the floor, a fireplace took up one wall, and a table and chairs had been placed in the center of the room under a glass chandelier. A thought tickled the edges of my mind: *Is the bedroom as nice as the salon?* I extinguished my grin as quickly as I could but not so quickly that Vincent failed to notice.

"Well, what shall we do now?" he asked in a teasing voice.

I inhaled deeply. *What indeed?*

I realized the time, and my courage evaporated. "I don't have long before I need to get back. Could we just talk for a while?"

He bit his lip. "Of course. I'm happy to be alone with you, whatever we do." He frowned. "I see you have a bruise on your cheek. I kissed it, but I didn't make it better. Do you want to talk about that? Or should I not mention it?"

I took a breath, wondering what to say. In the spirit of telling my truth, I said, "When I got home from painting with you, Germaine wasn't feeling well. Arthur was angry that I wasn't there to attend to her."

"Oh, my dear, I'm so sorry." He paled. "That was my fault. I didn't think about the time while we were enjoying the garden together."

"Hush. It wasn't your fault. It was Arthur's and his alone. I have the right to my own time. And Germaine was only a little sick. She got better quickly. Please, do not blame yourself."

He stared at the empty fireplace, taking a moment to reply. "He's a brutal man. I've thought that before, seeing the way you cower when he's around."

I nodded. "No more. He will not hit me again. If he tries, I will leave immediately."

After a long moment, his voice tentative, he said, "Uh, I don't want to pretend that I'm an expert in matters of the heart, because I'm not, but wouldn't it be better if you left before he wants to hit you?"

As usual, he'd cut through to the core of the issue with one thrust of his sword. "Yes. I know that. I'm thinking of how to arrange it."

He pursed his lips. "Louise, how can I help? I haven't been in a fight since I was a child, but I could call him out, at least. It would make my fist so happy to hit him. No one should ever strike a woman."

I closed my eyes, wondering if speaking my truth had made the situation better or worse. I remembered why I told people I'd walked into a wall. That way, they didn't feel as though they had to redress the harm and possibly make matters worse.

Stricken, I shook my head. "No. Please don't. I appreciate the thought, but I need to handle this in my own way."

"Yes, I see that. I apologize for causing you distress. But I cannot bear how he treats you." His voice caught on those last words.

I stood and walked to the table. *Away, away.* I wanted to feel his hands on me, his mouth on my own, and I also wanted to be walking through the woods with my hair down, feeling the breeze lift the locks and make them flow behind me as I strode. *What to do?* Like a bird when a human comes too close to its nesting place, I was torn between staying and going.

"I've upset you. I'm sorry. Please, let's speak of other things." He waited a moment for me to turn to him again. "I am thinking of putting on my own exhibit in Paris. Would you like to show some of your work too?"

I snorted, and the tension in the room released. "Surely you jest. I will come to your exhibit, but I'm not ready to show my work and may never be." I sat on the divan and reached for his hand. "Where will it be? Do you have a location yet?"

"Probably where I buy my art supplies. The owner has some of my paintings in his attic already." Scowling, he said, "My brother isn't trying to sell my works, so I've got to do his job and mine. I need to make money. I'm tired of being dependent on him. It's time for me to stand on my own feet so I can support a wife and children, if it ever comes to that." He gave me a meaningful look at which I smiled, but I didn't respond.

We talked more about our lives until an hour had passed, and I needed to leave. He took me in his arms and kissed me again. This kiss was even more passionate, with the promise of more.

"When can we meet again?"

I took a breath and considered. "I think we should keep our regular schedule, with painting lessons on Thursday afternoon. But on Tuesdays and Fridays, we could meet here if that works for you."

"Oh, yes." He bowed and kissed my hand. "I will count the hours until Thursday."

BACK AT HOME, ARTHUR was waiting for me, his face twisted into an angry scowl. I stopped for a second and straightened my spine then said hello and went about my business, sorting the mail that had arrived while I was gone.

He grabbed my arm. "Where have you been?"

I pulled away but didn't respond as I continued flipping through the letters and placing them in the baskets.

"I'm talking to you. Don't ignore me."

This was it, the moment for which I'd been waiting. Athena was ready.

"Not here," I said between clenched teeth. "In our room." I marched to our bedroom with him right behind.

Inside, I closed the door and turned to him. "All right. I'm tired to the bone about the way things are between us. I know about your mistress, so don't ask where I've been again, because I won't tell you." I beamed daggers at him.

He stumbled backward before righting himself. "Oh." Then, after a moment, he said, "I don't deny it. Many men have mistresses. Given how cold you've been to me, you can't blame me for looking for solace elsewhere."

"Oh no you don't," I snapped. "You will not blame your transgressions on me. Never again. At least have the integrity to admit what you're doing and take responsibility for your actions. At least do that." I stood straight, ready to scream my loudest and fight back if he came for me.

His face took on a puzzled expression. "All right," he said more quietly. "So you do not mind, then?"

"Oh, I mind. But truly, she's welcome to you. She can take your blows because I will not do it again." I shook my head. "In fact, I think it would be best if you leave now. Go to her. And feel free to stay. We don't need you here."

"I... I..." His words failed him. We stood like that for several long moments, glaring at each other.

Finally, he said, "No. This is my home. You are welcome to go if you desire. I will divorce you for deserting me. But you cannot take the children. Sophie and I will raise them, and you will never see them again. So go."

Sophie? So the mistress wanted my children. That shouldn't have surprised me. But I hadn't prepared for his response, and my heart beat furiously.

My answer burst from my lips. "I will not leave my children."

We continued glaring at each other, neither of us moving. I felt as though I was a tree, sending my roots into the ground. He would not move me.

Eventually, I said, "Very well. We are at a stalemate. I will sleep with Germaine, and you can do what you want. And we shall see how it goes."

He grabbed my arm. When I tried to pull away, he held on, his fingers digging deeply into my skin.

"Who is it? I can see you've changed. Who is the man you've been seeing?"

I'd expected this response. "Do you think I need another man to finally wake up to how you treat me? *No.*" I jerked my arm, forcing him to let go. "Now, leave me alone." I stalked out the door and slammed it behind myself.

In the hallway, I realized I was shaking. *Mon Dieu, did the entire house hear our argument?* Three male customers in the restaurant scowled at me when I walked in, but the women with them nodded and smiled faintly behind their hands.

I took a breath. So they had heard it, all of them. I continued walking into the kitchen.

Inside, the cook stopped chopping vegetables and said, "Good for you. It's about time you told him what's what." She calmly returned to her work.

I stood, dumbfounded. Edith had barely spoken to me in the months of her employment, other than to ask questions about the food. I'd been sure the woman didn't like me. But she'd just said, "Good for you."

I didn't know how to respond, so I stood there, rubbing my hands together. Despite the hot weather, they were cold, and I held them above the stove to warm them.

The cook stopped chopping again and gave me a warning look. "Now, stick to your resolve. He'll make it hard and maybe dangerous, but you can do it."

I nodded, grateful for the encouragement. To calm myself, I walked out to the back garden and pulled weeds from around my tomato plants. I carried the weeds to the chickens and continued walking down to the river, where I stood for many moments, watching boats drift by. Gradually, my breathing slowed, the trembling stopped, and my mind began working again. I wondered if everyone in my life understood the dynamics in my marriage, though they hadn't said a word. Anger, embarrassment, exhilaration—they all tore through me as I tried to decide which was strongest.

Edith had warned me this was a dangerous time. I would need to watch my back as I considered my next move.

Fortunately, the next day was Wednesday, and I'd arranged to have lunch with Hélène in Paris. I felt like a volcano, ready to expel all the rocks that had been pushed down inside for eons. I needed my friend to help me decide what to do.

Chapter 25

ON WEDNESDAY MORNING, I took the train to Paris and knocked on Hélène's door, feeling as though I was desperately fleeing an invading army. When my friend opened the door, I fell into her arms. Although I tried not to cry, tears streamed down my face.

"Oh, Hélène, I need your wisdom," I said between sobs. "And I need to talk to Claude too. Is that possible?"

Hélène rubbed my back and whispered, "Shh, it'll be all right. Let's go into the salon and have lunch, just the two of us, and then I'll have Claude come in so you can ask him your questions."

As Hélène pulled me into the house, I sniffed the faint scent of her fine perfume and was immediately comforted. If there was any place where I might find an answer to my dilemma, this apartment was the likeliest.

We sat together in the dining room, where a lunch of steak frites, salad, and soup had already been served. Hélène had remembered it was my favorite meal. I was so touched that I began crying again.

Hélène closed the doors and sat beside me then poured us each a large glass of white wine. "The children are at the park with the nanny, Claude is in his study, and the staff knows never to open these doors when I'm inside. You're safe, Louise. No one will interrupt us.

I want to hear the entire story, but first, why don't we eat? You'll feel better with food in your belly."

That was what I told my children when they were upset: "Eat, and you'll feel better." Usually, it was true. Unfortunately, my stomach roiled every time I tried to eat a piece of steak, so I focused on the frites and other dishes.

A cold fear stopped me. *Could I be pregnant?* I'd already thought the situation was as bad as it could be, but that eventuality would be far worse. After a moment, I realized that no, I was merely upset. My courses had come the previous week, and I hadn't had relations since then. That was a relief.

When I'd eaten all I could, I placed my knife and fork on the plate and turned to my friend. "Thank you, Hélène. You were exactly right. I feel calmer. Now, I can tell you the story."

When she nodded, I began, speaking first about the fight with Arthur and how he'd hit me and threatened to take the children from me.

She nodded. "I thought that might be coming. We'll ask Claude how to keep the children in your custody." She gave me a hard look as she patted my hand. "Go on. I think there's more."

I'd intended to talk about the problems with Adeline, but what burst from my lips instead was the story of how much Vincent had come to mean to me so quickly. "I may actually lie with him soon," I said, feeling the heat rise in my neck. "Do you think me bad for that?"

Hélène chuckled. "It's not something I would do, because Claude is plenty for me, but I can understand your situation. You need some fun in your life and someone who dotes on you, and it looks like you've found them both in Vincent." She hesitated. "But you must be careful. If Arthur finds out, you might as well kiss your children goodbye because he will take them from you in court. And who knows what else he'll do?"

She was right, of course. We exchanged bleak looks.

Hélène stopped to take a bite of her chocolate mousse. "Mmm, that's delicious. Please eat. Chocolate will calm your stomach and make your mouth happy." She smiled at me. "Don't worry so much. Yes, this situation is coming to a head, but we'll find a solution so you can rid yourself of Arthur and have your artist friend if you still want him when Arthur's gone."

"I—"

"I was joking, my dear. You may want him even more. You know you have a home here if you need one. Don't ask. Just arrive on my doorstep with your children in tow. But please do it before Arthur hits you again. You must decide what you're going to do and then do it quickly. Without hesitation."

"Yes, I know." That was essentially the same thing Vincent had said. "But I need help in making a plan."

"All right. Let's call Claude in now." She left the room for a few moments and returned with her husband.

He kissed me and sat down at the table, where the maid had placed another serving of chocolate mousse. "My favorite dessert." He took a bite and closed his eyes, delight on his face. "It's wonderful." Nodding at me, he said, "Hélène told me a little about your situation. We're not surprised that you've decided to leave Arthur. Good for you. He isn't worth your time and energy, especially since he broke his promise to never strike you again." His expression turned grim.

He took a breath and continued, "I think your best option is to disappear with the children, someplace where he can't find you. Far away. You can file for divorce in some other country that has more lenient laws." He paused. "I understand you also have come into some money that Arthur knows nothing about?"

I nodded. *Is he really telling me to leave France? Just take the children and run away?* "I have enough money, but where would I go that he couldn't find me?"

"Do you have relatives in another country?"

"My brother is in America, but I don't want to go there. It's a barbaric country. I truly don't want to leave France."

He scratched his chin, looking sympathetic. "I think you'll need to leave, my dear, if you want to keep your children and your money and live without your husband." His voice was gentle, but his words were firm.

We talked for another hour, discussing options. At the end, I thanked him and, choking on my words, said, "I'll need to think about this. I had hoped there might be better alternatives than running away to another country."

Hélène grasped my hand. "Dear Louise, I know this has been hard to hear, and I will miss you so much if you go. By the time you get back home today, Arthur will have left for a few days, no?" When I nodded, she continued. "You do not have to act today or tomorrow or even next week. You can take some time to choose the best course for you and the children. But please remember that you may not be safe with Arthur if he loses his temper again."

Tears welled up, but I nodded.

"I have a friend in London who owns an inn," said Claude. "He might be interested in hiring you as a manager." When he saw my look of dismay, he said, "I know you're independently wealthy, but I've never known you to be an idler. If not running an inn, then what appeals to you?"

My mouth was suddenly bone-dry, and I croaked, "I don't know."

Hélène smiled. "What you do in the future isn't as important as getting away with your children from your dangerous husband."

I couldn't deny the seriousness of the situation any longer. I would indeed have to leave—soon.

I suddenly realized how much time had passed, and I hadn't even started my weekly shopping. "Oh, I'm sorry to have stayed so long. I need to rush." I kissed Hélène and Claude. "I can't thank you enough for your friendship and the wonderful advice. And, of course, the marvelous lunch. I feel so much better."

I hurried through the shopping and caught a train that would take me back in time to put Germaine to bed. After I found a seat, I reflected on my conversation with Hélène and Claude. Although I'd daydreamed about leaving Arthur for years, I hadn't thought beyond the joy of not waking up to his bad breath or not having to cringe when he'd had too many drinks in the evening.

He was a terrible husband, but he loved his girls, especially Adeline, whom he'd subtly turned against me. I'd watched that happen, but so far, I'd assumed Adeline would eventually recognize his manipulation for what it was and come to appreciate my devotion. Now, I wondered if that was true or if it was another way I'd deluded myself into believing that all would be well if I just gave it enough time.

If... no, when *I leave Arthur, will I be able to convince Adeline to come with me?* Germaine was no problem—she was too small to care where she was as long as I was with her. But with Adeline, I would have to wait until the last moment to tell her we were leaving so that she couldn't go to her father.

Executing my plan was going to be far more difficult than I'd imagined. I took a deep breath and stared out the window of the swaying train.

Before we arrived at the station, I decided to go to America but just for a holiday first. Then I could decide whether it would be an acceptable place to live. I would be far enough from Arthur to feel safe, and my brother would welcome me. When I got home, I would write to him and ask his advice about the best way to travel there.

But I couldn't just pick up my things and leave, at least not today. I needed time to plan my escape. As both Vincent and Hélène had pointed out, though, I should leave before Arthur became dangerous, not after—not long, then. I thought I would be safe for another week or so.

Vincent. What to do about him? I was falling in love with him, but I didn't know him well enough to plan a future around him. Besides, he might not live a long life. If he was right about the timing of his seizures, or whatever they were, another one might be approaching that could land him back in the asylum. His health was uncertain, so I couldn't count on him to be with me for very long.

On the other hand, even a short period of happiness would be better than years of regret. And Vincent surely would provide me with extreme happiness, regardless of how long it lasted. I would ask him to accompany us, and it would be up to him.

I felt relieved to have made the decision to leave Arthur. An extended holiday in America, possibly with Vincent, would be a lovely thing as I considered whether to stay there or move to another country in Europe.

Chapter 26

Wheat is wheat, even if people think it is grass in the beginning.
–Vincent van Gogh

WHEN GÉRARD ENTERED the café the next morning, I dropped what I was doing to sit with him. He'd been in Paris for a few days to meet with some teachers at his lycée, and one thing had led to another, and now he was in Auvers for only a day before he needed to go back.

"How are things with Danielle?" I asked. "Was she with you in Paris?"

He shook his head. "She doesn't want to tell Cécile about our relationship yet, so she can't get away very often." Grabbing my hand, he leaned forward and asked, "Do you know if she's having second thoughts about us?"

I enjoyed the feeling of his hand on mine, so I left it there as I shook my head and smiled. "Not that I know of. She's just nervous about how things could work if she moves to Paris with you. She's been a widow for a long time, so it will be a big change. Give her some time, and I think everything will work out." I hesitated. "Have you proposed yet?"

"No. But I've hinted. I don't think Danielle is ready for marriage, even though I am. I'm so tired of being lonely, and this way, I get a ready-made family. I've been looking at bigger apartments, which I can afford if I receive the salary increase I've requested."

I beamed at him. Even if happiness wasn't in my future, I was glad it could happen for others. How lovely it would be if my two friends married and lived happily ever after, even if they moved to Paris. It couldn't happen to two nicer people.

A pang in my chest reminded me I wished it was happening for me too. But I wouldn't show any sadness to Gérard—he deserved a loyal friend who could enjoy his happiness.

Out of the corner of my eye, I spotted Adeline in the corner, staring at me in horror.

Oh no! She thinks I'm in love with Gérard. And she might tell Arthur.

I retrieved my hand and took a sip of tea, allowing those thoughts to percolate. If Arthur had the wrong idea about my lover, that would give me some cover, so it wasn't necessarily a bad thing. But I would need to look out for Gérard in case Arthur attempted to take out his vitriol with his fists.

"Uh, you're leaving tonight?"

He nodded.

"When will you return?"

"I'll be gone through the weekend if Danielle will come with me. If not, I might be back on Sunday afternoon. Why? Will you miss me?" he teased.

Flushing, I said, "Of course I'll miss you. I love having you around. You spice up my dull mornings." I glanced over my shoulder and saw Adeline staring fixedly at me, anger in her eyes. "But I must go, or else my daughter will immolate us with her gaze." I laughed and stood, patting his shoulder. "Thanks for coming by, and thanks for... you know." I felt my face heat up. "Tomorrow afternoon, then."

He smiled and nodded. "Tomorrow."

Oh no, did Adeline hear that? I couldn't be sure, but I hoped not. I wanted to give her just enough of the wrong impression to keep Vincent safe while we decided what to do. I was glad Gérard would be gone for the weekend.

THAT AFTERNOON, WHEN the time came for my painting lesson, I looked out the window and saw Vincent standing in front of the inn. I grinned, understanding he was doing it to show Adeline we had nothing to hide.

Because of my personal crisis, I hadn't painted since Saturday, and I'd cut up the painting I'd made that day. I was eager to paint something, but I knew for certain it would be a very long time before I painted flowers again.

I met him outside and said, as loudly as I dared, "I don't know what to paint. No more flowers. But what instead?"

This was a conversation anyone could overhear, so he sat on a rocking chair and gestured for me to sit beside him. When I did, he pulled the pipe from his mouth and asked, "What is it about flowers you suddenly don't like?"

"No depth," I said, fairly spitting out the words. "I want to paint something deep and brooding, maybe something ugly. Anything other than bright, happy flowers."

He puffed on his pipe and considered my words. "Are you telling me you're not bright and happy right now? Is that what this is about?"

"N-No," I said, biting my lip. "That's not it, exactly. I'm happy that it's summer and the flowers are blooming, and I'm happy to be taking lessons from you. But"—I paused as I worked through how to express my emotions—"I'm tired of painting flowers that express joy. I need to express other emotions, too, and I don't know how to do that on canvas."

"All right. That's good. Life has a vast range of emotions. Do you know what emotion you'd like to pursue this afternoon?"

"Uh, how about anger? And don't tell me I can paint angry flowers, because it's not what I want to do."

He chuckled. "You could paint something larger than a close-up of a flower, then—an entire landscape, possibly. That allows you to dab on heavy paint and use short strokes and dark colors and possibly even focus on something inherently upsetting. If we could paint a dead cow floating on the river, would that work for you?"

I glanced sharply at him and saw the twinkle in his eyes, then I batted him on the arm. "It doesn't need to be that bad." I laughed. After a moment, I said, "But I do like the idea of a full landscape rather than a close-up. And not Daubigny's garden again. It's too pretty." I thought for a moment. "What appeals to you today? I'm not the only one here, you know."

He nodded. "I've had my eye on this wheat field not too far out of town, where crows gather in the afternoons to eat the wheat. Sometimes, there are huge numbers of them, and it's a little spooky when they all rise together. The occasional farmer will shoot at them, but mostly, they use scarecrows, which do next to no good. I thought about going there, especially today when the clouds are gathering. What do you think?"

"Yes, that would work. Let me make sure Germaine is asleep and ask Adeline if she wants to join us." I rushed inside, eager to leave before something delayed me. Germaine was sleeping soundly, her nanny within calling distance. Adeline was polishing the silver, a task I'd asked her to do about a thousand times. I stood and watched for a moment, squinting in amazement.

"Well, it's nice to see you doing that, finally." I reached over and hugged her. "But do you want to go with Monsieur Vincent and me to paint in a wheat field? I could let you use my easel while I sketch, if you're interested."

Adeline wrinkled her nose. "I'm going to finish this and then go visit Cécile." She glanced at me. "Uh, if that's all right with you."

"Yes," I said, drawing out the word. "I assume if I ask Danielle tomorrow whether you've been there, she will say yes."

Adeline nodded.

"All right, then. You may do that as long as René isn't there."

Adeline bit her lip and shook her head. "He won't be there. I don't like him anymore."

I wanted to believe her, but I wasn't sure. She was going to need to earn my trust. Still, nothing would be gained by my fixating on the issue.

"Thank you for doing that job without me having to ask you again. That's a good girl." I kissed her on the cheek and walked out the door.

Outside, as I picked up my artist kit, I shook my head. "I swear, I'll never understand that child. She constantly surprises me."

Vincent smiled as we walked together down the road, master and student, innocently going to paint.

After a while, we came to the wheat field he had in mind and set up our easels.

"This is not inherently a pretty scene, so paint it as you feel," he said.

That was the only advice he would give me.

I painted a broad scene filled with yellows and browns. The wheat had ripened, and the stalks were heavy, so I tried to paint the heaviness those stalks must feel as they struggled to hold up the seed. They must have been frustrated when birds landed on the stalks to eat the wheat that had taken an entire season to ripen. I attempted to express the wheat's anger at the birds and the birds' delight at being able to eat to their heart's content.

After an hour, I glanced behind myself to check on how the sun had moved and saw something large—maybe a person—move in the wheat. I wondered who it could be—perhaps the farmer, come to see who was in his field. Or maybe it was that horrible René Secrétan, who I'd learned often followed Vincent in order to play practical jokes on him.

"Who's there?" I called out.

Nothing—no movement, no response. I stared until I saw a spot of black among the stalks. The only people who regularly wore black in the summer were those in mourning, and the only person in mourning who would follow me was my daughter, Adeline. *That little minx.* She'd turned down an offer to accompany us but instead had followed quietly, hoping to catch us doing something we shouldn't. She surely must've been acting on her father's orders because hiding and spying on me would ordinarily have taken a distant second place to visiting with Cécile. Well, she could stay there all afternoon, as far as I was concerned.

"Nothing, I guess," I told Vincent, who was painting a dozen yards away.

He shrugged and continued painting.

During the next hour, I occasionally glanced backward, only to see the same stirring among the wheat stalks. Adeline must've been getting tired of squatting or whatever she was doing. I deliberately drew out my painting time for longer than usual. Arthur wasn't home, and Germaine was feeling well, so I had no reason to rush.

Finally, when the shadows were long, Vincent laid down his brush and walked over. "Are you finished?" He glanced at my painting, which I'd actually finished a half hour before, except for dabbing some extra point to increase the texture. He stared at it for a long time and finally asked, "What do you think of it? Does it express what you want?"

I took a breath. "No, not well, but it's better than the flowers. I'm expressing the end of summer and the harvest and then the death of the plants." I glanced at him shyly. "Do you get that out of it?"

He squinted. "Yes, I do. But if you swirled the clouds a bit more, it would give more of an uncertain future to the scene. Do you mind?" He gestured toward my brush, and when I nodded, he took it and demonstrated. The mood I wanted to convey was suddenly present. He'd called it uncertainty, and yes, that was it.

Speaking more loudly than usual, I said, "Thank you, monsieur. You fixed it. Now, may I see yours?"

"Of course."

We walked over to his easel, and what I saw took my breath away. He had painted the wheat field with short strokes, with the path swirling through it and the clouds in circles. What made it even more remarkable were the crows flying over the field. Their blackness matched the black strokes of the sky, and a mood of danger was established—foreboding, uncertainty, death. The wheat was dying, and the birds would die if the farmer took his gun after them, then the snows would fall, and summer would be but a memory.

I hadn't even thought to paint the crows. To me, their presence and their sharp cawing had been nuisances that distracted me from the painting. Vincent, in his genius, had incorporated them into the scene.

After I absorbed the painting for a long while, I asked, hesitantly, "I'm sorry to ask you this, but are you sad or depressed? Does this picture represent your mood today?"

He busied himself refilling his pipe and lighting it. "I'm not sure how to answer that. In one sense, I do feel a sense of foreboding because I do not know what the future will bring. For example, in this scene, the farmer desperately needs to feed his family with the wheat the birds are stealing, so watching them doing it is painful for him and for me. In another sense, I can feel the birds' flight and freedom as they do what birds do: eat as much of the harvest as they can manage. We all must live, Louise, and sometimes, our goals conflict. So yes, there is uncertainty in my painting as well as yours."

"Oh, my goodness. I've never met anyone so eloquent." His depiction of uncertainty was far more powerful than mine. When I thought about it, though, his uncertainty was at a deeper level—he didn't know from day to day whether his illness would return or, if it did, whether he would live through the next episode. Also, he didn't know if he would have enough money to continue doing what he so loved or what he would do if he couldn't. And, of course, he didn't know how things with me would work out.

"It's amazing. I feel all that you convey and more. This might be your most brilliant painting."

He blushed. "Thank you, madame."

His formality indicated he had seen Adeline too.

After a pause, he said quietly, "I think you are worried about my sanity or maybe even my will to live when you look at this painting. I can assure you I have no intention of committing suicide. I am positive my paintings will sell, and I believe it will happen soon. So please, do not worry. I'm a bit... depressed... as you intimate but not dangerously so."

I didn't know how to respond, so I merely nodded.

"Shall we return?" he asked in a louder, more cheerful tone. "I don't want to keep you from your children for too long. You've done a wonderful job today. I think your painting is finished. Do not add a single brushstroke."

"Fine. But promise me you won't ever hang these two pictures together." I laughed. "I couldn't bear the shame of it."

"You know, you're improving every week. If you keep at it, one day you'll exhibit your paintings, and people will buy them. Maybe even before they buy mine, because yours are more... acceptable."

I grunted. Nothing was to be gained by arguing about whose paintings would sell first. I knew they wouldn't be mine and he was only being polite. We packed up our kits and carefully carried our wet paintings down the road.

As we walked, Vincent said, "You should title all your paintings. I'm going to call mine *Wheat Fields with Crows*. What will you call yours?"

I'd never considered giving my paintings titles. "Oh, I don't know. Maybe *Autumn Wheat*. How does that sound?"

"Fine. It's your decision. And by the way, you should sign them too."

"But you don't sign most of yours. Why not?"

"Because I'm not finished with them. I sign the ones I've finished and am pleased with. The others, well, I'll return to them one day, and then I'll sign them."

I considered his words. "I've seen you sign one or two 'Vincent.' Why not your last name?"

He laughed. "That one's easy—because hardly anybody who isn't Dutch can pronounce it. And I don't like most of my family. They don't like me either. So it's not a name I want to be associated with."

We were close to the inn when we ran into René and his brother coming from the opposite direction. Since Adeline was far behind us, they must not have been together. *Good.* I couldn't remember the brother's name, but he looked like he might be the nicer one. René was once again dressed in his cowboy clothes, but this time, the gun in his holster looked real. That was concerning. Who in their right mind would carry around a real gun when they weren't hunting? No, the boy had probably gotten hold of a toy gun that looked more lifelike than the one he'd had before.

As I was considering how to ask about it, Vincent said, "Ponjour, Puffalo Pill."

I couldn't help but chuckle at his play on the words "Buffalo Bill," but René clearly didn't consider it funny. He scowled and turned away.

Vincent shook his head and laughed as we walked on.

"I think he doesn't like you," I said.

"No, we're good friends. He likes to tease me, and sometimes I tease him back." He smiled.

I wasn't so sure, but I let it go.

As soon as we returned to the inn, we went our separate ways. The next day, I would know him in a different capacity—as a lover. I appreciated the painter and his pointed yet gentle observations, but I could hardly wait to get to know the lover. I hummed as I worked.

Adeline didn't appear until just before dinner. She arrived at the inn looking mussed, with her hair loose and pieces of grass stuck to her skirt.

"How was Cécile?" I managed to ask with a straight face.

"She's fine. We went for a walk out in the wheat fields."

I wanted to snort, but I held myself back. After all, I knew very well where she had been, and I had seen no evidence of Cécile. Apparently, Adeline was willing to risk that I wouldn't ask Cécile's mother if the girls had been together. Or maybe she'd seen Cécile for a quick visit before or after going to the wheat field. She was a wily one, for good or ill.

"Go change your dress and fix your hair, and wash up before dinner. I'll need your help to serve."

"Yes, Maman."

Chapter 27

Love is eternal—the aspect may change, but not the essence.
–Vincent van Gogh

THE NEXT MORNING, I awoke with a tingle in my toes. I rubbed my feet with lotion then moved up to my calves and thighs. When I reached my upper thighs, my entire body was aflame. I wondered how I would feel after making love with Vincent in a few hours. If I was this excited merely from anticipation, maybe my whole body would light up with an electrical charge when we came together, and I would glow like the sun.

Making love with Vincent.

Just thinking those words caused the tingle to run from my toes up my back and to the top of my head. I remembered a similar feeling when I was quite small and had fallen in love with a large stuffed panda in a shop window. I'd longed to hold it in my arms, to rub its soft fur and bury my nose in it. The panda was nearly as tall as I was, and I'd even anticipated dancing with it.

The moment I saw it nestled under the tree on Christmas Eve, I felt that same whole-body tingle. For a moment, I couldn't even run to the tree because I was so enthralled by that electric feeling. Of course, I knew nothing about electricity then. I just thought the tingle was caused by an immense joy.

I'd nearly loved that toy to death over the years. The tired old panda still sat in the corner of Germaine and Adeline's room. When I tried to throw it out, Germaine cried for days. So it stayed, a reminder of the greatest joy I had ever known as a child of five.

Now, after many years, the tingle was back, and it wasn't associated with a stuffed panda but with a man. A very special man.

When I finally got out of bed, I paid extra attention to my toilette, washing all those special places where Vincent might focus his attention and applying a light touch of my best perfume behind my ears, between my breasts, and just above my secret place. I felt like a bold woman of the world, something I had never experienced, and just thinking about it kept a smile on my face. I'd washed my hair the night before, and it hung in ringlets below my shoulders. I used only a few pins when I put it up, imagining how it might feel if he released it from its chignon and ran his fingers through it.

I didn't dare wear anything out of the ordinary because Adeline would notice and give me that squinty, judgmental look she'd perfected recently. Reluctantly, I donned a black shirtwaist and skirt, but only I knew that my underclothes were new and as white as snow. One day, if things went well, I would wear fancy clothes for Vincent, which would make him smile. Maybe we would attend his art exhibits, me in my finest gown and he in a suit I'd chosen for him. He liked to dress shabbily for his work, in case he spilled paint or poppy-seed oil on his clothing, but I imagined he would enjoy dressing up to attract buyers' money.

I pulled a gown from my wardrobe and held it against myself as I danced a few steps around the room. I wondered if Vincent danced. I'd never asked. Someday, when we had idle time, I would ask.

When I couldn't put it off any longer, I went into the kitchen and completed my morning chores. As usual, Vincent had picked up his breakfast and taken it with him to paint. We were to meet at Gérard's house at ten, and he'd promised he would get up early to do his painting beforehand. I wondered when he'd left the inn and whether he would return to change his clothes or meet me in his regular painting attire. Truthfully, what he wore made no difference. I was interested in the man himself, not his clothes. And I hoped he would soon be removing them anyway. Just the thought of that made me blush furiously.

Nothing unusual happened during the morning at the cafe, but I wondered why the cook didn't notice the raised color in my cheeks or my cheerful humming as I went about my chores. People rarely looked at one another—really looked—to see what was inside, I knew. They might notice me if I was nude—the thought made me giggle. No one commented that I was giggling for no visible reason.

At last, at last, the time came to leave the inn. I'd sent Adeline on an errand to pick wildflowers from the countryside for our table vases, and Germaine was with her nanny. The cook knew to expect me back before the midday meal, so I was free for a couple of hours.

Je suis libérée! I am free! I had so rarely felt free in my life. That was how my husband must feel when he ran to the arms of his mistress. He probably wasn't any happier in our marriage than I was, although he at least had some power in it.

I would not think about Arthur just then—only Vincent and the physical enjoyment we would share.

As before, I walked through Danielle's inn, stopping in the lobby to say hello to my friend's brother. We gave each other a wink as I walked through the lobby and out the back door. Glancing around, I saw no one in the alley, so I made my way to the fourth house on the right. The door was open, and I walked into the kitchen and through to the salon.

That time, the draperies were open a bit, allowing sunlight to filter in. Vincent was sitting on the divan, using a file to pry paint from under his nails and filing them to a smooth roundness. He had dressed up a bit, wearing a clean pair of pants and a shirt. His blue painting smock lay across the back of a chair. He had trimmed his beard and gotten a haircut. I studied him for a moment longer, noting that his face had filled out from eating my meals and that the perpetual expression of fear and mistrust on it had disappeared. He no longer resembled a scarecrow but rather a handsome, healthy outdoorsman.

He glanced up and smiled when he'd finished with his nails. "Did you enjoy your perusal? Do I pass muster?"

I flushed and grinned. "Yes, of course. So you were watching me too? Do I?"

He stood and grasped my hands. He was a few inches taller, so he leaned down and kissed the top of my head. "Always, my dear. You could dress in complete rags, and it wouldn't matter to me."

He let go of my hands and unpinned my hat to place it carefully on the divan, then he took me into his arms.

"Yesterday was fun, but it nearly drove me crazy not being able to touch you," he said, nuzzling my hair. "Umm, you smell good." His hands rubbed my back and shoulders. "Oh, where was I?" He laughed. "Yes, I remember now. I enjoyed painting with you and being outdoors together. But your daughter rather spoiled any possibility of closeness, and it was all I could manage to stop myself from doing exactly what I'm doing now."

He kissed me, and it was a kiss of familiarity. We knew what to do with our lips and teeth and tongues and which way to lean our heads. The kiss drew out and out. At last, panting, I pulled away.

"Um, I have only two hours. Could we..." Amazed at my own boldness, I gestured toward the bedroom. I was Athena, and goddesses could do anything, even have their way with the man of their choice.

"Ah, a woman who knows her own mind. I love that."

I was sure I'd turned bright red, both from the embarrassment of asking for what I wanted and because of the need for him. But

I wasn't unhappy about my tendency to blush. When we'd known each other longer and had more time to spend with kisses and hugs, I would happily allow each step to linger until I moaned with anticipation—but not today.

I'd never made love to anyone other than Arthur, and my experience with him had never lived up to what was described in risqué novels or photos. If I could ever trust a man to lead me along the path to my own satisfaction, that man would be Vincent. His eyes, hands, and body spoke of a rare sensuousness that I wanted to experience. I'd come close to making love with Denis, but he'd always stopped us—to preserve my reputation, he'd said. Now, my reputation meant nothing to me. Only this man did.

He led me into the bedroom and unbuttoned my blouse. He pulled off my shirtwaist then my skirt and, finally, my underclothes, and I stood before him, naked. I didn't know how my body compared with those of other women he'd known, but I didn't care. He would not be cad enough to compare me with others, at least not on that day.

His hands ran down my sides and around to my back as he pulled me closer. After a moment, he rapidly threw off his clothes, and I saw his chest was covered with soft, curly red hair. I ran my fingers through it down to his belly. His manhood was clearly ready for me.

He reached up to pull out the pins holding my hair but struggled with them until I pushed his hands away and did it myself. Then my hair fell below my shoulders, just as I'd imagined earlier, and I heard his sharp intake of breath.

"Oh, my dear, you are the most beautiful of women. I can't believe my eyes." He gave me another kiss, and we slowly moved onto the bed. He pulled away and asked, "Uh, does your friend mind if we use his bed?"

I giggled. "I don't think so. He knows why we're here."

"All right, then." He lay beside me. "Oh, my darling, you are my sun and moon, my everything."

We kissed again, and his hands were soon exploring my body, just as I'd fantasized. Mine were on him in the same way. His skin was rough and chafed where it was exposed to the sun and wind but soft and smooth in the areas usually covered with clothing.

My fantasies had been a poor prelude to the real thing, which felt like a symphony that he conducted. I might have been a violin, responding to his direction, but he, the conductor, pulled more beautiful music from me than I had any idea I could make.

When I could no longer stand his kisses, fondling, and rubbing, I reached down and pulled him into me. We fit as though we were two parts of the same mold. I gasped at the perfection. He held his position for a moment then began moving. I moved with him as the music we created swelled inside, outside, and around our bodies. My nails dug into his back, and I pulled him closer, deeper. Then the pulses surged through me, and I was unaware of anything but his sweet scent, his warmth. I cried out, holding him ever more tightly. I'd never experienced anything like this, and it was beyond my wildest fantasies. My consciousness floated somewhere near the edge of heaven.

His moan—a sound so sensual and welcome that I nearly cried from the ecstasy of it—brought me back into the room. The physical act was over then, but the feelings I'd discovered would remain with me forever. I now knew how physical love—not physical need, although that was there, too—felt, and I would never again settle for less.

He rolled over and pulled me on top of him. "I love you, Louise. My Louise."

I smiled and kissed the tip of his nose. "I love you too."

I collapsed on his chest, and we lay together, breathing, until I thought our time together surely must be almost over. A glance at the grandfather clock in the corner told me that, yes, I should go soon. But I couldn't just get up and throw on my clothes and rush out. I wouldn't do that. No, I needed to spend the coda with him just as much as I'd needed the main movement. Our symphony wasn't completed yet.

"I want to do this with you, over and over," he murmured dreamily.

"I too," I whispered. "Soon, we shall."

I leaned on an elbow and asked him something I'd been wondering about. "I told you about my first love, but you have said nothing about yours. Have you ever been in love?"

He sighed. "Yes, I was in love with my cousin Kee Vos. I'd always liked her, but after her husband died and left her with a son to raise alone, something happened to me. I fell in love and wanted to marry her." He paused, breathing hard. "I pushed her too hard and too fast, and she turned me down. She told me, 'No, never.' I didn't believe at first that she meant it, but I finally accepted it."

He rubbed a finger over my face. "Is this all right to say to you now?"

I nodded.

"I was so devastated that, shortly after, I fell in love with another woman, and we lived together for a while. But it didn't work out. She wasn't kind to me, and my family disapproved. Eventually, I left. That was years ago, and since then, I haven't dared to trust my heart to anyone. Except you. My heart feels safe with you."

I smiled. "It *is* safe with me, as I know mine is with you."

He leaned on his elbow and gazed at me with that searching look I'd come to love. He stroked my hair. "That deep chestnut color reminds me of the trees we sat under, where the sun touched the bark and brought it to life." His finger moved to my eyebrow. "And your brown eyes sparkle the way gold nuggets might catch the setting sun."

No one had ever said such things to me. I thought to be embarrassed but stopped myself. I would enjoy every second of my time with him. Our lovemaking might not happen again, and I wanted to remember perfection, not self-consciousness.

He kissed the tip of my nose. "And your nose turns up just the slightest bit. I love it."

His finger moved to my mouth and traced my lips. "I wish I could paint these lips. They are the fountain of youth for me." He paused. "Will you let me paint you sometime?"

I took a breath. "Yes. Sometime. Not today. Today, I must leave."

He rubbed his face and glanced at the clock. "Oh no. Sometimes time lags, but today, it has passed far too quickly." He sat up. "Yes, you must go. I do not want anyone to miss you and wonder where you've gone."

Sighing, I said, "Yes, I know. But I need to speak to you about something important. I'll tell you as I dress, if that's all right with you."

"I hate to see you cover your beautiful body with clothes. I'd love to paint you just as you are now." When he saw my expression, he hastened to add, "But I'll wait until the time is right."

"Well..." I turned my back and put on my underthings then turned back to him. "I plan to leave my husband, and I'll need to go somewhere far away, where he's not likely to find me. Would you be willing to accompany me?"

He stood, too, and pulled on his clothes. "Uh, where did you have in mind?"

"Not France, I think. Another country. Maybe even America?" I held my breath while I waited for his response. Vincent was a product of Europe, even more than I, and I struggled to imagine him anywhere else. "I know it probably isn't to your liking, just as it isn't to mine, but we would be safe there. My brother is in New Orleans, which he says is very cosmopolitan, and I'm considering taking the children and going to visit him soon. I'll stay for a few months and decide whether I want to remain. Would you come with us?"

He stood in the middle of the floor, stockings in his hand, as though he were a statue. "Oh, so far away." He paused. "Is there no other way for us to be together?"

I shrugged. "I don't know. But would you join us for a holiday? I can afford to pay your fare, and I would love for us to experience the New World together, even if it's just for a short time."

He stared at me, puzzled. "You have that kind of money?"

"Yes. I'll tell you about it later, but yes, and I'm happy to pay for your passage. Just please say you'll go with me."

"I do love you, Louise, but I'll need some time to consider this change in plans. I had hoped we'd go to the south of France somewhere, and we'd rent a house and paint together. Raise the children together. It's all I can dream of. And now, you have a different idea altogether. I must take a few days to consider it. Will that be all right with you, my dear?"

I stared into his anxious face for a moment. "Of course. Take the time you need."

I finished putting up my hair and pinned on my hat, then I spun around. "Let's put the idea behind us today. We'll speak of it later. For now, do I look like a woman who's just been loved so wonderfully that she's standing on a cloud in heaven?"

He laughed. "Only I can see that part, I think. To others, you might look a little excited, perhaps happy because you've found the right cut of meat at the market. Trust me, our secret is ours and only ours. I will visit the bathhouse before returning to the inn, to erase any trace of your perfume that might linger on my skin and give us away."

I threw him a kiss and ran from the room. "See you soon," I said before closing the door.

When I got home, I wrote to Hélène and asked her to have Claude make a reservation for four to leave for New Orleans, ideally early in August. That should give me adequate time to finish my preparations before leaving.

As soon as I knew the dates of our arrival, I would telegram Émile and ask him to meet us at the ship.

Vincent hadn't yet promised to accompany me, but at least he was considering it. I thought I could convince him to go on a holiday, though, and we would decide together whether to make it permanent. If he didn't come, I would lose the price of his ticket. But if he did, my greatest dream would come true. It was well worth the risk.

I twirled around the bedroom. After thinking about leaving Arthur for years, I'd finally decided to do it. In the end, his latest slap had made the decision easy. As I danced, a weight lifted from my shoulders, and I felt as light as air. I was young, happy, and in love, and the future was brighter than it had ever been.

I'd never wanted to go to America, but given the situation, it seemed exactly the right decision. It was a new world, and I was a new woman. I might not stay long, but I would have a pleasant visit with Émile and see if I liked it. While I was there, Arthur and I could surely come to terms about the divorce. I hoped he would be more reasonable when the children and I were across the ocean.

As I cooked dinner, I thought with joy about how Vincent and I would paint the scenes in New Orleans that Émile had so often described. Vincent's luck might change there, and he could become rich and famous for his paintings of America.

The children would like it there too. They knew only a little English, but I would start tutoring them. My English was reasonably good, and I was sure it would improve on the ship across the Atlantic.

The moon shone suddenly brighter, and even the pans clanking together sang a melody. My heart grew light as I thought about the life ahead of me.

Chapter 28

ARTHUR HADN'T RETURNED from Paris by dinnertime. I vaguely wondered what was keeping him, but I didn't really care. I was just thankful that the dinner crowd wasn't large and that diners ate quickly and moved on. In mid-July, the heat and heaviness in the air were enough to keep anyone from staying inside more than necessary.

Later in the evening, many couples strolled down the road, where the air was passably cool. A string quartet had set up on the grass outside the town hall, and people were dancing, twirling around and around to a waltz. I wondered where they got the energy in the stifling heat.

I took a break from cleaning tables and walked outside, where I held my arms in dance position and took a few steps to the left and right. Maybe I would see similar street scenes in New Orleans, and Vincent and I would dance until our feet were too tired to stand, then we would go to our rooms and make sweet, quiet love so as to not wake the girls.

If things worked out as I hoped, in less than three weeks, we would be on a ship bound for America. I could picture it, and the thought brought a broad smile to my lips.

Arthur staggered up the road and onto the porch just before closing time. Clearly, he was very drunk. Usually, he drank at home on Fridays after the dinner rush so as not to spend the money we couldn't spare but not that night. When he got closer, I smelled cheap perfume. *Oh*. Either the mistress or another whore had attracted his attention.

I sighed. *If only I were free of him already...* I greeted him coldly and went inside to finish cleaning tables and setting up for breakfast. The procedure had become second nature over the past months. I'd been the proprietress of the inn for nearly a year, and I couldn't quite remember how I'd spent my days before moving to Auvers. Maybe I would take that job Émile had written about: cooking at a French restaurant. It wouldn't be a bad way to spend my time and make a little money. I probably wouldn't ever be comfortable as a lady of leisure.

Arthur sat at the bar and watched me, his eyes narrowed. He addressed me in a mean but low-pitched tone so that the few remaining customers couldn't hear. "Did you enjoy yourself while I was away?"

I had prepared for his questions. "No more than usual," I replied mildly. "Nothing particular happened. All the rooms are filled, but the British couple will be leaving in the morning. Oh, the wine shipment will be a little late. It might not arrive until Monday. But that's all. You?"

"Never better." He squinted at me. "Did you have a good time with the boyfriend?"

I shook my head. Tiredly, I asked, "Do we have to go into this again? You're the one with the mistress. I'm just the hard-working wife who keeps the place together while you're out playing with her. Now, leave me alone." I walked into Germaine's room, where I'd grown comfortable sleeping.

Fortunately, he didn't follow.

WITH A SMILE AND A handful of wild bluebells, Vincent awaited me the next morning when I rose to set out breakfast. I was thankful Arthur was still in bed, although he would be up soon. Vincent
followed me into the kitchen. When the door closed behind us, he
leaned in for a kiss, his face alight with pleasure. I allowed a brief kiss
then pushed him away.

"That's dangerous," I whispered. "Someone could come in and
see us."

He grinned. "And then we would leave a little early." His blue
eyes sparkled as he nodded toward me.

Is he saying what I think he's saying? I grinned and reached over
to give him an enormous hug.

Then the maid came in for the coffeepot, and Vincent and I
moved apart. She gave us a brief glance but said nothing and soon
left.

After she was gone, he whispered, "I want to talk with you about
something delicious."

That sounded fascinating. I waggled my eyebrows. "All right.
Give me a few minutes, and I'll meet you at Gérard's house. He'll be
in Paris until tomorrow. I can't stay long, but I'm eager to hear what
is so *delicious*."

He grinned and walked back into the café.

Arthur was up and eating breakfast by the time I was ready to
leave.

"I'm going to the market for some peaches. Back soon." Picking
up my basket, I walked out, not waiting for his response.

Adeline might follow me, but I didn't think so. She'd been asleep
when I checked on her. Holding my head high, I walked up the
street and turned into the alley to Gérard's house. I wasn't quite bold
enough yet to enter through the front door. *Baby steps*, I thought and
chuckled. I was a woman in love, going to meet my lover.

As soon as I walked in the back door, Vincent hugged me and swung me around. We kissed, and he set me down.

After I caught my breath, I asked, "What did you want to tell me?"

"For one thing, I've decided to go with you. When can we leave?" He grinned, showing me the happy little boy he must have been.

"That's marvelous! I hoped you would. I'm so excited. We're going to have such a good time together." I paused. "I've sent a letter to a friend, asking her to purchase four tickets for early August."

His face fell. "So long. Why not now, today?"

"But... but I can't just leave today. I have to make plans and get the children ready."

He bit his lip as he considered my response. "I will need to send some of my paintings to Theo, but other than that, I can be ready in an hour. What plans do you need to make?"

Flustered, I said, "I... I'm not sure yet. I thought we'd wait until a couple of days before the ship's departure."

"But your husband... How can you stand to be around him one more day?" He sounded sincerely puzzled. "He abuses you, and I can see that you loathe him."

I rubbed my eyes and looked out the window. "I need to prepare for this tremendous change in my life. I'm sleeping with Germaine these days, so you need not worry about my having relations with him."

He was quiet for a long moment, and I dared not meet his eyes. Finally, he said in a soft tone, "I know this is difficult for you, my love. I am disappointed, but we will do it your way. I don't mean to push you. It's just that I'm so excited to be close to achieving my fondest wish—to have a wonderful family—that I want to do it *now*. I'm not a patient man, I'm sorry to say, but I will do my best to be patient for a few more weeks."

I hadn't agreed to his request for us to leave immediately, but instead of demanding that I do things his way or yelling at me or grabbing and hitting me, he'd accepted my wishes. For the first time in my life, I *counted*. I luxuriated in the warm feeling of being loved and respected. I could get used to that.

He was correct—if I needed to, I could probably have been ready to leave in an hour. I would grab the children and a few papers and walk out the door. I could always purchase what we needed in Paris. But I would rather take my time and plan to take a little more than the essentials. I'd lived with Arthur for many years, so I could manage a few more weeks.

Speaking gently, Vincent said, "My Louise, right now, I can only offer you my love and my paintings. I have something I wanted to give you today, but since you have to leave, I will wait and present it to you when the time is right." He paused. "Sadly, I have no money to provide for a family as yet. But I believe in my worth as an artist, and my paintings may sell more easily in America, where people are open to new things and different ideas. I wish we didn't have to speak of such things, but we do." He hesitated. "You said you have money? Is it Arthur's that you will take?"

I told him about my inheritance, assuring him that Arthur knew nothing about it. "I also have some money saved from the inn, and I will take that, but I won't be taking Arthur's money."

He nodded. "Well then, we shall see America and paint together and love together and parent together if you allow me that gift."

"Oh. The parenting aspect may need to wait for a while until the girls are more used to you. But I love the rest of your vision." I reached over to hug him, and we kissed.

When we pulled apart, I asked, "Is that the delicious thing you were talking about?"

He shook his head. "No. I think we should do something wonderful in our last days in France, something we've always wanted to do but have never done. We can share something new with each other." He grinned. "Here it is. Have you ever been to the Eiffel Tower?"

I squealed. "I wanted to go when it was built last year. But then we moved here, and my mother became ill, and other things happened. But I would love to go with you. Have you been?"

"Not yet. I was in the asylum during the *Exposition Universelle*. I was invited to exhibit with the Impressionists, but my health was too fragile to handle the stress. Unfortunately, I missed it, but I think we should go together while we can."

"Oh, yes, let's do." I considered. "Uh, would you mind waiting until Wednesday? I usually go to Paris on that day, so no one will be suspicious. We could meet there or on the train." I pulled his pipe from his mouth and gave him a long kiss. Afterward, I asked, "What do you think?"

He took a breath. "I can wait until Wednesday, but it will be a struggle for me. May we still meet here on Tuesday, as planned?"

I thought for a moment. "My husband is very suspicious, and he scrutinizes every move I make. He thinks I'm having an affair with Gérard. I don't want him to know the truth until we're ready to leave. I'll do my best, but it may not be possible. Even if Tuesday doesn't work, at least we'll have Wednesday in Paris." I fluttered my eyelashes at him. "And Thursday for painting. And next Friday for love. And soon, as much time as we want."

He laughed. "Oh, you are a little flirt. Yes, I will do as you wish. But understand I may not be at the inn as often as I have been. I do not wish to get into a fight with your husband and cause an uproar. So it will be best for me to stay away."

"All right. I understand. Do what you must." I gave him a quick kiss but pulled away when he tried to make it last longer. "I must go now, or Arthur will wonder what happened to me. À bientôt."

"À bientôt, my love."

I went out the back door and ran to the market, where I bought a few peaches. Next, I would have to make something with them. *A peach clafoutis, maybe?* Just thinking about warm peaches covered by a crêpe-like batter made my mouth water.

Chapter 29

Love always causes trouble, that's true, but in its favour, it energizes.
–Vincent van Gogh

DURING THE NEXT FEW days, I quietly sorted through the girls' clothing and placed the items I would take with us into a special drawer. I did the same with my own clothes and retrieved a couple of valises from the shed. I was doing the preparations I'd told Vincent were necessary before we could leave. *Leaving* had such a magical sound. The thought made my heart sing and my feet want to dance.

On Tuesday, I received a letter from Hélène containing four tickets on the steamship *Abyssinia*, departing from Le Havre on the eighth of August. I placed them inside one of the valises, along with other important papers.

This is going to happen. I felt a little nervous and quite excited when I thought about starting a new life with Vincent in America, but I didn't dwell on either emotion. I had much to do before we left and much to get through with Arthur, so I would take my current life a day at a time.

On the morrow, I would visit the Eiffel Tower with my new love.

WE'D ARRANGED TO MEET at the foot of the giant tower. Vincent arrived first, and I spotted him through an opening in the

"

crowd. He was dressed in a suit I hadn't seen, and he looked like a prosperous business owner. I, too, had dressed in my best. Unfortunately, I was still in mourning, so my dress was black, but I was sure my excitement overcame the dull clothing.

We kissed as one of many couples in love visiting the most romantic place in Paris. Craning my head to look up, I could barely see the top.

The tower had been a hugely ambitious project, designed for the previous year's *Exposition Universelle*. It was the tallest building in the world and could be seen from anywhere in Paris. Many Parisians thought it ugly, but I loved how it towered over the city. I could hardly believe I was there. For once, my personal struggles seemed insignificant. I vowed to enjoy that special day without worrying about a single thing.

"Let's go inside," Vincent said. "It's lunchtime. Would you like to eat in one of the restaurants?"

"I don't know. I've heard the food is mediocre and quite expensive. Maybe we should look around first and then decide."

The lift we took to the first platform was huge, reminding me of a giant railway carriage. For months, the system had been inoperable, and visitors had had to walk up the 328 stairs, but it was working that day, fortunately, although the clanking was so loud that we couldn't talk over the noise.

We stepped out of the elevator and walked onto the platform. A strong wind whipped our hair, and we laughed with delight. The city spread before us, and it was the grandest thing I'd ever seen. We held hands and walked along the platform, looking at the splendid view on all sides. I wasn't worried about seeing someone I knew—at least, not much. I didn't think any of my friends would be there that day, and even if they were, I was beyond caring. If Arthur found out about us, we would just leave earlier. I looked over my shoulder a few times but saw no one I recognized. Soon, I relaxed into the experience.

As we walked, I saw many landmarks I recognized. "Oh, there's the Arc de Triomphe. It's so beautiful from here." We walked a little farther. "And the Seine is so lovely, like a ribbon of water."

He squeezed my hand. "You love this city, don't you?"

"More now than when I lived here. I can see its beauty now whereas before, I mainly saw the grime. I could look at this view all day."

Laughing, he said, "Well, you could take a while longer. But would you like to eat? It's my treat."

I'd expected to pay for the meal, but I didn't argue. He must've had enough money to pay for it, or he wouldn't have offered. Smiling, I said, "Well, then, how about the Café Brébant? I've heard the food is reasonably good."

The French restaurant wasn't crowded that day, so we were seated on the open-air veranda. As we'd heard, the food was only fair—the soup was watery and lukewarm, and the lamb was tough.

"Shall I send it back?" I asked after taking one bite. "I can't believe they're serving such poor food."

Vincent laughed. "My dear, the food is far from the quality of yours, but look around you. We're paying for the view, and the food is secondary."

He was right. Despite the mediocre food, we laughed and talked through the meal, pointing out buildings we recognized and speaking of what we would like to do in New Orleans. Neither of us knew much about that city, other than that the people spoke French, and it was supposed to be beautiful.

"What more is there to say?" Vincent asked. "We shall be together, making art and making love."

I smiled until my face muscles ached. I could hardly wait to start the next chapter of our lives. I would indeed miss Paris terribly, but this spectacular day was a perfect way to experience its charm one last time. Besides, maybe after Arthur and I divorced, Vincent and I could return to France, perhaps with the children, as a warm and loving family.

When we finished eating, we looked at the steep stairs to the second level and hesitated.

I laughed and said, "Let's take the lift again."

He didn't argue.

At the top, the wind had strengthened, and the sun had disappeared behind the clouds. The day had turned nasty, and the city had lost its luster. The time had come to leave.

"Why don't we walk down?" Vincent suggested. "It's a lot easier than going up, and we'll be out of the wind. And we'll be together longer."

The walk down wasn't so bad, and we paused several times to view the city again. When we finally reached the ground, I was barely out of breath, and Vincent appeared to have taken a promenade in the park. Those long walks around Auvers were doing us both good.

We were unwilling to part yet, so we walked to the Seine and strolled across the Pont d'Iéna, holding hands and watching the water gently flow beneath us.

Vincent murmured, "I wish I could paint this. I haven't taken an entire day away from my easel since the last time I was sick."

Sick. Suddenly, my exhilaration shifted toward something more ominous. We might be on the precipice of escaping from my terrible husband and loving each other indefinitely. On the other hand, we could be in the final days before Vincent's horrible malady returned and left him incapacitated for weeks, if not months—if not forever. *How could I forget the reality of our situation?* I hadn't really forgotten it, of course, but merely ignored its threatening presence because I couldn't do anything about it.

Vincent looked at me, his face stricken. He grasped my hand so tightly that I needed to pull it away and massage my fingers.

"I'm sorry, my love," he whispered. "Sometimes—especially on wonderful days such as this—I'm so afraid of what the future brings that I'm tempted to leap into the water and bring all the waiting and the fear to an end." He shook his head. "Not that I would ever do it, but I love you so much, and I want this to go on for years." Speaking softly, he continued, "And I'm so afraid it will only be today. Tomorrow, the end could come."

I rested my head on his shoulder and grabbed his hand. "Oh, Vincent, I feel sure we'll have many more days like this one. You seem so much better than when you first came to Auvers."

"I hope so." He glanced at his timepiece and took a breath. "I'm sorry to have our day end on this difficult note, but I believe it's time for you to leave." He let go of my hand and stood back a few inches. "I'll be fine. Sometimes after a wonderful day, I grow a little morose. Don't let it worry you, my dear."

We hugged and kissed once more, and I headed toward the train station, considerably chastened. Life with Vincent was going to be a little more complex than I'd envisioned.

Chapter 30

UPON MY RETURN TO THE inn, I discovered that Germaine was feeling poorly again. She was running a slight fever, and her runny nose had returned. I gave her some willow bark tea and put her to bed then sang songs and read books to her until she fell asleep.

I wasn't particularly worried since this illness wasn't bad, but as I stood and stretched my back, I realized that this was the second time she'd gotten sick while I was out with Vincent. I wondered what would happen to her when we left the life she knew. Her health had always been fragile, and if she became really ill while we were in America, that would be terrible. Maybe we should stay in France, close to medical care.

I pushed the thought away. My daughter's illness had nothing to do with Vincent, and I deserved some joy in my life. Besides, there were probably good doctors in America too.

Dinner was long past, but Adeline had made a pot of French onion soup and had left what remained to warm on the stove. I'd taught her how to prepare it months ago but had thought she wasn't paying attention. However, when I tasted it, it was delicious. I complimented her on the excellent soup, but she merely stared at me with an accusing look and said nothing.

A tingle rose up my spine. That look couldn't have been about the soup.

As I swept the floor, and Adeline set the tables for the next day's breakfast, I cleared my throat. "Honey, are you all right? You seem... quieter than usual."

Adeline grunted and shot me a look that might've been either disappointment or disgust.

I grabbed her shoulders. "Did something happen while I was in Paris?"

Adeline wouldn't meet my eyes. Finally, she said, "You have no right to tell me what I can and cannot do. No right." She broke out crying and ran into her room.

I sank into a chair as understanding seeped through my veins. I didn't know how she could've found out about Vincent and me, but I had little doubt that she knew. Adeline hadn't been in Paris with us, and he and I had traveled to and from the city separately. Thus, her knowledge couldn't have come from that day.

I let my mind float backward. Nothing inappropriate had happened with Vincent during the painting lessons. The two of us had kept up the charade of only being teacher and student. So that wasn't it.

The only time the girl could have seen us together was at Gérard's house. But Adeline hadn't been in the house with us, and she hadn't followed me—at least I hadn't *seen* her following me. I wondered if she could've done it without me noticing. It was possible, I thought, my heart sinking.

Something niggled at the corners of my mind. Finally, I remembered the draperies in Gérard's parlor, which had been open a bit when I met Vincent there on Friday. *Could Adeline have seen us through that slight opening?*

My blood turned to ice as I realized Cécile might've let slip that I was meeting Vincent. Danielle wouldn't have told her daughter about the assignation—of that I was sure—but Cécile could've over-heard her mother discussing it with Gérard.

I shook my head. Right then, how my daughter had found out didn't matter. *Adeline knows now.*

The next question was what the girl would do with that informa-tion.

My vision went blurry, and I thought I might faint. I leaned over and put my head between my knees, and my vision gradually cleared. My confident attitude from earlier in the day had dissolved into mist, and I was a worried mess.

When I sat up, my mind worked feverishly. I needed to do some-thing about Adeline and quickly, but I didn't know what. I couldn't ask Vincent because he was staying in Paris for the night. He planned to visit the shop where he stored some of his paintings and purchase art supplies. He'd told me I shouldn't worry if he didn't show up until the next evening.

This was an emergency. I couldn't allow Adeline to tell her father what she knew. Just the thought of Arthur's fists pounding my body made everything ache and my hair stand on end. I needed to leave immediately, to grab the girls and take them to Hélène's apartment. My friend had invited me to show up any time, day or night, so I would do that. *Now.*

I stumbled into my bedroom and began throwing things into a valise, but then I heard a small "Maman" coming from the girls' room. Germaine didn't sound well.

I flew into the room and felt my little girl's forehead. It was burn-ing hot despite the willow bark tea. She began coughing, and the barking cough was unmistakable—the croup that had made her so sick the year before had returned.

I turned to Adeline, who was sitting on her bed. "Help her sit up and lean forward while I boil some water. We won't call a doctor yet, but I need to get her over some steam."

Adeline nodded, and I rushed into the kitchen. As I went about stoking the stove and pouring water into a pan, I wondered if I'd missed some signs. Yes, Germaine had had a cold the week before, but her breathing had been fine, and she hadn't been coughing. Earlier in the evening, her fever had been so minor that it might've been because of the hot day rather than illness.

When the water boiled, I carefully poured some into a bowl and carried it and a clean towel into the bedroom. I held the little girl in the steam and covered her head with a towel, letting her breathe it in.

Over the next hour or two, the barking cough came less frequently, and the wheezing stopped. The fever decreased. When I set her down, both Germaine and I were wringing wet. I dried her off and changed her nightgown then placed several pillows on the bed so that she could sleep propped up. I made more willow bark tea, and she drank a few sips before falling asleep.

I massaged my aching back as I watched my younger daughter sleep. Her breathing sounded good. By the time I was convinced that all was well, it was the middle of the night. Adeline was still awake, watching me with a pale face and large eyes. I felt her forehead, but she was fine, for which I was thankful. I told her to call me if Germaine coughed again, and I went into my bedroom.

It was strewn with the clothing I'd been in the process of packing.

Sighing, I picked everything up and replaced it in its proper places. I would not be leaving that night. Depending on Germaine's health, that might not be possible for a few days.

I refused to accept this health crisis as anything other than a temporary delay of my plans. Everything was going to work out. I still had weeks until the ship sailed, and we would be on it.

IN THE MORNING, GERMAINE felt somewhat better. I made her spend the day in bed, and I sent Adeline to call for Dr. Mazery, the village doctor. When he arrived, he examined her and told me to continue the steam treatment and to keep her in bed until she felt completely well. He left some medicine to help relieve the fever, but he warned me that sitting in drafts or moving around too much could worsen her symptoms.

I'd been through all that a year before. If Germaine's illness progressed in the same way, she might not be able to travel for a week or more. I walked out with the doctor.

"We were planning on going to stay with some friends in Paris for a few days. Might she be all right to travel?"

He shook his head. "Are there small children where you're going?"

I nodded.

"No, croup is very contagious, and you don't want to expose other children to it. Besides, outside air isn't good for her. She needs to stay in bed—here—for a few days, at least. Let's see how she does tonight. I'll come back tomorrow."

"Thank you, Doctor."

After he left, I collapsed onto a chair and tried to decide what to do. I had no choice but to stay there until Germaine was well. If Adeline accused me of being with Vincent, I would deny it, but Arthur would surely believe her instead of me. I prayed the situation wouldn't come to that, but if he hit me, I would run to Danielle's inn and take the children with me, even if Germaine was still sick.

That was the best plan I could make at the moment.

Adeline had said nothing yet about what she might or might not have seen. I could only hope the girl would keep her mouth shut for a few days longer.

I would avoid Arthur when he got home the next night. As soon as Germaine was safe to travel, I would gather the children and leave.

If Vincent hadn't yet returned from Paris, I would leave a note under his door with Hélène's address.

But I didn't have a good feeling about the entire situation.

VINCENT DIDN'T RETURN until the next evening, just before dinner. He set his painting supplies in the Artists' Room and gestured toward the shed.

As soon as I could, I followed him out there.

Once inside, I closed the door and rushed into his arms. He held me as though I was the only thing keeping him from collapsing.

After a moment, I realized he was upset. I pulled back a little and said, "What happened?"

He kissed my forehead. "I'm sorry, *ma belle*. Nothing is wrong. It's just that I'm unused to things being right, and I was afraid you wouldn't be here when I came back, or you would have changed your mind about us."

He paused. "I met with a couple of friends in Paris, and a journalist found me. He wanted to interview me about 'my new success.' I didn't know of what he was speaking, but he told me I was the talk of Paris, and he was writing a glowing piece about my work."

I started to congratulate him but stopped when I saw the tortured look on his face, and I gave him a questioning look.

"I couldn't help myself—I fled. All my life, people have disliked me. I've never understood why because I try and try, but people always turn against me. And for years, no one has liked my work other than me. And now you. So here I am, with all my dreams coming true, and I can't believe it will happen. I rushed back here so I could hold you in my arms."

He shook with tears.

"I am with you, my darling," I said. "I love you. And soon, the world will love you too."

After a moment, he took a breath and moved away to sit in a chair. "Thank you. For everything." He looked at me. "But you are upset too. I can see it in your face. What has happened, my dear Louise?"

I told him about Germaine's illness and Adeline's anger. "The look on her face when she stares at me is horrible, like I've betrayed her trust so much that she cannot stand for me to be her mother."

"Oh no." He stood and held me while I cried. When my tears finally stopped, he asked, "What shall we do now?"

"I want to leave immediately. But the doctor says it isn't safe to move Germaine just yet. Oh, Vincent, I'm so afraid of what will happen when Arthur gets home. If Adeline tells him, I don't know what he'll do."

Vincent thought for a few moments. "Let us hope you are wrong about Adeline. We have no choice but to carry on as usual until Germaine is well enough to travel." He paused. "When do you think that will be?"

I'd thought about this. "If the weekend goes well, Monday will work. I'll tell Arthur I need to take her to see Dr. Garnier in Paris and that Adeline should come too. I can say we'll stay the night with Hélène. He won't say no, I think." I paused. "You can leave during the day, and we can stay with my friends until the ship sails."

"All right," he said with a smile. "We have a plan. Just three more days. On the fourth day, we'll be together."

I gave him another hug and a tremulous smile then made my way back to my customers. I ignored Adeline's nasty looks and carried on with my duties.

That night, Germaine's cough returned, and I was up half the night again. But that time wasn't as bad, so I hoped we could still leave by Monday.

On Monday, my new life would begin.

ARTHUR ARRIVED ON FRIDAY evening, later than usual and drunk again. I shivered when I saw him but didn't bother castigating him for his lateness. On the contrary, I appreciated every hour I didn't have to deal with him. Since he was so drunk, I thought he might pass out quickly, and I would be done with him for the night.

Over and over, my mind repeated, *Two more days. Saturday and Sunday. And then we'll leave on Monday.* I told myself I could do this. And if I needed him, Vincent would be there.

When he closed the bar, Arthur settled onto a barstool. I braced for what was coming.

"I hear you've been having a good time with the schoolteacher," he said. "Monsieur Gérard, is that right? Did the two of you enjoy yourselves while I was away?"

I breathed a sigh of relief. Either Adeline had misunderstood what was happening, or she hadn't yet told her father what she'd seen.

"I don't know where you heard that, but you heard wrong," I said, scowling. "Gérard is my friend. I have no idea where he is. He certainly wasn't with me. Besides, he's seeing Danielle. Didn't you know that?" I snorted. "You're imagining things."

He gasped, squinting in confusion. After a moment, he asked, in a strained voice, "Are you telling me the truth?"

"Ask anyone. It isn't exactly a secret. I suspect they'll announce their engagement soon." As soon as the words were out of my mouth, I realized I shouldn't have uttered them. Gérard was my cover. But he was a nice man, and I hated to hear him maligned.

Arthur seemed to become instantly sober. He stood up quickly, kicking the stool backward. "Uh, I'm going out for a few moments. I'll be right back." He unlocked the front door and ran outside. He stood in the road for a moment, looking around frantically, then disappeared.

Now, why on earth would he do that? I didn't really care because my ruse had worked, at least for the moment. Maybe he would stay out for the rest of the night—anything to get him away from me.

At bedtime, he still hadn't returned. Relieved, I retired to Germaine's room, where both girls were asleep. The transcendent experiences with Vincent had erased any illusions I might have harbored that my marriage was tolerable. I saw my life clearly as the wasteland it had become.

In a few moments, Arthur burst into the children's bedroom and hissed at me, "Get out here now. I need to speak with you."

My heart lurched. I shushed Germaine, who had awakened at her father's tone, and wrapped my robe around myself as I went into the bedroom I'd shared with Arthur until ten days before.

"What is it? I was asleep."

"You're my wife, and your place is here." He pointed at the bed.

Warily, I sat on the bed. He was slurring his words, which meant he was even drunker than I'd realized. In the past, he'd been the most dangerous at such times. If I said even the slightest thing that he could take in the wrong way, he might slam his fists into my body.

I took several breaths as I decided what to do. "What's happened?"

He leaned forward, and the sour stench of whiskey on his breath almost bowled me over. "If not Gérard, then who are you fucking?"

I hated when he spoke with such crude language, and he knew it. That was probably why he did it. I ignored the word because his question meant he still didn't know about Vincent. *Good.* I shook my head. "I've told you there's no one. You're imagining things." I tried to give him a small smile, but my face didn't want to move in that way. I was trembling, and my body wanted to curl into a ball. I couldn't allow that to happen, because then I would be too vulnerable to his accusations and his fists. But I didn't think my legs would support me if I tried to walk away, so I continued to sit.

He went on and on, yelling at me for my supposed infidelities. At one point, he grabbed my shoulders and shook me until my teeth rattled and I bit my tongue. Still, I refused to say a word. Finally, after time interminable, he stopped and pointed at the bed.

"You'll sleep here, beside me, as usual. And if you ever try to leave me, I'll kill you and him both. Do you hear me?"

I knew not to argue at that point. If my survival required me to sleep beside the monster for a few more nights, I could manage.

He lay on the bed and began snoring almost instantly.

I pulled off his shoes but didn't bother with the rest of his clothes. He could sleep in his own vomit if it came to that. Then I lay, gingerly, on the bed beside him.

The night was long, but I eventually slept and woke with his arm around me.

Chapter 31

SATURDAY WORE ON, AND nothing new occurred. Vincent went out painting early and didn't return until dinner. When I saw him, we spoke only of trivial matters because I didn't want to upset him more than necessary when nothing could be done about the situation. Germaine slowly recovered. By Saturday evening, the little girl was demanding to get out of bed and play. Even though I wouldn't let her, that was a good sign of her healing.

I kept thinking, *Monday morning. Monday morning.* On the day after next, I would leave and never return to this place of stress and heartache. My only worry was how Adeline would react when she learned we weren't coming back. But I would deal with that when the time came. I only had to survive one more day before my new life would commence.

AS USUAL, SUNDAY WAS filled with routine. After attending church and serving the midday meal to our guests, we family members went our own ways. Arthur played billiards with a friend, I played dolls with Germaine, whom I'd finally allowed to leave her bed for a while, and Adeline stayed in her room and appeared to be reading a book, although she never made progress, as far as I could tell.

In midafternoon, Cécile knocked on the front door and asked if Adeline could go out for a while. The older girl seemed unsettled, and her voice was unnaturally high and thin when she asked for Adeline. I sent her into my daughter's room, and the two girls came out a few moments later, eyes big and shoulders hunched. They disappeared down the road without explanation.

Adeline came back an hour later and retreated to her room. After a while, I went to check on her and found her lying on her bed, sobbing as though she'd lost her last friend.

"Honey, what's happened? Tell me." I gathered the girl up and held her on my lap.

Adeline was nearly as large as I was, but she wrapped her arms around my shoulders and continued sobbing.

"What's going on? Did something happen with Cécile? Whatever it is, maybe I can help."

"No. You can't help. Please don't ask me anything else."

I sat beside her, rubbing her head as she cried. Maybe something other than my behavior was bothering the girl. I wasn't sure I had the fortitude to deal with anything more just then, so I smoothed her hair and brought her some tea then left her alone to brood in her own way.

Arthur was acting strange too. After his friend left, he sat in a rocking chair on the porch and nursed a single glass of beer as he stared vacantly across the street at the empty town hall. When I asked him what was wrong, he ignored me, so I let it go.

Outside, another storm was brewing, which would probably hit after sunset. Meanwhile, the air was stultifying as dark clouds gathered on the horizon. Soon, the wind would pick up and blow away the heavy air, then drops as big as saucers would fall, followed by thunder and lightning. Storms came and went several times a week, but that Sunday felt different—heavier, darker, more ominous than usual.

I served a light supper for my family. I hadn't seen Vincent since midday, when he came in for a quick meal then went back out.

As the hours slowly passed, my mind repeated, *Tomorrow. Tomorrow.* It was all I could think about.

After the sun set, the clouds gathered, and the evening turned blustery. Arthur and I sat on the porch, waiting for the storm to arrive and force us to enter our stifling abode.

I watched as Vincent approached on the darkened road. He was without his bag or his easel, and he wasn't carrying a canvas. That was strange—he was usually loaded down like a pack mule. He staggered along, holding his belly, and he seemed to be limping. He passed us without a word and walked up the stairs toward his room.

Arthur and I exchanged puzzled glances. We hadn't yet lit the gas lamps, so I couldn't see my husband clearly, but he seemed pale, and his breathing was fast and uneven.

"What is it, Arthur? Do you know what's wrong with Monsieur Vincent?"

He shook his head. "I'll check."

We walked into the building together, and Arthur quickly lit the lamps. We stopped at the foot of the stairs. A thin line of blood stretched across the room and up the stairs. We heard moaning.

My breath caught in my throat as my eyes followed the trail of blood. I felt split in two—part of me wanted to run to my darling and soothe whatever ailed him, and the other part wanted to pretend nothing was seriously wrong. I wasn't sure I could cope with one more thing that night.

Glancing at Arthur, I saw that his face had contorted into a rictus. I placed a hand on his arm, but he jerked it away.

"I... I should see what's wrong," he said in a tight voice.

"Yes. We'll both go."

VINCENT'S ROOM WAS at the top of two flights of stairs. The door was open, but the room was dark, so I quickly lit his lamp. Vincent lay on the bed, curled into a fetal position, his face contorted in pain.

I turned to Arthur. "We must get a doctor. I'll try to do what I can here while you run for Dr. Mazery." I hoped the village doctor would be in that night, not delivering a baby or doing something else from which he could not extricate himself.

Arthur clumped down the stairs.

I turned to Vincent, who opened his eyes when I touched him. "My darling, what has happened?"

He groaned. "I'm so sorry, my dear." He held his stomach.

"Are you hurt? Ill?" I gently pulled his hands away and saw blood pouring from a small puncture wound.

My mind flashed through the possibilities. Maybe he'd gotten caught on a barbed wire fence while he was walking through a farmer's field. But he had only one wound, and it appeared to be deeper than barbed wire would make. Or he could've been stabbed, but if so, it was with a tiny knife.

"Shot," he said between gritted teeth.

Shot? How can that be? No one is ever shot around here.

"Who did this to you?"

For an instant, he stopped squirming and looked into my eyes as he grabbed my hand and murmured, "If I die, please think of me now and then." He groaned again and covered his stomach with his hands. Despite my questions, he said nothing more.

Not knowing how to help him, I ran to the kitchen for a basin of warm water and a cloth to wash his wound. When I returned, he allowed me to clean it. A hole the size of a pea appeared just below his ribs, and after a few moments, the bleeding gradually stopped.

Vincent closed his eyes and remained silent. I squeezed his hand, but it lay limp in mine.

Soon, Dr. Mazery arrived and asked me to leave the room while he examined the patient. Downstairs in the café, my daughters were clearly terrified. I asked Adeline to put Germaine to bed and then to remain in their room. They retreated silently.

Arthur sat at a table, his head in his hands. "Is he all right?"

I sank into a chair. "I don't know. Dr. Mazery is examining him."

A few moments later, the doctor came down the stairs and sat on a chair. "Someone shot him with a small-caliber pistol, but beyond that, I cannot say. The bullet appears to have missed his major organs and blood vessels, and it didn't hit bone. I think I could feel it toward the back of his abdomen, but it's too deep to remove. It could have punctured a lung or hit an artery—I can't say for sure. We'll have to wait and see how it goes. He could survive this."

"But who shot him?" I asked.

"He won't say. I don't think he did it himself, though, because the bullet came from farther away than he could have held the gun. And the angle was odd. It looks to me like an accidental shooting. Instead of answering my questions, he asked me to prop him up and give him his pipe." He thought for a moment. "Were there any witnesses?"

Arthur didn't respond, so I said, "We don't know. He just came stumbling in. He'd been out painting."

"I'll return to the patient. Would you mind bringing up a chair or two?"

"Certainly."

He went back upstairs, and Arthur carried two dining chairs up to Vincent's room. Several of the other boarders stepped out of their rooms to ask what was happening. Arthur told them what he knew and asked them to remain in their rooms for the evening.

Before long, Dr. Gachet appeared at the door, accompanied by his son. "What has happened? I heard Vincent was shot."

I frowned, wondering how the news could've spread so quickly. "Yes, we believe that is what happened. Please go on up to his room. Dr. Mazery is there too."

He gestured for his son to stay in the café while he rushed up the stairs. I followed him but remained on the landing so that I could hear and not be in the way.

"Vincent, what is the problem?" asked Gachet.

The answer came from Dr. Mazery. "Hello, Dr. Gachet. Gunshot wound. Here."

After the two men talked for a moment, Vincent asked, "Is no one going to remove this bullet from me?"

After a long silence, Dr. Gachet replied, "We don't have the ability to do it here. If we could transport you to Paris, we could try it there. But we don't know exactly where the bullet is, and you might not survive the trip."

No one spoke. Eventually, Gachet continued, "I'm sorry, Vincent. You can survive for a while with a bullet in your belly. When you improve, we'll do surgery then."

Vincent grunted.

In an exasperated voice, Dr. Gachet said, "Now, will you tell us what happened?"

Vincent waited a long time before saying, "I shot myself," in a strange tone.

After a long pause, Dr. Gachet said, "No, I don't think so. Who are you shielding?"

No answer.

Dr. Gachet huffed. "Were you trying to commit suicide?"

"I suppose so."

"For God's sake, man, why would you do that?"

No answer.

I crept down the stairs. Whatever had really happened, Vincent appeared to be sticking to his story. I found my rosary and began to pray. Our plans had clearly been upended, but that was not my major concern just then. More than anything, I wanted—needed—Vincent to live and be all right. The man deserved to live, whether or not he was with me. I prayed harder.

After a while, it occurred to me that someone should contact Vincent's brother, Theo. I checked in the mail basket but found no letters, either to or from Theo, and I didn't know his Paris address.

Dr. Gachet came downstairs and asked for pen and paper so that he could write to Theo. When I provided them, he wrote a brief letter, but neither of us knew where to mail it. Dr. Gachet went upstairs and asked Vincent for the address, but he refused to give it, saying he didn't want to bother his brother.

Just then, Tom Hirschig, the Dutch painter whose room was next to Vincent's, arrived at the inn, and he quickly learned what was happening. "I don't know where Theo lives, but I know where he works, so I'll take the letter there first thing in the morning."

The doctors agreed to that plan. They were fairly certain Vincent would make it through the night, but they were absolutely certain Theo should come. No one knew what the night or the next day would bring.

After that, both doctors left, saying they would return in the morning.

Dr. Mazery stopped at the front door and asked, "Is Germaine doing better?"

"Yes. She's well."

"Good." He nodded and left.

Struggling to control my tears, I brought up some warm bone broth and spooned it into Vincent's mouth. Over and over, I asked him what had happened, but he would give no more information.

"My darling, was it because of me?" I whispered, hoping Arthur wasn't lurking outside the bedroom door.

"No, not at all," he said, softly. "I had planned to go with you to America. But now... I don't know if I can. I'm sorry."

Tears formed in his eyes, and he rubbed them away with the back of his hand. Even the slightest movement caused him to groan with pain, so I dabbed at his eyes with a cloth.

"Was it... was it because of your illness, then? Has it returned? You said you don't harm others, only yourself."

"No. Not that." He grasped my hand. "I want to say something while I still have my wits about me. If I survive this wound, I will join you in America. But please, I beg you, do not wait for me. You must flee while you can."

He paused and licked his lips. "If I don't survive, take some of my paintings with you. That way, you might remember me from time to time. And I had something else to give you, but now I can't find it. If you come across it, you'll know it's for you."

I took a breath and started to interrupt, but he held up a hand. "If I don't survive, please don't grieve for me too long. I'm just a scruffy artist who would've been nothing but trouble for you. But I do love you. You're worthy of love, so find someone else who will love you as I do." He paused. "And please do not ask me again what happened. It is better that you not know."

My knees crumpled, and I sat heavily on the chair beside his bed.

Vincent closed his eyes and replaced his pipe in his mouth. He puffed away, seeming to be content.

Just then, Arthur appeared in the doorway. He appeared not to have heard our interchange, so I breathed a sigh of relief.

"Louise, come to bed now. Monsieur Hirschig has volunteered to be available if Monsieur Vincent needs anything during the night. It's late, so let's allow him to rest now." He spoke as gently as he could, given who he was. "I've cleaned the stairway, and the girls are asleep."

"Good night, madame," said Vincent. "I shall be fine tonight. You need your sleep."

I started to argue but quickly realized that would be futile. "All right. Please have Monsieur Hirschig wake us if there is a need."

Vincent's room was extremely hot, so I opened his skylight so that he could feel the breeze and see the stars, since the storm had passed. I wanted to kiss his pale, dry lips, but of course that would not be acceptable behavior for a landlady. Instead, I leaned over to pat his head then walked out the door, leaving it open behind myself.

Chapter 32

I LAY STIFF AND SILENT on the bed, as close to the edge and as far from Arthur as I could get, but my mind soared up to Vincent. His brother would surely arrive in the morning, so I might not have another opportunity to be alone with my lover. I was tempted to return to Vincent's side, but whenever I moved, even the slightest bit, Arthur would snuggle close and throw his arm around me. *Does he suspect? Yes, probably.* I had no idea if he knew anything for certain.

Vincent, you must live, my darling. I need you, and the world needs you. How can I lose you just when I finally found you?

I crept from the bed once during the night and went outside to the privy. Back inside, I stood at the foot of the stairs and listened for any sound. *Nothing—no, wait, is that a moan?* I couldn't be sure, and the stairs would creak if I tried to climb them to check on him. So I went back to bed, to toss restlessly until morning.

When I awoke, daylight had arrived, and Arthur had already risen. I dressed hurriedly and walked into the kitchen. Fortunately, my husband was nowhere to be seen. I checked on the children. Germaine had no fever and only a slight cough, and Adeline was still asleep.

Monday. We were supposed to leave for Paris that morning. I'd known the night before that it wouldn't happen, but the realization that all my planning had been for naught was devastating. I stood for a moment, holding back the tears for my dear love. I would stay with Arthur forever if Vincent could live, but I didn't have the power to choose who would live and who would die.

Dreading what I would find, I made a tray of food and carried it up the stairs.

Vincent lay in the same position in which I'd left him hours before. I could hear him breathing, so I still hoped for a miracle. The room smelled of oil paints and turpentine but also blood and urine. The poor man had been unable to get to his chamber pot during the night. I would change the sheets and clean his room—that was the least I could do for him.

He woke when I neared his bed. Dull eyes stared at me in the morning light.

"Louise? Is that you?"

"Yes, my darling." I sat on the chair beside his bed. "How was the night?"

"I'm so sorry—the bed." He gestured toward the wet sheets.

"It's nothing. Please don't fret. I'll change your sheets. Can you move? I brought you some tea."

He rolled to one side—so I could replace the sheet and tuck it under him—then to the other side. With each movement, he groaned, but when I finished, he sighed. "That's so much better. Thank you. I hate to be a bother."

Brushing my fingers across his face, I leaned over to give him a quick kiss. "Just get well quickly." I paused. "I'm so sorry, my love. If we'd left when you first urged me to, none of this would have happened. It's all my fault."

He didn't respond for a while. Eventually, he said, "Not your fault. Don't ever blame yourself." He glanced around the room.

"Your husband was in here earlier. He instructed me not to talk to you any more than necessary. Is he still here? In the corner, perhaps?"

I took a deep breath. The room was small, and if Vincent had been in his right mind, he could've seen that Arthur was not in the room. I wondered if Arthur had really said that or if Vincent's mind was wandering. I might never know.

"No, darling, he's not here. I don't know where he is."

We sat together for a while, and I held a teacup to his mouth as he slurped the tea. After only a few sips, he shook his head, showing he was finished.

"Would you like some breakfast?"

"No, thank you." He grabbed my hand. "Gachet told me he will summon my brother today. Is that right?" When I nodded, he frowned. "I wish he wouldn't do that. Theo has more than enough concerns already. But listen to me. When Theo comes, let us not behave as lovers but as innkeeper and tenant. I don't want to ruin your reputation in the community. If he finds out about us, others may too." His eyes pierced into mine. "Will you do that for me?"

He wants to deny any connection with me. I felt a stab in my heart, so deep and painful that it almost stopped my breath. His words made some sense, but surely his brother could keep a confidence. Still, this might be his dying wish, so I had no choice but to comply.

"Yes. I understand. I wish you would tell me what happened, though."

He shook his head. "It is for you I remain mum."

I didn't understand but wouldn't argue. "All right. We will be landlady and tenant until you're well, and then we'll leave together." I squeezed his hand. "I must go now. When I can, I will check on you." I handed him a small bell. "Use this if you need to summon me, and I'll be here."

"Thank you." His voice was strained, and he closed his eyes, clearly worn out from the interaction.

I tiptoed out, carrying the soggy sheets.

AFTER BREAKFAST, FIVE of our seven boarders checked out, saying they were sorry to leave, but responsibilities called them. Only Vincent and Hirschig remained. I was as pleasant as I could be in the face of the polite lies. I should've realized they would all leave. No one wanted to stay at an inn where a boarder had been shot.

Then two gendarmes arrived. They stood in the café, shuffling their feet for a moment, before telling me they'd heard about the shooting.

"Who told you?" I asked.

They glanced at each other. "Uh, we're not allowed to say, madame."

It could have been anyone. Surely, the whole town knew about it by then.

"Would you like to see the patient, then?" When they nodded, I led them up to Vincent's room. "Uh, he isn't entirely lucid," I said. "Please keep in mind that he's in terrible pain, and keep your questions short."

They agreed and entered Vincent's room. I listened in the hall while they questioned him.

"Who shot you?"

"I may have shot myself."

"*May have?* Sir, can you be more specific?"

He didn't answer. After a long pause, one asked him if he was trying to commit suicide.

"Yes, I suppose so."

The same answers he had given the doctors—they sounded rehearsed, rote. I wanted to intervene and tell the officers that what he said wasn't the truth, but I had no idea what was true. Maybe I had pressed him too hard to leave with me, and shooting himself was his response. After all, he'd spoken of hastening his end when we stood on the bridge over the Seine, saying he wasn't used to good things happening. Or maybe his illness had returned, and he'd been trying to spare me from having to care for him.

So I remained quiet. After all, Vincent must've had some reason to tell them what he did, even if I didn't understand it.

He ignored all further questions, never saying another word to the officers. Eventually, they trooped down the stairs and asked to speak with my husband. Since Arthur was nowhere to be found, I served them coffee and sat with them, answering their questions as best I could.

No, Monsieur Vincent hadn't been acting differently before the incident. No, he hadn't mentioned wanting to commit suicide, but I was only his landlady, and he probably wouldn't have said anything like that to me. Yes, his brother had been summoned. Yes, two doctors had seen him, and they thought he could survive the shooting. No, he had no enemies that I knew of. He was just a painter who lived quietly, drank a bit, and spent most of his time outdoors with a paintbrush in his hands.

They thanked me and left.

In the afternoon, Theo arrived. He seemed terribly distraught and rushed immediately to Vincent's room. I brought them lunch then lingered on the stairs. Vincent seemed to have been roused by his brother's visit, and soon the two of them were speaking intensely in Dutch. I left them to it.

The two doctors came and went, checking on the patient. In the late afternoon, Dr. Gachet came down the stairs, a stethoscope around his neck, and shook his head at my questioning glance.

"I don't think he'll make it," he said, his voice ragged.

I pursed my lips, nodding. With Vincent's death, the world I'd constructed in my mind would end, too, and I could do nothing to patch it back together.

Arthur finally arrived home, wild-eyed and drunk. He'd apparently been looking everywhere for something or someone—he wouldn't say what or who—and he grabbed Adeline's arm and pulled her outside. They spoke for a few moments, and Adeline shook her head several times before she shrugged and walked back inside.

What is going on? Did Arthur and Adeline's conversation relate to Vincent's situation, or is there something else I don't know?

By late afternoon, I'd let the staff go for the evening and closed the restaurant. No one came to dine, anyway.

In the early evening, a knock sounded at the door. Arthur answered it to find a portly gentleman.

"I am Monsieur Delépine," the man said, "and I have just purchased the inn. I wanted to come and introduce myself."

When Arthur cast a glance at me, I could almost hear his thoughts: *Now you come, amidst this crisis?* He inhaled deeply then held out a hand. "Welcome, Monsieur Delépine. I am Arthur Ravoux, and this is my wife, Louise." He offered him dinner and a glass of wine or a tour of the premises—anything he wanted.

The new owner accepted a glass of wine, and we all sat at a table in the café. Monsieur Delépine had heard about the shooting. "What do you know about the circumstances?" he asked. "And how is the victim doing?"

"I know nothing about the circumstances," Arthur said. "I've been out most of the day, trying to learn what happened, but I discovered nothing. No one knows where he was when he was shot or why it happened or where he got the gun. I can only assume he brought it with him and has had it in his possession all this time, waiting for the right time to turn it on himself."

My husband was lying. I could tell by the tone of his voice that he was hiding something, but I had no idea why. He couldn't have shot Vincent, for he'd been at home all day on Sunday. He must've known who did, though.

I wanted to say I'd cleaned Vincent's room many times and had never seen a gun there, but I didn't dare speak. If Vincent died, we might have to close the inn. No one would want to sleep where a man had breathed his last. Even if a miracle occurred and he lived, people probably wouldn't be willing to stay there for a long time.

That wasn't any business of mine, though, since I still planned to leave—someday. Still, I felt a pang of sympathy for Arthur, who would have to manage the fallout on his own—or not, I supposed, depending on how this meeting went.

The three of us spoke for an hour, and I brought out the accounting books I meticulously updated every month. They showed that the inn had made a good profit during the summer, but unless business improved during the coming winter, it was unlikely to be a sustainable enterprise for the long term.

The man eventually left, thanking us for our honesty. Arthur locked the door behind him and poured himself a serving of cognac. "Well, damn. Your painter friend has probably bankrupted us. I hope you're happy." He glared at me.

"Don't blame me. This isn't my doing." I was tempted to continue talking, to tell him everything I thought about him, but I bit my tongue. We would have time for that later—or not.

In the evening, I put the children to bed. Germaine clung to me as I read a story about a mouse, but the little girl eventually fell asleep. Her fever and cough were both gone, which was some consolation. Adeline was in her bed, pretending to read, when I sat beside her.

"Now, will you tell me what's going on?"

Adeline shook her head. "I can't, Maman. Don't ask me why, but I just can't."

"All right, honey." *Now what am I supposed to do?*

I heard a voice calling my name. "Madame, madame?"

It was Theo, and I hurried out to find him standing in the café.

"Madame, he's cold. Do you have a quilt?"

Cold? That was dire news. The downstairs was sweltering, and Vincent's room would be even hotter. If he was cold, he was probably running a high fever, which indicated a terrible infection, one he was unlikely to survive.

"Yes, monsieur. I'll bring one right away. Is there anything else? And may I look in on him?"

"No, there's nothing else. I wouldn't mind having a break and some food. Anything you have in the kitchen will be fine. I'd appreciate it if you would stay with him for a while."

I served Theo some bread, cheese, and wine and left him to eat in peace while I carried my best quilt up to Vincent's room. He was breathing more shallowly and faster than before, and his face was as pale as the sheet upon which he lay. He shook as if freezing.

"Oh, my darling." I leaned forward and laid my face against his. He was burning hot, and he turned his head away, seemingly unaware of my presence.

"Just remember I love you," I whispered to him, my lips close to his mangled ear.

"Perhaps there will be a child," he whispered back to me. He spoke so softly that, if my face hadn't been close to his mouth, I wouldn't have realized he'd spoken.

I stood, stunned, both that he was speaking rationally and also by what he'd said. A child—that had never crossed my mind.

"No, I don't think so. I'm already thirty-three."

"My mother was thirty-seven when she had me, and she had five others after me."

I took that in. He was right. It was a possibility. "Then you must live to see what happens."

He smiled at me weakly. "I wish for that."

I covered him with the quilt and tucked it around him. He stopped shaking and seemed to be more peaceful. Then he turned inward, neither moving nor speaking while I sat with him, holding his hand.

Theo returned in a few moments. "It won't be long now," he murmured.

"Oh, I'm so sorry, monsieur," I choked out. "Will you let me know when it happens?"

He nodded.

I had no acceptable reason to remain in Vincent's room. I was not family—not a wife or a sister or a cousin, even—and certainly not a fiancée or lover. I was nobody but a landlady.

Downstairs, I began cleaning the inn. Since I could do nothing for Vincent, I might've gone out of my mind if I didn't do something, and cleaning gave me an outlet for my nervous energy. I started in the kitchen, washing, sweeping, mopping. Tears blended with the mop water.

Arthur went to bed, and when he requested that I join him, I shook my head and gestured for him to leave. He did, without speaking.

When I finished with the kitchen, I cleaned the restaurant, the billiard room, the hallway, and the Artists' Room. Still, no word came from Theo.

I wasn't tired, but I felt strangely separated from my body. *What should I do now?*

Cook, of course. There would be a need for food. There was always a need for food in trying times. Despite the death of one body, the remaining bodies would need to be fed.

Just after one in the morning, Theo came downstairs, wheezing, and sat in a chair. He looked unwell, like he might keel over at any moment and join his brother.

"It's over. He died in my arms. His last words were 'I want to die like this.' And then he did." He dropped his head into his hands.

I'd known this would be his news, of course, but a part of me had hoped for—had longed for—a reprieve, for Vincent to live, to cast off the infection and come back to life, to travel with me to America, where together we would create a new, better life.

I moaned, and tears ran down my cheeks.

"Madame?" asked Theo, clearly confused that I was taking the news so badly. "I'm sorry this has happened in your inn. I will—"

"No, monsieur. It's not that. I respected your brother very much. He is... was... a brilliant painter and a true gentleman. I took painting lessons from him, and I enjoyed our time together." Vincent probably wouldn't mind if I told Theo that much, and it would explain my oversized grief.

"He hadn't shared that with me. You've lost a friend and a teacher, then, just as I've lost my dear brother, the person who understood me the best."

We sat quietly together for a long time. The gas lights flickered, their shadows dancing, showing no regard for the anguish required to merely breathe—in, out, in. Theo picked at his nails, one after the other, left hand then right. The stringent aroma of mop soap thickened the air. Our clock kept time, each second a resounding reminder that time went on... one tick at a time.

Finally, in a strained tone, he asked, "Do you know what happened? Do you think he committed suicide?"

I shook my head, but my insides somersaulted. "He seemed fine, looking forward to his life." After a pause, I asked, "Do *you* think he did?"

"I... I don't know." Tears formed in his eyes. "He and I had been having problems. I'd told him I might not be able to continue supporting him. There are so many concerns. I might not remain in my current employment, and both my wife and my child are ill, besides my own precarious health. I didn't see how I could continue giving him money. He was very upset with me." He held out his hands, palms up, as though offering a supplication. "I don't know if that was why he did it or if there was something else."

I wished I hadn't promised Vincent not to discuss our relationship with his brother. I was tempted to do it anyway but held my tongue in deference to Vincent's wishes. *On Friday, he was full of life and love, and on Sunday, he shot himself?* No, I would never believe it.

"I don't want to speak out of turn, but I don't think that was it. He seemed so hopeful about the future. I can't believe he did it to himself."

"But he told us all he did." He shook his head. "It's hard to believe, I admit."

"I don't know why he said those things. And now we'll never know."

We sat in silence for a long time. Nothing more could be said.

Finally, he roused himself. "Is there somewhere I can sleep for a few hours? I'm exhausted, and there will be much to do tomorrow." He shook his head. "I mean today, I suppose."

"Oh, I should have told you. I made up the room two doors down from his for you. Sleep for as long as you want. There's no rush. We can handle everything in the morning."

"Thank you, madame." He slowly trudged up the stairs.

I walked out the front door and stood in the road, staring up at the stars. Vincent would have painted those glorious stars with his swirling brushstrokes. But the world would have no more of his wonderful paintings. And I would have no more of his love.

Finally, I was alone and didn't have to pretend to be only a student or landlady. I longed to howl in misery or scream at the Fates for doing this terrible thing to my beloved. But the grief was too deep and too fresh to allow me to even break down into sobs. That would come later, I knew.

But right then, my body felt numb, as though it had died with him.

Chapter 33

Adieu, accept in thought a handshake, and believe me. Yours truly,
Vincent.
–Vincent van Gogh

THE NEXT MORNING, THEO began planning for the funeral. There was no Protestant church in the area, so he went out to visit with the local priest but came back shaking his head and dropped heavily onto a chair. After I placed a cup of coffee before him, I sat down at the table.

"It was bad?" I asked, as delicately as I could.

"It was terrible," he burst out, spitting a bit of coffee toward me. He touched his mouth with his napkin. "I'm so sorry, madame. That was uncalled for." When I nodded, he continued. "He wouldn't do a service or allow my brother to be buried in the church's cemetery because word has gotten around that Vincent committed suicide. It didn't matter to him that we don't believe that's true. He just shrugged and told me it was impossible then showed me the door." Theo's face was contorted into a furious mask. "And to think that our father was a pastor his whole life. He buried anyone without asking about the manner of death. Bah!" He slammed a palm down on the table.

We sat without talking for a few moments.

Finally, I asked, "Shall we have the funeral here, then? I don't think my husband will object. We have only one boarder, anyway, and he was Vincent's friend. We might as well do it where Vincent lived. And died." I paused. "Would that be acceptable, monsieur?"

He exhaled deeply and grabbed my hand. "Oh, madame, that is what I so hoped, after the priest turned me down. Vincent was happy here, and it would mean so much if we could mourn him here. Thank you so much."

We continued talking about the arrangements. The funeral would be held the next day, Wednesday, July 30, at two thirty in the afternoon. Theo would make sure that Vincent's friends in Paris were notified in time to attend. I would prepare a meal to serve before the funeral, and the inn would be available if people wanted to return after the burial.

Theo headed out to find a coffin maker and a cemetery plot while I began preparing for our first funeral. The nanny, the chambermaids, and even the cook had resigned, so I would be in charge of everything, along with Adeline, if I could find my daughter and put her to work.

She was in the Artists' Room, looking at Vincent's paintings. The other artists had taken theirs with them when they left, so all that remained were Vincent's. She'd also brought in the paintings he'd stored in the shed, along with his paint supplies. The paintings made a lovely arrangement as she leaned them along the walls. We decided to display them in the same way around the coffin. Vincent was, more than anything, an artist, and he would probably prefer mourners to look at his paintings rather than his pale, lifeless body.

Adeline looked as depleted as I felt, and we had minimal conversation as we planned a small meal for the next day. She agreed to make her French onion soup, while I would put together plates of Vincent's favorite cheeses and breads. That was all we had the heart to do.

Germaine was in her bedroom, and Arthur was with her. She wasn't quite back to her normal self, so I'd made her remain in bed for another day. Arthur sat on her bed, reading a book aloud to her. As I watched the two of them, I realized that he'd spent very little time with our younger daughter. This was the first I remembered of him reading to her. I appreciated that they could have a few moments together before we left forever. Maybe she would even remember it and treasure the memory.

Sadness overcame me, so I went to take a nap.

THE NEXT DAY, THE UNDERTAKER laid Vincent out on a board on top of the billiard table. To stare at the face of my beloved would have pitched me into a dark abyss, so I glanced at him out of the corner of my eye. From what I could tell, he seemed to be at peace.

Adeline and I covered the bier with sunflowers, yellow dahlias, and other yellow flowers. Yellow had been Vincent's favorite color, so that seemed a fitting way to say goodbye. Theo nailed some of Vincent's paintings around the table. The sharp smell of embalming fluid filled the room, competing with the sweet scent of flowers.

Theo had dressed him in his good suit, the one he'd worn for our visit to the Eiffel Tower. No photographer worked in town, so no photographs would be taken. I didn't have the heart to draw a picture of his dear, dead face, so his self-portraits would be the only images left of Vincent. I had none of them, so all I would have would be my memories.

A dozen or so of Vincent's friends arrived to take part in the ritual, along with Dr. Gachet and his family. I recognized the artists Pissarro and Lauzet, among a few others, and was pleased that some people from the community had decided to attend. Theo and I greeted them all somberly. Theo's wife wasn't able to return from Holland in time, and he needed someone to stand by his side, so I did it. Few people ate any of our food, and I was relieved I hadn't gone to much trouble. Everyone milled around, mostly admiring his paintings and the flowers but saying little.

Before the funeral, Vincent was placed into his casket. One by one, the mourners filed past it. Some wept, and others tucked additional flowers around him.

Vincent lay amidst all the flowers, his paintings surrounding him. I finally looked at him closely. He was pale, of course, his startlingly intense eyes were closed, and his face was without expression. In a way, though, he was victorious in death. He had lived life on his own terms, and his glorious paintings gave tribute to the most unusual and creative man I'd ever met.

If he'd been alive, he would surely have painted the scene in bright, hopeful colors—maybe oranges or greens or violets. He would laugh at the long faces, telling people not to grieve for him. I could almost hear his raspy voice telling us he'd had a hard life, but it had ended on a high note, so we should wish him well as he traveled amongst the stars. Also, he might add with a wry smile, we should buy his paintings so that the world wouldn't forget him.

I couldn't help but compare his funeral to my mother's. Many more mourners had attended hers, but Vincent's was the one that would stay with me. He'd been the love of my life, but I couldn't share that with anyone, nor the depth of my grief. I did my best to control my tears, and mostly, I was successful. I knew I would revisit that day over and over, and then I could cry—but not then.

Several men closed the casket and carried it to a horse-drawn funeral coach, and everyone walked behind it, led by a sobbing Theo. In the hot sun, we climbed the hill to the burial site, a sunny spot among the wheat fields. Without a priest to lead the ceremony, no one knew what to do.

After we stood there silently for a while, Dr. Gachet spoke briefly. "I admired Vincent enormously. He was an honest man and a great artist who had only two aims: art and humanity."

I could've echoed those words and added to them that he loved deeply, but of course, saying anything aloud wouldn't have been appropriate. So I said the words to myself only.

The day was hot, and the sun beat mercilessly down upon us, so in a short while, the men lowered the casket into the grave. Then the group dispersed, some back to the inn and others to their regular lives. But for me—and for Theo, too, I suspected—life would never be the same.

After everyone left, Theo packed Vincent's belongings. I cleaned the inn again. Even though it was spotless, I knew of nothing to do other than to clean it over and over.

On Thursday, Arthur went to Paris, where he would stay the night. We hadn't said much to each other since before Vincent was shot. When he left, I was vaguely relieved he was gone.

By Friday, Theo was nearly ready to depart. He met me at the front desk and glanced around the empty room, looking as though he was going to cry. "I am so sorry that my brother's death has ruined your business. If I could change that, I certainly would."

Everything meaningful had already been said, so I just nodded.

Finally, he cleared his throat. "What are the charges, madame, for our food and lodging? And the flowers. I am ready to settle the bill."

I had the means to pay for my lover's funeral, and I wanted to do it. I couldn't tell him that, though, so I did the best I could. "No, monsieur. It was my honor to serve your needs and those of your brother. You owe me nothing."

"Please, I insist."

The matter seemed important to him, so I didn't object further. He paid in full and added some extra for our trouble.

Also, Theo invited me to choose as many of Vincent's paintings as I wanted. I didn't tell him Vincent had offered the same thing, but in addition to the portrait of Adeline, I took three that I'd watched him paint: the rosebushes behind the inn, the houses with thatched roofs, and his last landscape of Daubigny's garden. I ran my hand gently over the other paintings and committed them to memory before Theo packed them for transporting.

Surely, the death of such an amazing artist would bring buyers, and Vincent's labors in obscurity would be justly rewarded. Unfortunately, he wouldn't be there to revel in his glory.

I wondered if he would have celebrated overly much, anyway. He'd been embarrassed by the articles praising his work. To date, only one painting had sold. Vincent had seemed to want to be famous and rich, but he was frightened of changing his identity from a struggling, misunderstood artist to a successful one. America might've been good for him, but I would never know.

When Arthur returned on Friday evening, he gave me a wide berth. He and the children sat in the empty café and stared at me, their listless mother.

My world was gray. Vincent had taken the colors with him.

Chapter 34

I am seeking, I am striving, I am in it with all my heart.
–Vincent van Gogh

ON SATURDAY, I AWOKE with one overriding thought—although I was terribly sad to be doing it without Vincent, I still intended to be on that ship to America in six days. Having no time to waste, I would need to discover what had happened to Vincent right away. Despite what he'd told everyone, I didn't believe he'd committed suicide. I'd known him better than anyone in the days before his death, and he was not suicidal.

No, someone had shot him, and I meant to find out who. And why.

My mind was awhirl with thoughts. Neither Adeline nor Arthur was likely to tell me what they knew, although they clearly knew something relevant. I'd asked them both several times and had gotten nowhere. I wouldn't talk to them about it again until I had more information. I considered who else might know something.

Then I remembered that Cécile had come over to talk with Adeline on Sunday afternoon, and she'd seemed upset. I would start with her.

I dressed and went into the kitchen. Only Tom Hirschig was in the café, and he stood when I entered the room. "Madame, I will be leaving too. I'm sorry to do this to you, but—"

"Of course. I understand." I walked over to the counter. "Is there an outstanding bill?"

"Yes." He paid his bill and picked up his bags, which were sitting by the door. Just before stepping out, he turned to me. "I loved him, not just because of his tremendous talent but because he was so sensitive and caring. I will always remember how gracious he was."

I nodded. "Yes. I'll miss him too."

He bowed and walked out of my life.

No more boarders remained, and despite the nice summer weather, we were not likely to have more soon. For once, I had all the time in the world. I'd given the remaining staff the day off, and I considered telling them not to bother returning.

I ate eggs and bread and drank coffee that I barely tasted as I idly wondered whether Gérard would come in that morning. He must have returned from Paris. I waited, but he didn't come. After I spoke with Cécile, I would stop by Gérard's house and tell him the sad story.

Arthur and the children were still asleep when I left. Having no reason to wake them, I would let them have a day to recover from all the stress. I pinned on my hat and set off.

At Danielle's inn, I was surprised to see her brother instead of my friend. "May I speak with Danielle?" I asked him.

He shook his head. "She's staying in Paris for a while. In fact, she's selling me her share of the inn and moving in with Gérard. They'll be married next month." His face was set, and his tone was not exactly friendly.

"But why so soon? I'm not surprised they're marrying, but I'd thought she would let me know." I hesitated. "Is something wrong?"

He shrugged. "It's not for me to say."

I sighed in frustration. "What about Cécile, then? Could I speak with her?"

He shook his head. "She's in Paris too. I don't know when she'll be back."

I stared at him, puzzled by his attitude. "And you won't tell me what's going on? I have a feeling it's something I should know."

He shook his head and returned to his work.

I turned and left, wondering why Danielle had cut off our friendship so quickly without giving me an opportunity to talk about whatever was upsetting her. It must've had something to do with Vincent's death, but I couldn't understand why my friend would be angry with me. I'd done nothing wrong.

Back home, my family was awake and moving around the empty rooms. Arthur read the local newspaper while I made them breakfast. Vincent's death and funeral were covered in a few paragraphs on an inside page.

I tried to think through what had happened. Arthur had acted strangely the afternoon of the shooting, as had Adeline. And Arthur had seemed to think I'd been having an affair with Gérard. I wondered who could have told him that falsehood.

Adeline. Must have been.

Suddenly, the pieces fell into place. I turned to my daughter. "Would you take a walk with me?" I tried to keep my voice light so as not to frighten the girl, but we probably both knew it wasn't an invitation Adeline could turn down.

"All right. Let me finish my tea."

In a moment, the two of us headed out the door. We walked across the road to the town hall, where we sat on an empty bench. Adeline stared straight ahead, not looking at me.

That behavior wouldn't work any longer. I took my daughter's arm and held on lightly. I didn't want her to run away when I asked my questions, and my grip could quickly strengthen.

"Adeline, I know you're close to your father. He must have asked you to keep an eye on me while he was gone. Is that right?"

Adeline shrugged.

"Honey, a man has been killed, so you need to talk to me. This has gone far beyond loyalty to your father. Do you understand?"

She took a deep breath and let it out in what sounded like a sob, then she stared down at her hands.

I needed some way to convince my stoic, determined daughter to tell me the truth. I would have to threaten her with something. That was harsh, I knew, but if that was what it took to get answers, I would do it.

"If you don't answer my questions, I will take you to the police station and tell them you know more about Monsieur Vincent's death than you're saying. Now, tell me what you know."

Adeline finally raised her head, and I saw her pale face and terrified eyes.

I grabbed her hands. "Tell me."

She turned to look across the street at the inn, where her father was standing on the porch, watching us. "Please, could we go somewhere else?"

I rubbed my eyes. Of course she was afraid of her father, and most likely, her fear was justified. "All right, where would you like to go?"

Adeline turned big eyes on me. "You know that place where you and Monsieur Vincent had your last painting lesson? Under the tree in the wheat field? Could we go there?"

Pain stabbed my heart. I'd had such a fine time with Vincent that day. "Yes. We knew you were watching us. Let's go."

We hurried down the road to the path that meandered through the field. When we came to the tree, we sat on the ground beneath it.

I faced my daughter. "Now, talk to me. Don't leave out a thing."

Adeline hesitated for a long moment but then began to cry. "Oh, Maman, it's so terrible. I've been so frightened. I wanted to tell you, but I didn't dare." The words flew out of her mouth and tumbled over one another. "Papa thought you were having an affair with Monsieur Gérard. He—"

"You told him this, yes?"

She nodded. "I saw you going into Monsieur Gérard's house one day. Papa promised to buy me grown-up clothes if I kept an eye on you, so I told him what I saw." She looked down at the ground then rubbed at her eyes with the back of her hand. "But I was wrong to do it."

Bile rose in my throat. I swallowed several times until I could form words. "Did your father plan to do something terrible to Monsieur Gérard?"

She nodded. "I didn't find out until Cécile came to see me on Sunday." She breathed hard and began sobbing again. "She had run into that bastard René Secrétan in the afternoon. He had Papa's gun and—"

"Wait. He had your father's gun? The pistol he uses for shooting?"

"Yes, that one. I didn't realize it at the time, but I think I saw Papa give it to René one day while you were in Paris. It was in a box with a lock, no?"

I nodded.

"Oh, Maman, I didn't know what it was. Papa also gave him some money. I didn't know what was happening." She covered her eyes with her hands and sobbed as though she might never be happy again.

I didn't speak. My heart had turned to stone.

Finally, Adeline removed her hands and continued. "Anyway, Cécile had just seen René, and he'd bragged that he was going to kill someone but not Monsieur Gérard. Papa had found him on Friday night and said he had the wrong man, so Monsieur Gérard was saved from dying. Cécile said that René seemed to think that was hilarious.

She was afraid he would shoot Monsieur Gérard anyway, just for the sport of it, so she came to see me."

I struggled to understand her words. "So you're saying that Papa gave René his gun and some money to kill Gérard because he thought he was my lover? That whole thing is crazy. Why would your father do that? And why would René agree?"

She considered that. "I don't know about Papa, but René is pretty strange. It's why I stopped seeing him, because he scared me. His papa wouldn't allow him to have a real gun for his holster, but Papa made a deal to let him have the gun if he would kill Monsieur Gérard. I heard them laughing and saying it would be called an accident."

She shook her head. "René's mind doesn't work like other people's. He probably thought he could get away with anything because his family is rich." She paused and took a breath. "I don't think he would have given back the gun even if Papa asked for it." After a moment, she said, "You should probably ask Papa about all this, if he'll tell you."

I gasped. This news was horrible. "All right. Let's go back to Sunday afternoon. After Cécile told you, you two walked around for a while. What were you doing?"

"We tried to find René, to make him stop. But we couldn't find him. I told Cécile to tell her mother what was going on and have them all leave town, in case René killed Monsieur Gérard anyway." She stared at her hands, clenched in her lap.

There must be more. Instead of shaking her, I forced myself to wait.

After a long moment, she burst out, "Maman, I did something bad. I saw you with Monsieur Vincent in Monsieur Gérard's house one day last week, and I told Cécile on Friday. She might have told René about that so she could save Monsieur Gérard." She took a deep breath. "I've thought and thought about it, and here's what I believe happened. When Papa found out that Monsieur Gérard wasn't your lover, he went after René to stop him from killing him. Papa didn't learn about you and Monsieur Vincent from me, but René might have told him. I think René must've decided to go on and kill Monsieur Vincent so he could keep the gun and the money. I don't know if Papa told him to do it or not."

I was too stunned by her story to say a word. *Could René be that evil, that he would kill someone who hadn't done anything to him just to keep a gun?* That didn't seem possible, but it was what Adeline thought, and she knew the boy better than I did. I suddenly felt lucky he hadn't targeted me instead of Vincent. I'd been angry at René and had kept him from seeing my daughter. Also, he'd killed that bird. Could a bird and a man be the same to this deranged boy?

I shivered.

Adeline sobbed uncontrollably and threw herself into my lap. "If I could undo everything, I would. It's all my fault."

I didn't try to stop my daughter's tears. The fault was Arthur's and, of course, René's. But Adeline wasn't blameless. Lifting her up, I asked, "What, exactly, did you see happen between Vincent and me?"

Adeline spoke between sobs. "I saw you kissing him." Then she threw her head down again in my lap.

The draperies in the salon had indeed been open that day. Thank God that was all she'd seen.

"Did you tell your father that?" I asked.

Adeline shook her head. "Oh, no. By that time, I understood Papa might do something dreadful. I wanted to talk with you about it, but I didn't dare because I shouldn't have been following you."

We sat together, neither of us speaking. Gradually, Adeline's tears stopped.

I finally understood that Vincent's claim about shooting himself was made to save my reputation. He'd known that, if the truth came out, my reputation in the community would be ruined, and people might even blame me rather than Arthur for the murder since I'd cheated on my husband. Arthur could easily have divorced me and taken the children, and Vincent wouldn't have been able to protect me, since he would be dead.

The dear, dear man.

In my entire life, no one had ever been so generous toward me.

I wiped away the tears that had formed. I would have plenty of time to grieve later, but right then, I needed to make some decisions. I considered my options.

First, I could tell the police what had happened, and they would arrest both René and Arthur. But that would lead to a situation in which the community might turn against me, just as Vincent had feared.

Second, I could ignore the entire situation and follow my plan to flee to America. That made my stomach roil. No, I would leave, but I would not run away.

Third, I could tell Arthur what I knew before I left him. After Adeline's confession, I had leverage to protect myself that I hadn't had before, but whether I could use it depended on Adeline.

I would have to take the risk.

"Honey, sit up now. I need to speak with you very, very seriously." When the girl sat up and dried her eyes, I continued, "I know you regret what you did. And I regret putting you in the position of having to choose between your father and me. We'll have plenty of time to speak of this later. Right now, though, I need to tell you something, and I'm taking the risk that you won't immediately tell your father. Can I trust you with that?"

"Oh, Maman, I never want to tell him anything ever again. He isn't to be trusted."

"Yes, we agree about that." I took a deep breath and stared at my daughter. *This is the time, and* mon Dieu, *please let this be the right decision.* "Okay, I have a plan. I had hoped not to tell you about it before it happened, but I'm going to do this now. There are two options. We can go to the police and tell them everything, and your father and René will be arrested. I will do that if you want." I paused, seeing the shock on her face.

"But I have a different idea. Hear me out before you respond. I want to tell your father that we know what happened, and we won't go to the police if he allows us—you, me, and Germaine—to leave quietly. He must agree to never bother any of us again, at least until you and Germaine are grown and can make your own decisions about whether you want to see him. If he breaks the agreement, we will tell the police what we know about Vincent's death."

Adeline stared at me, uncomprehending. I took a breath and continued. "I have tickets for us to sail to America to see your uncle Émile on Friday."

"Oh, Maman, really?" Her eyes shone.

"Yes. I hadn't told you because I thought you would prefer to stay with your papa."

"Oh, no. Not anymore. I'll be so happy to leave France. I can't get the memory of Monsieur Vincent lying in the coffin out of my mind, and it was all because of Papa. And René. I want to be far away from both of them."

I released the breath I'd been holding. "All right. This is what we'll do. We'll go back to the inn, and I want you to go to your room and begin packing whatever you can carry. We'll leave today and go to Hélène and Claude's house. We'll take only a few things, and we'll buy the rest in Paris."

I paused, searching my daughter's eyes. "Will you do this for me? We'll need to leave quickly, as soon as I talk to him." I tried to put the next words together correctly. "Now, listen. If he strikes me, I want you to run to the police station and bring the officers right away. If you don't, he might come for you next. Will you do that?"

"Yes. I will."

"All right. Let's go now, while we still have the courage."

We walked back to the inn, feet dragging, fingers entwined.

Chapter 35

BACK AT THE INN, ADELINE took Germaine into their room and closed the door. I hoped Adeline could hear me if I screamed, for I would definitely scream my loudest if Arthur tried to hit me.

How has it come to this, that I have to enlist my children to protect me from their father?

To confirm that Adeline had been correct in her assessment of the situation, I walked into our bedroom and opened Arthur's wardrobe. The place where he'd kept the gun box was empty—no box, no gun, and no bullets. I took a breath then slowly closed the wardrobe and walked back to the café, where Arthur was still reading the newspaper.

I stood just inside the door, one hand on the knob, and told him, "We need to talk."

He glanced up. "Okay. Sure. But would you get me some more coffee first?"

I bit my lip but brought the coffeepot from the kitchen and re-filled his cup. I hoped it wouldn't scald me if he threw it in my face.

"What is it?" He smiled as though what was left of our world hadn't been destroyed.

I called forth Athena, the warrior goddess. "Where is your gun? I just looked in the wardrobe, and it wasn't there. Where is it?"

His smile faded, and his face paled. "I... I gave it to someone. I was tired of hunting and gave it away. The damned gun wasn't reliable, anyway." His eyes didn't meet mine.

I moved closer to him but stayed beyond his reach. "Was the person you gave it to René Secrétan?"

"Yes. How did you know?" He thought for a moment. "Of course. You know we used to hunt together. But did you know the boy and his family have left Auvers? They left Saturday evening, I believe."

I wondered if he could be telling the truth. If that was the case, René might not have been the one who killed Vincent on Sunday. He could've given the gun to someone else to do the dirty deed.

No. Cécile had seen René on Sunday afternoon. His family might've left town on Sunday evening but not Saturday. Arthur was lying.

I wasn't sure how to proceed. I'd thought Arthur would admit what he'd done, but apparently, he wouldn't. I took a breath and called forth the fury I'd tamped down for so many years.

In a firm voice, I said, "Arthur, I know you paid that boy to kill Gérard. And I know you or someone else warned René off when you found out I wasn't having an affair with him."

He slowly set his coffee cup in its saucer and folded the newspaper. He wore the blank expression that suggested he was thinking as fast as he could.

After a long moment, he said, "I had nothing to do with Monsieur Vincent's death. If René killed him, it wasn't my doing. I didn't go out of the house on Sunday, as you know, because you were with me. So don't try to pin that death on me. *No.*"

This was harder than I'd thought it would be. I considered giving in and waiting to leave until the next time he was in Paris. But no, I owed Vincent's memory the truth.

I shook my head and steeled my resolve. "I won't argue details with you. Not here, not now. I know you paid René to kill the man you thought was my lover. When Gérard turned out to not be the correct one, he killed another innocent man. And he did it with your gun."

Arthur started to speak, but I interrupted. "It doesn't matter whether or not he was my lover. A good man, and our boarder, was murdered. Even if you didn't pull the trigger, you were behind it. I have witnesses to all this and more."

I took a breath. "Furthermore, what kind of father turns his own daughter against her mother, giving her gifts to spy on me? I didn't think even you would sink so low."

He pushed his chair backward and rose to his feet. His fists were clenched, and his eyes assumed that crazed look I associated with the beating he'd given me the year before.

I spoke forcefully before he could come at me. "Here's the agreement I will make with you. If I tell the police what really happened, both you and René will hang. I'm willing to do that, but I'm going to give you one chance to save your neck."

I had his complete attention. He stared at me with the angry look that meant his fists would soon follow.

I was sorely tempted to tell the police what I knew and watch them drag him away. *But no.* "Do not even think of hitting me, or the police will find out everything."

He tensed as though preparing to spring at me.

"The girls and I are leaving," I said. "Today. Right now. If you try to stop us, I will tell the police what I know. You'll be arrested, tried, and convicted, and then you'll hang. But if you allow us to go with no problems, and you do not attempt to find us—ever—I will leave my share of the inn's resources to you. There isn't much now, I know, but you might want to have your mistress come and run it with you. I don't care what you do as long as you leave us alone. When I get to where I'm going, I will file for divorce, and you will not fight it."

I paused, breathing heavily, having finally found the right words. "Do you understand me?"

He lowered himself onto the chair, where he sat, rigid, for several long moments, looking down at the table in front of him. I shifted uneasily from foot to foot. Regardless of my fatigue, I would not move from the door, which I would open and run through if he made even the slightest movement toward me.

His reign of terror in our family was over. I knew it, and he must have known too. He raised his head at last to look at me, shrugged, and said with a snarl, "Get out of here. Whatever you think you know, it's wrong, and I can prove it. But I'm sick of you and these bratty kids too. Leave now, before I change my mind."

He stood and pushed back his chair then headed for the cellar. "I need to do an inventory of the wine for the new owner. I'll be down there for an hour, and I want you all gone when I get back." He paused. "Do you understand?" he asked, mimicking my tone.

I didn't respond but just watched him until he'd gone downstairs and closed the door. Then I leaned on the table and took a long, deep breath.

I was free.

Chapter 36

New Orleans, Louisiana, July 1940

It must be good to die in the knowledge that one has done some truthful work... and to know that, as a result, one will live on in the memory of at least a few and leave a good example for those who come after.–Vincent van Gogh

SUDDENLY, A HORN HONKS outside, and I start and open my eyes. Looking around, I realize that, instead of being back at the inn or even aboard ship, I am sitting in my little apartment in New Orleans. A small part of my mind has been aware of my surroundings as I spoke, but I ignored it while I was immersed in telling the most important story of my life.

Danielle—the young one—must've turned off the fan during the afternoon, presumably to not interrupt my story, and turned on the lights when it grew dark.

My legs are stiff, so she helps me stand and make my way to the washroom. After I've finished, I look down at my hands. They are the hands of a very old woman, not those of the young Louise who packed up the children's clothes and her other possessions to sail to America.

When I return to the living room, I notice a tray of food on the table and smell gumbo. I've swapped my traditional French cooking for Cajun, and I'm not sorry. Gumbo is now my favorite food. Young William always brings me dinner, and he's apparently brought enough for two.

"Your grandson delivered this food an hour ago. You didn't stop talking, so I whispered to him to set it here. He stayed for a few moments and listened to part of the story, and he seemed surprised to hear you talking about Vincent van Gogh. He had no idea you were acquainted with him."

I draw in a breath sharply. "How... how much did he hear?"

She smiles. "That the two of you were in love. He left before you described your wonderful love scene."

I exhale and stare at the bowl of food. The day has been long, and I'm hungry.

"Does he know?" she asked, her voice gentle. "He looks very much like van Gogh. Same hair, eyes, and the same intense gaze. He's even around the same age as the Vincent you describe."

I shake my head. "I've never told anyone. When we first arrived and I discovered I was pregnant, Adeline gave me lots of questioning looks, but she never outright asked, so I didn't have to lie. My family thinks Arthur was my son's father."

Danielle nods, looking pensive. "Your dinner is ready to be warmed. Shall I do that for you?"

She takes the dishes into the kitchen, and I hear clanking. My grandson is such a sweet young man—much like his grandfather. I wish he would try his hand at painting, but whenever I suggest it, he laughs and says cooking is creative enough for him.

Danielle shares the meal with me, and we eat in silence. After she has washed the dishes, she asks, "Do you mind if I look at your paintings?"

"Be my guest."

They cover every wall, in both the living room and the bedroom. I wait, knowing what she will see, but I don't stop her. The time has come for all my secrets to be told. My days on this earth are few, and I don't want my family to throw away the valuable paintings when I'm gone.

After a while, she sits beside me and holds my hand. I'm happy for the human touch. It's such a rare thing these days. She licks her lips and stares at the far wall, which has the most paintings.

"Uh, I see you copied some of his famous works."

Nodding, I smile. "When we first arrived, I went back and re-painted the ones I'd painted with Vincent. I wasn't able to bring mine with me, but they meant too much to me to forget them. And then, as the years went by and his paintings became more famous, whenever I saw a photograph of one I didn't recognize, I would try to copy it. Doing that made me feel closer to him." I point at one. "That's my favorite. It's of the cherry blossoms when he was in Arles. It's such a hopeful painting. I prefer to remember Vincent as hopeful rather than despondent or mentally ill."

Danielle stands and looks at the paintings again. She points at three that grace the wall above the dining table. "But these are original van Goghs, are they not?"

I chuckle. "You are definitely an art historian. I wondered if you would recognize them." I take a breath. "During the days before the ship sailed, Aunt Ella returned to the inn and took the paintings I had hidden under the bed. They came with me to America, rolled up safely in my trunk. They are irreplaceable."

I stand and walk over to them. Up close, I can see more texture, the different colors of paints he used, and the energy with which he painted them. I've never grown tired of gazing at them and remembering him hard at work.

"The art world doesn't even realize these exist," Danielle says. "They're a major find. Even though they're unsigned, they're clearly works by van Gogh." She points at one. "This one of Adeline is much like another one that Theo had, but it's a little different."

"Yes, and now you know why that is."

She moves to stand in front of another painting. "I've seen several renditions of the houses in Auvers but not this one. And I loved hearing your description of how he painted Daubigny's garden. It was clearly this painting." She gestures toward it.

She turns and smiles at me. "Actually, I loved your descriptions of all the paintings. I could have pictured them in my mind's eye as you spoke, even if I hadn't been able to see them on your wall." She hesitates. "I know you didn't just paint copies..."

"I painted many other things in my career—it's true. After I stopped being angry, I returned to painting flowers. I kept the Vincent copies for myself, though."

"Now that I know your story, I can see why. When I first came in, I wondered why you would have copies of van Gogh's works in your apartment when you are so famous for your flowers."

I shake my head. "I'm not *so* famous. Thank you for that vote of confidence, but you exaggerate."

We sit in silence for a few moments before she asks, "I can have the van Gogh paintings authenticated for you. And you should insure them. They're surely worth many thousands, if not millions."

"Yes, I'll do that. But not tonight. I need to feel them around me tonight. I'll let you take them with you tomorrow."

After a moment, she changes the subject. "What happened when you arrived here?"

"My brother was waiting for me. I took the cooking job he'd saved for me, and I found I liked it well enough. I thought I'd return to France after a few months, but with the new baby and the new restaurant, I never found the time. Aunt Ella came over to help, and she stayed for five years, until her death. I so appreciated her presence." I shrug. "I divorced Arthur within the first year. That was easy because he disappeared from the inn and from Auvers only a month or two after we left. We never heard from him again. Good riddance." I rub my sweaty palms on my dress. They still sweat every time I think of Arthur and those horrible days with him.

"I split the money from our mother with Émile, and he and I opened our own restaurant. All our family members worked there. We did well for forty years, but the Depression killed it. I was ready to stop cooking, anyway. But I was sorry to lose my beautiful house. Still, this apartment is adequate. My son wants me to move in with him and his wife, but I've been happy to live alone for so long." I pause. "I believe I'll take him up on his offer soon, though, if they'll have me."

My voice tapers off. I don't need to go into what is staring me in the face. If she can't see that my time is short, she's obviously not looking.

I clear my throat and continue, "After I retired, I finally wrote the cookbook of my family's French recipes, and that was what led you to me. So, it has all worked out after all." I chuckle.

"Did you marry again?"

I shake my head. "There were suitors over the years, but none of them measured up to my Vincent. I learned early on that it's better to have no husband than to have a bad husband." I pause, chuckling again. "I even wrote to Denis a few years after I came here. He wrote back and sent a photo. He'd turned into someone I didn't recognize—rotund and red-faced, with many children and grandchildren. In the end, I was glad we hadn't married." I shake my head. "It's funny how life turns out. Often, it's for the best, even though we don't realize it until much later."

"And your children?"

I sigh. "Adeline was never entirely happy with me. After a while, she blamed me for breaking up our family, which I suppose was true, in a way. As soon as she finished school, she moved back to Paris. She became a chef and married but had no children. I rarely hear from her. And now that the Nazis have occupied France, I don't know if I ever will again. I pray for her every day."

The sadness overwhelms me for a few moments, then I let it go. Adeline was never easy to be around, even when she was young. She probably isn't any different today. "Germaine was another story. She was always cheerful. She married young and moved to Baton Rouge, where she lived a happy life until the cancer took her. She gave me four grandchildren, and they visit me regularly."

"And the other child?"

"William was born about eight months after we arrived here. I didn't dare name him Vincent, although I wished I could. William was Vincent's middle name, so it sufficed. He was an easy baby and a peaceful man. He lives a few blocks from here." I glance at her. "He looks more like me than his father, but every time I see William, Jr., I can't help but smile. His grandfather would've been so proud. If Vincent had lived, what a wonderful life we would've had." Tears form, though my heart is warmed at finally being able to speak freely about the loss that still inhabits my soul.

"Thank you for telling me your story, Madame Ravoux. I wish I had recorded it on my tape recorder. I didn't ask before we started because I didn't know what you would say. But now that I've heard it, I'd like to write an article about your life. It's historically important. Would you allow me to interview you on another day and have you speak into the tape recorder?"

I shake my head. "You took notes, and that's enough. I don't want my old voice to be recorded. But you may use the notes to write your article." I pause. "I didn't know if you would believe me," I say quietly.

"I do. Every word." She bites her lip. "You know, when I write the story, your family will know the truth about you and Vincent."

I nod. "Yes, I understand that. It's time."

She takes a deep breath. "I'm sure you need to rest, and I'll leave you soon. Before I go, though, I want to ask you about my Grand-mère Danielle. It seems that you two parted on bad terms."

"No. I visited her in Paris before I left, and we reconciled. When she understood what really happened, she thanked me for letting her know. She was sad about Vincent, of course, but there was nothing to be done. Gérard lived on instead of him. Neither of us had any say in that. So we hugged goodbye, but we didn't keep in touch."

"Ah. I understand. I can give you the little package now."

She pulls it from her bag and hands it to me. It's small, about the size of a ring box, and wrapped in brown paper. When I open it, a small note is folded up inside. It's written in French.

I'm sorry I didn't get to give this to you in Paris. We found it after you left, when we went back to Auvers to pack Gérard's things. It was sitting on the bedside table. I've waited all these years to return it to its rightful owner. It's all I can do.–Danielle

I smile and look inside the box. I see not a ring, as I expected, but a locket and chain. It must have been the gift Vincent had intended to give me. After his death, I searched his room but found nothing. I decided later that he must've been out of his mind when he mentioned it to me.

I open the locket, and inside are two miniature paintings—one of each of us. Vincent smiles at me on the left, and I smile back at him on the right. The likenesses are tiny—only about an inch across—but they are perfect renditions. He must've stayed up many nights painting them, straining his eyes as he looked through a magnifying glass and dabbed paint with a paintbrush the size of an eyelash.

I can't stop my tears, but they are tears of joy. Vincent must have planned to give it to me when we were at Gérard's house, but I ran off so quickly that he didn't, then he forgot it was there. If we'd had other times together at the house, he would've found it, and it would've been around my neck for the past fifty years.

Wordlessly, I pass the locket to Danielle. She smiles when she sees what it is and reads the note. Then she passes it back to me.

"Would you like me to fasten it around your neck?"

"No. Not yet. I want to look at it. But you could bring me my reading glasses. They're in the kitchen." When I put them on, I see the faces even more clearly. How young we were and how hopeful.

Danielle clears her throat. "You said earlier you had no proof that you and Vincent were in love. I think you do now."

She's right. Vincent's son and grandson will have the proof they will need after I tell them the story.

I smile. "Nothing in my life has pleased me more than this. I wish I could thank him for painting it and thank Danielle for making sure I received it."

"I think she knew how much it would mean to you. I imagine she's smiling at us from heaven."

Soon after, the young woman leaves, promising to return in the morning to pack up the paintings for authentication.

I will treasure the locket for the rest of my days, but I don't need it to remind me of our love. Vincent is a major part of who I am, and I will never forget him. Still, knowing that he painted this gift for me warms my soul. He had no money, but he gave what he had, and that was his heart. And his art.

I sit for a while longer, holding my locket, before I stand and prepare for bed.

Author's Note

BESIDES BEING A WRITER, I am also an amateur painter. Vincent van Gogh is my favorite artist, and I've tried for years to emulate his style. But I didn't know much about the man himself until I read *Van Gogh: The Life* by Steven Naifeh and Gregory White Smith during COVID lockdown. After finishing that definitive biography, I became obsessed with learning more about van Gogh, so I read everything I could lay my hands on. Van Gogh became "Vincent" to me, and although I didn't like much about him, I was fascinated by this complex character.

The thing that intrigued me the most was Naifeh and Smith's idea that Vincent didn't shoot himself but instead was shot by René Secrétan, a young man in the village. The evidence they presented was not definitive, but they thought it explained the shooting better than the suicide hypothesis. And they didn't speculate on why René might've done it, other than to say it might've been an accidental shooting. Biographers don't speculate much, other than to explain the data they've found. Speculation is the purview of fiction.

I'm a fiction writer, so that was where I began. I couldn't stop wondering what would convince René to shoot Vincent. *A woman!* I thought. When I learned that the innkeeper, Louise Ravoux, was about the same age as Vincent, I was off and running. I could visualize Vincent falling in love with Louise and her husband being so angry that he paid René to shoot him. And there it was, the plot of the story.

I also wanted to give poor, suffering Vincent something positive to brighten his last days. In many ways, he was a difficult human being, but his art is the most amazing I've ever seen. He deserved something good to happen to him in his life. Fiction gave it to him, not reality.

I did my very best to stick to the historical narrative. Specifically, Vincent lived at the Auberge Ravoux for seventy days, and those were the days depicted in this novel. He went to see his brother on a certain date, which is in the novel. He was shot on July 27, died on July 29, and was buried on July 30, 1890. In short, I tried to put everything that has been documented about Vincent's last days into the novel—everything other than the affair with Louise, which is fiction.

If you're interested in more reading to learn about the real man instead of the fictional character I've made him out to be, start here:

Murphy, Bernadette. *Van Gogh's Ear*. New York: Farrar, Straus and Giroux, 2016.

Naifeh, Steven, and Gregory White Smith. *Van Gogh: The Life*. New York: Random House, 2011.

Van Gogh, Vincent. *Ever Yours: The Essential Letters*. Edited by Leo Jansen, Hans Luijten, and Nienke Bakker. New Haven, CT: Yale University Press, 2014.

Walther, Ingo F., and Rainer Metzger. *Van Gogh. The Complete Paintings*. Cologne, Germany: TASCHEN, 2015.

These lengthy tomes are enough to get you started. After that, you can take off in any direction. Van Gogh was a fascinating figure who has been written about more than most people in human history.

Let me repeat—this book is fiction. After studying Vincent's life intensively for more than a year before I started writing, I still didn't know whether I believed he was murdered or committed suicide. I can actually envision either scenario happening. I'm no expert, merely a novelist who made up a story to go along with the biographers' suppositions.

I tried to trace Louise Ravoux's life, but not much is known about her. As far as I know, she didn't have an affair with Vincent, didn't leave her husband to immigrate to America, and wasn't the victim of domestic violence. I made that up because I wanted to write a story about a woman who found her true self through the love of an unknown artist.

I hope you enjoyed it.

Acknowledgments

WRITING A NOVEL THAT takes place in France during a global pandemic when you can't travel to scout out locations is a difficult thing. I can't adequately thank my research assistant, Alina Tylinski, who was the niece of a friend and happened to be in France during COVID. She enthusiastically agreed to work with me, even though we'd never met. She read and critiqued several drafts and visited most of the sites in the book when I couldn't. She literally made this book possible. Any flaws are mine, of course, but I couldn't have even tried without her.

Thank you to my critique group, Tall Pines Fiction Writers, for reading this book over and over and offering support and critiques through the trying times. So many Zoom meetings. I can't thank you enough, Josh Pollock, Heather Starsong, Lily Larson, and Jenn Perez, for your dedication to helping my writing be as good as it could be. Although we've disbanded and gone our separate ways now, I'll never forget our years together. I think we all learned to write by being together.

Numerous people read drafts and offered comments: Kathy Dolan, Suanne Shafer, Lael Har, Rachel Dacus, Margaret Wallace, Daniel Booth, Jaki Wilsun, Susan Haught, and probably others that I'm not remembering just now. Thank you so much. A writer needs beta readers like a sunflower needs the sun.

Thank you to M. M. Finck for her help in sorting out the plot and the first chapters. That was awesome. And thanks for the support of the Women's Fiction Writers Association. I've learned so much from you.

I'm grateful to Daniel Booth for your ongoing support through all the years and all the books.

Thank you to my ever-loyal critique partner, Judith Bula Wise. You read so many drafts and talked about this book for years, and you never once showed any irritation with my one-track mind.

Thank you to Red Adept Publishing. This is the fourth book of mine you've published, and I love how you support your authors. Thanks to Lynn McNamee for accepting the book, to Sara Gardiner for all your insightful content edits, to Kelly Reed for the line edits, and to the rest of the staff for all your careful work on this project. You are heroes. And geniuses, in my mind.

And finally, thank you, dear readers, for reading my work and making it possible for me to keep publishing. This is a work of my heart, even more than the others, and I hope it touches your heart too.

About the Author

Diane Byington has been a tenured college professor, yoga teacher, psychotherapist, and executive coach. Also, she raised goats for fiber and once took a job cooking hot dogs for a NASCAR event. She still enjoys spinning and weaving, but she hasn't eaten a hot dog or watched a car race since.

Besides reading and writing, Diane loves to hike, kayak, and photograph sunsets. She and her husband divide their time between Boulder, Colorado, and the small Central Florida town they discovered while doing research for her novel.

Read more at www.dianebyington.com.

About the Publisher

Dear Reader,

We hope you enjoyed this book. Please consider leaving a review on your favorite book site.

Visit https://RedAdeptPublishing.com to see our entire catalogue.

Check out our app for short stories, articles, and interviews. You'll also be notified of future releases and special sales.

www.ingramcontent.com/pod-product-compliance
Lightning Source LLC
Chambersburg PA
CBHW061518210726
48287CB00006B/1733